Ro[illegible] M[illegible]rs

PL[illegible]

Return

Lost Army Gold

by
Dan Willis

Stick Horse Press
www.stickhorsepress.com

About the Author

Dan Willis has spent a lifetime as a cowboy, growing up in Central Texas. He draws on his vivid memories and love of history to take the reader on a journey into the Old West.

Willis was a top all-around rodeo cowboy, winning Rookie of the Year honors in the Rodeo Cowboys Association (now the Professional Rodeo Cowboys Association) in 1965. He also qualified for the National Finals Rodeo in the bull riding that same year. He has worked as a rodeo announcer and rodeo clown in arenas across the country.

Following his career as a rodeo cowboy, Willis has worn a number of hats, including auctioneer, rancher, cattle buyer and host of his own farm and ranch news show. He has also served on a number of boards of directors including the Texas Rodeo Cowboy Hall of Fame. Willis is also a 1997 inductee into the Texas Rodeo Cowboy Hall of Fame.

ISBN - 978-0-9814903-1-1

Printed in the United States

All inquiries regarding this book should be addressed to
Stick Horse Press
PO Box 3 • Walnut Springs, TX 76690
Telephone & Fax - 254-797-2629
Website - www.stickhorsepress.com

Chapter 1

The late summer evening was hot and muggy as I crossed the nearly dry Brazos River and rode slowly down First Street, Waco's busiest route. Cotton wagons were waiting to be unloaded and music was filtering out of the *Brazos Queen* and the *Cotton Palace*, Waco's two sin dens. As night approached, a strange mixture of folks mingled on the sidewalks. Farmers and field hands idled away the hours, waiting to be unloaded. Soldiers from Fort Fisher bumped elbows with trail drivers and a few Indians loitered in the willows that were growing on the banks of the Brazos River.

My mind was nursing on uneasy peace. Vocations had wandered for me from Civil War Veteran, a losing cause, to homestead farmer, cowboy and now Indian fighter.

Officially, I was Bill Fowler, Army scout in charge of delivering payrolls quarterly to Fort Graham, Fort Griffin, Fort Concho, Fort Gates and Fort McKavitt. My mind pondered this last job. I'd homesteaded a ranch a few miles north of Waco in the fork of the Bosque and Brazos rivers. This was flat bottom land, with good grazing and huge pecan trees. I finally felt at home after a lifetime of drifting.

Starting out broke, just back from the war, money had been real scarce. I'd made the first couple of years by hiring on with trail herds crossing the Brazos on their way to Kansas City. I learned from experience that large herds drew stray cattle like a magnet. When cows and heifers mixed with a steer herd, it was like a new whore in an old bar. This always caused a lot of fighting. Trail bosses would let you cut the herds at a crossing and sell them for a song.

Waco was a favorite crossing and I'd been "singing" for a couple of years. I had accumulated a pretty good herd of cows but needed a few more to make a living. I'd taken this job for the Army for the past year, but this was going to be my last trip.

Reflecting on the past, I had mixed feelings for the Indians I'd been fighting and trying to elude. I figured the government should have honored their treaties and left the West to the Indians. Hell, this country was big enough for everybody. Buffalo hunters were the problem. The Army should have shot all the buffalo hunters and made peace with the Indians. Buffalo killers were what kept the Indians stirred up and the settlers moving west were the ones paying the big price.

The Barnhart brothers, who had a big trading post south of Waco where the Tehuacana Creek entered the Brazos, had worked out a treaty between the government and Indians. The whites were to stay east of the Brazos and the Indians were to stay west of the river. Hell, it was only a week until someone crossed the river with a wagon train and all hell broke loose.

I rode slowly to the fort, uneasy about tomorrow. The Comanche had really been on a tear and we were going right through the heart of their country.

Captain D. Bradford Mills sat at his desk studying my request for a troop of soldiers to escort us to Fort Graham. I suggested a troop from each fort to escort us to the next and then drop off and return to their home fort. This suggestion would allow each troop to return to their home fort instead of one troop being gone for the full month it took me to make the rounds.

Mills was a West Point graduate, temporarily assigned to Fort Fisher, a Texas Ranger post. He had been a decorated hero during the Civil War but he knew nothing about Indians and wasn't about to let a Southern rebel call the shots. Having not been assigned a post of his own, his temporary commands had given him a great sense of insecurity.

With a large show of authority, Captain Mills stated that as usual; two soldiers would assist in the delivery. If I was afraid of Indians, maybe I should resign my duties. Stating that he had no fear of an attack between here and Fort Graham, he might consider an escort from Graham to the other forts, if horses were available.

Smarting over his rebuke, I drifted back to the Brazos Queen and after a steak and a pitcher of beer, settled in for a game of chance. Not prone to gamble, I was just killing time and waiting for Ginny to come down from her quarters. I was Ginny's favorite since the night I'd shot a riverboat dock hand that was going to carve her up with a large knife in a jealous rage. While waiting for Ginny, I began reminiscing. She had told me about how she had come to the Brazos Queen.

Ginny, like me, was adrift after the South lost the war and hard times had turned her to the world's oldest profession. She was the toast of the town. She had a long mane of mahogany hair that framed porcelain skin and blue eyes as big as saucers, and could leave you wondering how in the hell could she be what you knew her to be. As she sat brushing her long red hair, she approached the same question. Flickering lamp light struck the mirror before her, causing flashes of light, similar to the thoughts flashing through her mind. Her thoughts raced back to the battle at Vicksburg and the sheltered life she had led before the war.

The daughter of one of the wealthiest planters in the delta, which lay just north of Vicksburg, Ginny had been christened Virginia Louise Wancloth and cradled in a lap of luxury.

Growing up in the slow cultured South, where her days were spent studying foreign languages, etiquette and planning for the next party to attend, she was unprepared for the fall of the South and what happened afterwards.

Rumors of the North's raging Army were drifting down the Mississippi via the steamboats and runaway slaves that traveled the river frontier. War seemed far away until the dying scream of her father awoke her in the chill of the early dawn. Ginny told me, "A troop of Northern soldiers and riffraff that had attached themselves to the unit, were plundering and looting *Scarlet Oaks*. This plantation had been my only home and world until I was fourteen years old."

Ever the gentleman, Danford J. Wancloth, greeted the officer in charge, and invited him into the house and asked his pleasure. With all the arrogance gained from his latest victories, the officer spat in Danford's face and fired point blank at close range, thus closing a chapter on the Wancloth family's grandest times.

As if seeing it again, Ginny told me, "I watched as my mother was stripped and raped repeatedly by the soldiers and the other riffraff that were there. When the soldiers were finished, the slaves gang raped my mother. The Northern officer had released the slaves and they took their vengeance of being in bondage out on my mother until she died."

Ginny stated, "I guess, because of my youth and the commanding officer's obsession for Southern belles, I was reserved for the officers and their pleasure. One sordid day followed another until the war miraculously ended and I slipped away in the still of the night. I drifted from place to place, penniless and hungry 'till a gambler made me a deal." After endless and nameless men she had found her niche at the *Brazos Queen*, Numero Uno in Waco's "best" pleasure palace.

Bates banging on the piano was Ginny's call to service. From where I was sitting, I could see Ginny's expression as she slowly started down the hall toward the stairs. Her grimace was one of resignation to her station in life. Feeling guilty for resenting where she was, she silently thanked God for Bates.

Tormented by the demons that drove him, Bates had been a preacher before the war. As he began to softly finger the piano keys, he looked up the stairs to see if Ginny was coming. "Ginny is the last woman I ever intend to love," Bates thought, "If love is a word I can still use."

Sweat started pouring off his bald head as the tune brought back haunting memories that he'd just as soon leave buried - visions of him preaching hell-fire and brimstone to a crowded church in Atlanta. The largest congregation in town had been under his spell. He recalled the flash of rage that caused him to kill a young man he had caught in the act of adultery with his wife. He relived the trial and the heartache, the infidelity of his wife had wrought. Even when he was cleared of the crime, his ministry was over. Turning his back on his calling, he gradually drifted downhill ever since.

Joining the Army had been his refuge and turning his hate into action had made him known as "Charge Hell General Bates." A fight in a bar where he killed an enlisted man was killing number two. He said "After that, who keeps score?"

Not a gunfighter but a dangerous man to cross with a knife, derringer, or sawed off shotgun - his specialty, Bates was a first class card-shark, a pimp and a saloon keeper. Bates feared no one and respected none, except Ginny. Bates wondered what was his thing for Ginny? His thoughts went back to their first meeting.

Bates had told me the story of their meeting. "Ginny had stepped off a paddle wheel steamer that ran sometimes 'round a trip to Galveston. It depended on the water flow in the river. There were two dry docked, loaded with cotton and waiting for the river to rise. They would go down stream on the next high water."

Ginny was in the company of a "natty" dressed New Orleans gambler named Tom May. They had sat in on games Bates was running and with a keen eye, Bates studied the pair. Ginny was a beauty indeed and May had the smoothest bottom card deal he'd ever seen a gambler use. May had a flawless delivery and a brilliant mind for cards. Business flourished for them as trail hands, farmers and river boat gamblers were picked like a chicken. Ginny sat in as a stooge or distracted players with her good looks as May ran the cards. Bates approached May for a cut of the profit and an argument broke out.

Bates said, "They both pulled a shoulder holster and if I wasn't the fastest, I was definitely the straightest shooter, and when the smoke settled, May was dead, and I was shot through and through, but recovered. Ginny assumed the role of nurse and has been here with me five years this spring."

I saw Bates flex his fingers, and he looked old and his fingers were stiff. Hell, he couldn't shuffle cards any longer, but he could still play the piano with ease. Looking up, Ginny was descending the stairs. The crowd had gotten quiet and she started singing as if on queue. Ginny was Bates' greatest resource and a funny arrangement. She sang for her room and board, entertained a few preferred customers of her own choosing and kept all the money. Watching as Bates looked at her now, I was wondering if he'd been younger, would he have made an honest woman out of her? He had told me, "Her kind has always been my downfall. Even in the ministry," he said, "I'd have to fight lust and it was always the prettiest that drew my attention, never the also rans." Bates and Ginny had a platonic relationship - like father and daughter kinda, but you could tell, he loved her somewhere in between.

Glancing across the table, Ginny smiled as I winked at her. Bates saw her smile and caught my wink out of the corner of his eye. Bates wasn't jealous of me as he was so many of Ginny's guests. First, he knew I minded my own business and second, I covered all the ground I stood on. I was also from the same South that Bates and Ginny had come from and this made us nearly kin. "Too damn many 'Blue Coats' in town now," Bates had said, "Yankee soldiers with their damn Northern brogue. I'm a good mind not to serve the bastards, but money is money."

Ginny had even been keeping company with Captain Mills, unknown to his wife. Bates played tirelessly, Ginny sang all the tunes she knew several times and I was lucky with the cards. As the night wound down, men dropped out and the game broke up. I'd won a lot of money for an honest poker game. Ginny was tired and wanted a hot bath. Summoning a black chambermaid, she retreated to her room, knowing I'd be along shortly.

As Ginny crested the stairs, I turned to Bates and handed him my winnings. Bates was my banker, a dangerous killer, but honest to a fault in money matters. As Bates counted my winnings, I told him of my concerns for the upcoming trip and reiterated my conversation with Captain Mills.

"Mills is a jackass and wouldn't know an Indian if it bit him on the ass," Bates said, and repeated a conversation he'd had with a trapper at the bar earlier in the day. He said, "The trapper had stopped to visit a homesteader between here and Glen Rose and found the whole family scalped. Comanches!" I nodded thoughtfully.

I followed Ginny up the stairs and bathed in her bath water. Reservations about the trip evaporated as Ginny snuggled in my arms. I thought how life had been good lately, and as I made love to Ginny there wasn't an Indian in the world and dying was the last thing on my mind.

I awoke alert, like a man does who lives dangerously. Lying quietly for a few minutes, taking in my surroundings, I breathed in the soft fragrance of Ginny's body and wondered if a man might get used to this. Quietly dropping my hand down to the gunbelt that lay by the bed, I watched dawn come a-creeping up on the night. I rose softly so as not to wake Ginny, I dressed quickly and stepped out into the new day.

Chapter 2

Walking quickly to the livery stable, I reached for my bridle and a curry comb then unlatched Old Blue's stall door. Blue nickered softly as I poured a generous feeding of oats in his trough and began to brush the loose hair and hay from his back. Old Blue was another story. He was a gray Thoroughbred stallion I had purchased from a wagon train headed west from Kentucky. Hell, nobody in his right mind rode a stud, but Old Blue was a "gentleman's gentleman." He never squealed or fought when saddled and was the best horse I'd ever ridden. Tireless under the saddle, I'd ridden him a hundred miles at a stretch and he could outrun anything in the country. I had bought him for a breeding horse to cross on some mustang mares and draft horse mares that I had accumulated, but he doubled as a riding horse during the off season. Slipping a bit in his mouth, I checked the curb chain and headstall, making minor adjustments. As I threw my saddle on Old Blue's back, I glanced at the girth and latigos. This might be a day when I couldn't afford a breakdown.

Leading Old Blue out into the street, I mounted and rode toward Fort Fisher as dawn turned a chilly pink in the east. Two guards were mounted and a pack mule was loaded with gold — pay for the soldiers scattered at forts across the Indian country. The last frontier was sparsely staked by this outcropping of forts across West Texas. Cole Badger, a corporal, was my regular guard, a damn good shot and a soldier through and through. The second guard was new. A black, buffalo soldier as the Indians called them, and I damn sure wasn't pleased to have him along. He was a private, a remnant from the war that went from slavery into the Army. He had proven himself under fire, but I wasn't sure he'd stay and fight if things got tough. I told him, "I don't really like having a coward on this trip. If the Indians attack, I need someone that will stay and fight, not run."

Deke Williams answered softly, "I learned a long time ago that actions speak louder than words and I am a man of action. As bad as I hate to risk my life to serve a Southerner, I took an oath as a soldier to do my duty." No love was lost between us as we left the fort.

As the day approached, we were riding down First Street while Corporal Badger and I discussed the route to take. I wanted to take the west bank of the river, getting out into the prairie where I could see what was happening. As commanding officer, Corporal Badger said, "We are going to follow the stream bed since the water is low and that is the shortest route." By the time we reached the river bank, there was a real cuss fight taking place and neither of us would budge. Bringing Private Williams into the argument was Corporal Badger's way of winning because Deke was Army and no soldier was going to vote against a commanding officer. This was like having a piss fight with a pole cat, you "ain't gonna" win.

Cussing Army, Indians, and buffalo soldiers under my breath, I let Old Blue have his head and taking the lead, led out for Fort Graham. Fort Graham was a hard day's ride away and located on the east bank of the Brazos. It was the next fortified encampment.

The morning went slowly by as Corporal Badger and I rode along in grudging silence. Private Williams followed leading the pack mule. Flies droned round the horses' ears and deer flies would bite viciously causing the horses to duck under low lying branches that grew along the bed of the river to dislodge their tormentors.

I rode warily along the middle of the river. Damn, I didn't like this sitting duck position. If there were an Indian in this country, we were dead ducks. Not stopping for lunch, I handed out hardtack and jerky and stopped to drink at the springs. Relieving ourselves before remounting, we kept on riding. The bluffs rose on the west bank, throwing a shadow on the river bed as the afternoon wore on. I was uncomfortable as the sun began to slip behind the bluffs. The rays blinded me and there was still an hour or two of daylight left.

Calling a halt, I once more made my plan clear. Corporal

Badger laughed at my concern saying, “Hell, we’ll be at Fort Graham by dark and we haven’t seen an Indian sign.”

I hadn’t seen them, but I could feel something in the air. As we rounded a bend in the river, limestone bluffs sprang up from the river on the east bank and the bluffs on the west sloped down to ground level. White Rock Creek fed into the Brazos on the east and there was a buffalo crossing that came out of the Bosque country and went up White Rock Creek. I reined Old Blue off to the right toward White Rock Creek, putting as much distance as possible, between us and the deep shadows and dense brush that lined the Brazos. Day was slipping away and if there was going to be Indian trouble, it was going to be in the next hour because Indians hated to fight at night. They were very superstitious. As I rode to the right, Corporal Badger begrudgingly swung in behind me with Williams following suit with the pack mule.

Shots rang out from the west bank, and fifteen Comanche braves splashed into the river. Deke Williams took the first hit, a bullet just above the belt that left a big hole. Corporal Badger caught two bullets and the pack mule two arrows. I caught an arrow in the thigh that lodged against the bone.

Screaming like hyenas, the Indians were in hot pursuit. Deke coolly fired his Army issue and reloaded as they gained the mouth of the creek. For a minute we had the bend in the creek for cover and we took out five Indians as they entered the creek. A large dark cloud had been building to the north all day, and lightning began to crack and thunder boomed. We were hoping to reach Fort Graham before it hit but our plans had been rudely interrupted. Large rain drops splattered in the river as the battle raged. The Indians had three old guns they had stolen from the settlers. All single shot muzzle loaders and they didn’t know how to reload them. The Comanches threw the guns away but kept up a steady deadly arrow attack. When their attack cost them five braves, they retreated back across the river and gathered their dead and wounded.

I shouted for Badger to take the lead and dropped back and

whipped Deke's mule into a dead run. I shouted for Badger to look for a cave or outcrop of rock to make a stand in and to "ride like hell." If the Indians split into two groups and came up both sides of the creek, we were in a death trap.

A mile or two up the creek, with rain falling in sheets, we rounded a bend in the creek just as lightning flashed. Corporal Badger spotted a cave in the west bank of the bluff. It was high enough to be out of the water if it flash-flooded, and there was a limestone bluff on the east bank made it impossible for a frontal attack. The rock overhang gave some protection for the horses and prevented anyone from dropping down from the top. We rode straight for it as night settled in. Williams stepped off his horse and faded into the dark, covering me and Badger as we unloaded the gold and got the horses and mule into the mouth of the cave. As Williams dismounted the bullet hole gaped open and I had to admit I was wrong about this buffalo soldier. Hell, he didn't know what quit meant. I'd seen lots of men fight wounded, but this man was dying and still fighting. Calling softly to Deke, I covered him while he crawled back to the cave. Slipping farther back into the cave, we rounded a bend and discovered a larger room with dry wood and decided after a while to build a small fire and survey our wounds.

Deke was breathing real shallow and had lost a lot of blood. The worst part was there was nothing you could do for him. Badger wasn't in much better shape. He had a bullet in his lung and was slowly drowning in his own blood. He had another bullet in his kidney and was passing a lot of blood. The arrow in my thigh was against the bone and grinded every time I moved. The only chance I had was to push it on through because the shape of the arrowhead prevented backing it out. Hobbling back to the mouth of the cave, I heard muted voices and realized the Indians had stolen the horses and mule. The Indians had taken refuge under a limestone overhang down the creek, just out of rifle range. They had built a fire and killed the pack mule and were feasting and waiting until morning to smoke us out.

I knew we were in a hell of a fix. If I had Captain Mills by the neck, I'd have choked the bastard to death. Mills and Corporal Badger and all their damn Army intelligence was the cause of all our trouble. Viewing the circumstances, I knew the Indians couldn't overrun us, but as soon as morning came and the wood dried out enough to burn, they would build a fire at the mouth of the cave and smoke us out or roast us alive.

While plotting a plan of action, I began to push and rotate the arrow. I finally bypassed the bone and by hammering on the shaft with a rock until I would be on the verge of fainting, I'd stop until the dizziness would pass and then do it again. The arrow was finally forced out the bottom of my leg and withdrawing it slowly I must have passed out. When I came to, water gurgled through the bottom of the cave.

Picking up a seasoned limb with a forked top, I whittled a crude crutch of sorts and padded it with strips I had cut from my saddle blanket. Using the crutch, I began to search the cave for the source of water or another way out. Hearing water falling, I followed the sound and discovered a hole in the rock just large enough for me to wiggle through.

I went back to check on Williams and Badger and found them in a pain racked stupor. I knew they weren't long for this world and decided I'd better "get while the getting was good." I vowed to come back and get them, but neither answered. Swallowing hard, I turned and started on the long journey to Fort Graham.

Going back to the cave opening, I barely squeezed through and crawled out in a cedar thicket. Rain was falling in buckets as I slowly stood and got my direction. My leg was bleeding pretty bad as I stood and watched the Indian's fire glowing from under the overhang beside the creek below. I didn't think they would move in this storm, but decided I'd better travel, storm or no storm. The rain would wash out my tracks if they tried to follow me. I cussed myself for not bringing my Henry rifle. I could have taken a good many of the red bastards to hell with me from the top of this bluff, but the throbbing in my leg forbid another climb in and out of the rain filled cave.

Slowly hobbling toward the river, I stepped into the longest night of my life. Rain made it hard to keep my direction. Only the rumbling of the river kept me on track. Fighting brush with one stiff leg and crutch took its toll on an already exhausted body.

Daylight. The rain still fell in sheets as I rested under a large oak tree. Not a quarter-of-a-mile up the swollen river, the nine remaining Indians sat under a tree arguing about whether to cross. Evidently, another one had died during the night. Five had been killed in the first attack and lay tied over their horses.

My leg felt red-hot and throbbed. The swelling made my pants so tight, I took my knife and split my pants leg front and back. Blackish blood seeped from the wounds on both sides. But worse than the pain in my leg was the sight of the Indian war chief riding my blue stud. Damn! Indians and armies both. I waited to see what the Indians were going to do. Finally, with much discussion, the chief rode Old Blue off into the raging river and the other eight braves followed suit.

Knowing Indians like I did, I did not move for a full hour following their departure. My leg was nearly immobile now. I waited until the rain and visibility was nearly zero.

Throughout day and early evening the rain continued to fall. Flood waters rose and the Brazos was bank to bank. About midnight I reached Fort Graham, barely coherent from exposure, loss of blood and fever. I stumbled through the fort's gate and tried to explain the situation. The guard summoned the camp doctor and the commanding officer. They took me to the infirmary, where I met Dr. Crawford. When the commanding officer arrived, I told him how to find Private Deke, Corporal Badger, and the cave in White Rock Creek. He assured me that first light would find a patrol unit en route. I vaguely remember Dr. Crawford cutting off my pants and appraising the situation. Infection had a hell of a head start and he said amputation might be the next step. I drifted into a fevered stupor as the commander left and Dr. Crawford tried to work magic.

With limited equipment and supplies, the doctor began by scrubbing both sides of the wound with lye soap and whiskey. He was hoping to make the wound bleed. Because my leg was so swollen, he was not successful. Red streaks were extended in every direction, infection rampant. Pulling a fifth of good whiskey from his black bag, he poured it down me until I passed out. In my condition it didn't take much whiskey.

Rousing up once, he plied me with whiskey again. This time I passed out for good. Dr. Crawford sent for the blacksmith and had him bring an iron rod from the back of a wagon. He then fired it in the wood stove, drew it to a cherry red. Enlisting the blacksmith to assist him, they laid me full length on the hospital bed. They tied my hand and foot to the four poster bed putting a pillow beneath my wounded leg, began the difficult process.

In my stupor I vaguely remember the blacksmith laying across my body and the doctor thrusting the red-hot rod through the wound real slow, cauterizing it. I passed out again from the pain. Chills ran down Dr. Crawford's spine as I screamed in my drunken unconscious state, but it was either this or amputate. This was a picnic compared to amputation.

I awoke again screaming, but was once again rescued from the pain by unconsciousness. All night and the next day drifted by in a fog of pain and sleep. Finally I awoke around midnight. Weak from fever and stress, I was hungry but my hands shook so hard, I had to be spoon-fed the broth. All I had eaten for three days and nights was a little hardtack and jerky the first day.

The first thing I asked was, "What about Williams and Badger?" I tried to get up. I explained to the doctor, "I told them I'd be back to get them," I got a blank look from Dr. Crawford.

Sergeant Ray had been assigned to the task, but a hurried trip to the area found the Brazos overflowing its banks and the water backed up into the White Rock Creek. No cave was visible. It was still raining and twelve inches fell before the flood stopped.

No sign of the cave or Williams and Badger was ever found once the flood had abated. I couldn't imagine how in the hell the detail could miss the cave with the directions I gave them.

Removing the bandages on my leg everyday, Dr. Crawford would smell to see if gangrene was present. "Once you smell it, if the patient is going to survive you must amputate at once," he told me. Every hour on the hour he would check the wound. Time stood still as the wound drained and festered. Finally on the seventh day, it began to show some healthy pink color and the swelling began to go down.

I began to hobble around the fort for a few minutes each day, but I had lost a lot of weight and strength, plus my leg had gotten awfully stiff. Gradually my strength came back. I thought of returning to Waco.

During one of the examinations, I told Dr. Crawford, "I need to get back to my ranch in Waco. Do you think I could get a horse, saddle and gear for the trip?"

Dr. Crawford was adamant. "You are not to get on a horse, or expose yourself to any more germs until your leg is completely healed," he ordered. "Due to the arrow hitting the bone, there is the danger of bone infection as well as tissue damage, and you are a long way from being healed!"

The commanding Army officer at Fort Graham finally dispatched a horse-drawn buggy to Waco and transported me back to Fort Fisher. "When you get to Fort Fisher, you report to the doctor and have him continue checking for infections and keep the dressing changed," Doctor Crawford told me.

Chapter 3

Reporting to Captain Mills, I gave a brief account of the attack and the situation in which I had left the two soldiers. I also reminded the son-of-a-bitch that I had requested troop protection. Ignoring my comment he dispatched a company of men to go to White Rock Creek and look for the cave, the soldiers and the lost gold. I chomped at the bit to go along, but was cut short by Captain Mills. I was rudely informed of my dismissal as an Army scout and was relieved of any charge of finding the bodies.

I left the fort and caught a ride with a hack driver, slowly making my way down First Street to the *Brazos Queen*. Surprise filled Ginny's eyes when she saw me enter the saloon. No one knew about the Indian attack and they weren't expecting me to be back for a month or so anyway.

Ginny was thrilled to have me back in town and insisted I stay with her and let her nurse me. This suited Bates, too. He'd taken a likin' to me.

I mended slow and my leg bothered me as summer turned to fall and then to winter. I lived at the *Brazos Queen* and Ginny and I spent all of our time together. Bates began to pay Ginny by the month for entertaining the crowds and brought in another girl that took Ginny's local clients. Things settled into a routine. Bates and I closed up after Ginny quit singing every night. Each day started at noon.

Captain Mills came by the saloon after a week to see Ginny. She told him she was busy. A man accustomed to not being ignored, he wouldn't take no for an answer. Grabbing Ginny's arm and jerking her around, he pulled his Army rank as if she were a soldier. Ginny slapped him full in the face.

I stepped in as Mills raised his fist to hit her. The trouble boiled between us that had been simmering a long time. Talking real low and plain, I said, "You best walk out the door and never come back if you like living and breathing."

Mills choked on rage and as his face turned purple, he said, "When I get through with you, you'll wish the Indians had killed you instead of the soldiers you deserted." He hinted that I had led them into a trap and deserted them. He stated, "There is no trace of a cave anywhere along White Rock Creek and no trace of the gold." He further stated, "I am thinking about filing Federal charges for cowardice in the line of duty and for stealing the shipment of gold."

Since the cave and the gold couldn't be found, circumstances looked to be in Mills' favor. Blind with fury and faster than rain, I slapped Mills over and under twice. With blood flying from his nose and mouth, I grabbed him by the collar and the seat of his pants and threw him out into the muddy street like a sack of trash. Bates was furious. He had raised up his shotgun to kill Mills when the Captain hit Ginny. I had saved Mills' life, but in turn had made an enemy for life.

Talk began to circle around Waco that I had killed the two soldiers, stole the gold and faked the accident. As I sat by the wood stove in the saloon each day and ached from the long cold winter, I thought I'd sure done a hell of a job faking it with all the pain I had endured.

Chapter 4

Some mornings I'd forget the Indians had Old Blue, and found myself heading to the livery stable to feed him. Then I'd recall the picture of the brave crossing the flooding river on Blue and would remember how Blue felt underneath me when he ran. I had his first crop of colts at the ranch, three year-olds now, and they needed breaking. Getting restless as spring approached, I hired a surrey and took Ginny and Bates out to the ranch.

Willie, my top hand and former slave, greeted us. Willie looked after the ranch and ran things just as good when I was gone as he did if I was there. He was sure glad to see me. We were damn near family even if we were different colors. The story about the Indian attack and stealing Old Blue really fired him up. He sure did like that blue stud and breeding season was just around the corner.

Willie was my right hand man. Top horseman, farmer, and in his younger days he and I had fought Indians and survived lots of life's wrecks. His gray hair and shuffling gait surprised me. Hell, he was getting old. Recalling the thirty years he'd been my main man, he wasn't a colt when I bought him from the plantation owner and gave him his freedom. Willie never forgot it. Hell might freeze solid, but Willie would never leave the ranch.

Everything was in order, even though I had been gone eight or nine months, those three year-olds of mine were halter broke and had been ridden a few times. Nice colts, but there wasn't a replacement for Old Blue. I told Willie to pick out a couple to leave for studs. There was one gray with lots of muscle but he was out of a cross-Percheron blooded mare and it showed. The other was also a gray, but a too little light boned and muscled. His momma was a real fast, small light boned Thoroughbred match race mare that came out of Mexico.

I left Willie some money to run the ranch and pay the hands. My heart wasn't in the ranch, I couldn't get the Indian attack and losing Old Blue out of my mind. Needing a horse in town, I had Willie catch a big dun gelding and tying him to the back of the surrey, took him back to town with me. I needed something to do with my time and thought maybe riding would loosen up my stiff leg.

At first I just rode around town, but as my leg healed, I began to stretch out my rides. Slowly my leg strengthened and I was nearly back to normal.

Talk was floating around about the soldiers and the missing Army gold. I fretted about this, although I knew the facts. People would get quiet when I walked in and I knew they were talking about me. People always want to believe the worst. Hell, I wouldn't have went through what I'd been through for the whole rotten stinking Army, much less a piss ant load of gold. I knew what I had to do and at first light I eased out of bed and headed for the livery stable. Saddling my dun gelding and buying a good brown mule and pack saddle, I set out for White Rock Creek, the missing soldiers and gold. I felt like my reputation was at stake. Hell, I knew where they were, these bumbling assed soldiers couldn't find a bell and it a ringin.'

I rode north slow and easy. There hadn't been any more Indian raids since the night of our attack. Thinking back over that last year, I felt like I had slept a year and had lived a nightmare. As I rode off into the Brazos bottom, I noticed the buffalo trail hadn't been used this year and most likely last year either. "Those damned buffalo hunters! They're going to kill all the buffalo and the Indians are going to starve. Then it's going to be up to the white man to feed them. Damn, life was getting complicated," I thought. One minute I was feeling sorry for the Indians and the next was wanting to kill the red bastards for wounding me for life and stealing Old Blue.

I crossed the river just before dark, right where the attack had taken place. The river was running knee deep on my horse and the mule, but was cool and peaceful. Riding up the creek and around the bend, everything looked the same. The small stream flowed along the white limestone creek bed and the world seemed at peace. Hobbling the gelding and mule, I turned them loose to graze while I built a small fire and fried some bacon. Coffee boiled on hot coals as I made camp and dinner came together. It was hard to imagine the violence here just a year ago and the flood producing rain, compared to the full moon and peace that was here tonight.

My mind raced back to that ill-fated day last year with regret. Badger and I spent the last day in bitter silence and even when I knew Badger was dying, I didn't make amends. He had been a top soldier and died like one. Worse was the way I treated Private Williams. This wasn't like me. Probably just my Southern raising, I reasoned, but hell, Old Willie was black and he's nearly family.

Visions of Williams covering me and Badger with a hole in his back as big as your fist made me ashamed of the way I'd treated him. I wondered what Williams thoughts were when he died. I wondered, did he hold it again' me for the way I treated him. I can't believe I doubted whether he'd stay when it got rough. Hell, he was all a soldier could hope to be and what did color have to do with it? Red, black or white, we all try to survive with what we have to work with. Deke might have been someone's "boy" most of his life, but he sure as hell died like a man.

Drifting off to sleep, I dreamed off and on of Private Deke, Corporal Badger and the Indians. They kept getting mixed up in my mind. Sometimes it was Deke and Badger on Old Blue crossing the flooded river and once again, I'd be running and slipping in the rain on one crutch. As dawn approached, I awoke more tired than rested as reality replaced the nightmares of my sleep.

Washing my face and hair in the cool spring water brought focus back to mind about the cave, the missing soldiers and the Army's lost gold.

Dreading what this day might bring, I caught the mule and dun gelding, and slowly brushed them and saddled them. What would I find? Did the Indians find Badger and Williams before they died?

Did they endure a scalping before life escaped them and what about the gold? Did the Indians take it? Or wouldn't I have noticed it when they crossed the river in the rain?

Mounting my horse, I pulled on the mule's lead rope and started up White Rock Creek toward the cave. Rounding the next bend, everything looked different. There were huge boulders laying in the creek bed along with dead trees and mud from a slide. Nothing looked the same. How far did we run that night before we found the cave? Thinking back, it seemed a blur. Rain was falling in sheets and the Indians were in hot pursuit. The creek looked different in the bright sunlight than it had from the lightening flashes. I thought I would remember the limestone bluff across from the cave, but every curve in the creek had white cliffs rising straight up. Mud slides had changed the face of the west bank and no cave was visible, as I rode north. The creek became more shallow as I rode all the way to the head, where a spring babbled constantly as it made its way toward the river.

Dismounting and taking a long drink, I tried to remember some landmarks from that night a year ago. Suddenly I decided to search for the other entrance that had allowed me to escape that night. I hobbled the mule to let him graze while I searched through the brush with no results. No cave, no soldiers, no gold! As night began to fall, I caught the mule, I rode back to my old camp, and was puzzled over the disappearing cave. "Was this the right creek?" I wondered. Rounding up wood for a fire, I began to doubt myself. After a quick cold supper, I rolled up in my blanket, away from the fire and promptly fell into another night of dream plagued sleep. Indians and soldiers and former black slaves kept stealing my horses and Willie and I couldn't stop them, then we were all lost in a dark cave.

Dawn finally came and I was back to the hunt. First I crossed the river and made damn sure this was the right buffalo crossing and setting on my horse a minute, made sure this was the right creek. Riding through my camp, I made sure this was where we had made our stand. As I rode slowly up the creek, searching, I rode under one of the huge pecan tree that shaded the creek. I heard a squirrel chattering loudly, and looking up saw Deke's old Army issue hat, caught and held by the stampede string, in the tangle of limbs. Hell, I knew for certain, this was where we had run.

Dismounting I walked slowly along the creek bed knowing that the cave had to be here somewhere. The rock slides had changed the look of the bank and nothing looked the same. Going over the same terrain I'd covered the day before, I backtracked up the bluff and again searched for the narrow hole in the top. With no landmark to go by all the brush looked the same and cedar was so thick you couldn't walk in it. Rattlesnakes were plentiful and I had killed four or five by night each day.

I spent a week just riding, walking and looking. Finally I knew the country like the palm of my hand. I had a map of it in my mind. The creek cut the valley half into with about a hundred acres on each side. Huge pecan trees covered the gullies and creek banks and several small springs flowed toward the river. A nice bottom rolled around the mountain and ran up the river a mile or more. I thought if I hadn't already homesteaded a place, this would be ideal.

To the east on the top of the bluffs, the range opened up into real good grasslands with lots of buffalo wallows. This explained the buffalo trail from the west. When the fly season came, the buffaloes would travel to the east side of the river, to the blacklands and wallow in the black mud. The mud would dry and be like a shield that the flies couldn't penetrate. Too bad they couldn't find some protection from the damn hide hunters! It was a pure waste to kill a whole buffalo and just take its hide. Hell, the Indians used it all, plumb down to the shoulder blades for hoes and the bladder for water jugs. Damn, here I was feeling sorry for the Indians again, when they had stolen my best horse! If me and Willie ever got a shot at this buck riding Old Blue, he would be through riding stolen horses or hunting buffaloes.

Finally, giving up, I rode slowly back to Waco. Questions

haunted me as I traveled. How did they die? Were they scalped and mutilated? Did the mud slide damn up the entrance and the running water fill the cave, drowning them? Or did their battle wounds take them first? What if I had stayed, would they have lived? Or would I have died? Again the battle raged through my mind, as I relived the agony of the fight and escape. Once again, I assured myself that I did the only thing I could have done, and the rest was fate.

Chapter Five

Waco was once again full of cotton bales waiting to be loaded on barges and paddle wheel steamers. They would go down stream to the coast, on the next high water. Business was booming at the *Brazos Queen* and Bates was raking in the loot. I stopped at the *Brazos Queen* to see Ginny. During the course of our conversation, Ginny said, "I'm worried about Bates. He looks bad. I wonder how old he is, he has never told me and I'm sure not going to ask!"

In a world where fast and tough ruled, old was a disadvantage, but Bates' reputation with a sawed off shotgun kept most of the trouble at a minimum. Most of the trouble was from the soldiers, young, hotheaded and a lot of them still fighting the Civil War. When you mixed that with the South that had lost the war and a lot of their pride, it didn't take much to start a fight. When you mixed liquor and women with all of this, plus gambling, hell, you couldn't keep it from happening and the *Queen* had her part of it.

I began to spend more time at the ranch. The ranch was a full-time job. Waco was growing and housewives wanted a fresh supply of tender beef and not old tough four and five-year-old trail beef just during trail drive season. Butcher shops were opening in town and with my proximity to town, I'd found a market for my yearling and two-year-old beef, right here at home. Once a week, Willie and I would cut out a dozen or so of the fattest yearlings and two-year-olds, and drive them to town. Willie had made a bumper corn crop and we'd taken to chopping ear corn with an axe and mixing cotton seed with it. Feeding this combination, the steers got fat in a hurry and beef was worth a lot more than the feed would bring.

A year went by and trouble began to brew around the *Brazos Queen*. Captain Mills had been doing a lot of talking about the lost Army gold. A reward was being offered for information concerning the lost gold and the missing soldiers. Nothing was mentioned of the Indian attack or me being wounded. You could see a difference in the soldiers that came to the bar. Ginny had been hearing a lot of talk and the soldiers began dropping clues of someone knowing where the gold was hid.

Ginny snuggled in my arms one night after closing, and as I drifted off to sleep, once again former slaves and soldiers riding gray stallions began to invade my dreams. Jerking to full awake, my gun was in my hand and the demons of the night rode off into the darkness. As I lay there, I began to tell Ginny of the cave that disappeared, the suffering I'd endured, and how I was struggling with the death of Deke and Badger. Ginny listened attentively and then confided in me the gossip that was circulating around town. She begged me, "Bill, you've got to leave town until this blows over. I'm afraid someone will say something and you or Bates will get killed. Or you will kill someone else and hang."

She finally cried herself to sleep as I stared at the ceiling, lost in thought. Sleep evaded me as night crawled into day and rising at the first light, I rode to the ranch without saying goodbye. It seemed my best thinking was done at the ranch. As much as I liked Ginny, I couldn't get used to living in town. The noise of the wagons and boats coming and going was just too much. Dang, I wished I could have her and the ranch both at the same time, but Ginny was a town girl and would be bored to tears at the ranch.

Chapter Six

Willie was milking when I rode up. Large buckets of milk were foaming as Willie squirted milk from the Shorthorn cows he treasured. I had managed to buy a few Shorthorn cows and a couple of bulls from homesteaders traveling west. Willie guarded them jealously. I grinned as I recalled the old days and our first milk cow. I'd gotten a heavy springing longhorn, from a trail herd that was wilder than a peach orchard boar. Willie needed a milk cow. When she calved, Willie penned her and the fight was on. About the third time she kicked him, Willie invented "whipped cream." She'd kick Willie and he'd whip her when she did. The more I thought about her, the better I liked the Shorthorns' gentle way.

Whistling softly, I rode into the barn and Willie knew from the way I whistled something was wrong. I finally began to tell Willie about the rumors, the missing gold, and the cave disappearing. "It just disappeared off the face of the earth," I told him.

Willie was a great tracker and thinking deeply on the subject, he suggested, "Mr. Bill, why don't us'ns rides back up thata way and lets me help you look for that there missin' cave."

I missed the blue stud. I'd had Willie geld the two gray studs he wanted to keep. I was just hard to please after riding the big gray Thoroughbred. I was never one to keep "pretty good" breeding stock, and after having the Kentucky Thoroughbred around, a mediocre stud wasn't going to work. Hell, a stud was half your herd. I'd done this with my cattle, buying every Shorthorn bull I could find to run on my Longhorn and milk cow stock. This had really paid off. Willie and I had kept every crossbred heifer and had improved my herd using the Shorthorn bulls, plus the steers were quick to gain and mature.

Dawn found Willie and me on those two gray geldings riding out toward White Rock Creek. The Bosque River flowed from the west and the Brazos flowed from the northwest. I used my dun gelding as a pack horse to carry our supplies. I'd spent part of last night in Ginny's bed, but rode out to the ranch just before dawn so we could get an early start. I decided to take Bates and Ginny's advice about getting out of town for a while and letting things settle down. Ginny was in my thoughts as I rode slowly through the tall prairie grass and crossed Childress Creek. Women had always just been a convenience for me. Someone to cook and clean, romance or dance with, but never anything more. Ginny was crowding my thoughts.

Taking stock of the little gray gelding I was riding, he was not as big as his sire, but really quick and alert. He was not as flighty as he was before we cut him. Likewise the other gray that Willie rode had become more settled and sure suited Willie. He was heavier than Old Blue, maybe not as quick, but had a lot of bone and stamina and all heart. These are the kind of horses I wanted to raise. I thought about the blue stud the Indians had stolen. Damn, I hated to loose him!

The sun was getting low as Willie and I rode off into the Brazos bottom. Once again the buffalo trail showed no use except for small game and deer. Those damn buffalo hunters were killing them all. "Pretty soon there won't be a buffalo in the country," I said, and again I pitied the plight of the Indians.

The Brazos was low and moving slowly south as it wound its way from West Texas to the Gulf of Mexico. Riding out into the current a ways, I stopped and let the horses drink. It had been a hot day for that late in the fall and the horses were tired and sweaty.

Looking off to the northwest, Willie studied the clouds that were building. He told me, "Mr. Bill, falls a'fixin to be here. I feels it in my bones." The squirrels that were busy gathering pecans and storing them in the hollows of the huge trees, seemed to agree.

The night was still hot as we fixed a small fire in the creek bed, but about four o'clock the next morning a strong wind blew in, scattering the coals from the fire and waking us both. Pushing the coals back together and building up the fire and making coffee, I filled Willie on the details of the landscape.

Dawn broke as we saddled our horses and moved up the creek. Things pretty much looked the same. Deke's old hat still hung in the tree branches where the flood had deposited it, large boulders still littered the floor of the creek, and the west bank was strewn with downed trees, that had been uprooted by the flood. Erosion had caused little gullies and washes in the new soft dirt. Again, nothing looked like it did the night of the flood. As we rode up the creek, no cave was visible. Riding up from the creek we canvassed the west bank from top to bottom. Evidently the sticks and debris carried by the flood had covered the small opening. Brush and weeds had evidently grown over the entrance. I was flustered and the cold dry wind had chapped our faces and hands as we prowled through the brush in search of the entrance.

Dark approached and the cold settled in. Wind blew, making it hard to light a fire. Moving up the creek, we made a new camp behind two of the large misplaced boulders. When these two had fallen they butted up against each other, and formed a crude "V." While Willie hustled wood and tended to the horses, I got a good fire going and our bedrolls spread. Out of the wind and with a good fire, I told Willie about the attack, and once more relived it in my mind.

I told him, "I really don't see how Private Deke Williams continued to fight with a huge hole blown in his back. While Badger and I ran for the cave he continued to cover us."

I got real quite for a minute and reminisced about the insulting remarks I'd made to Deke. After a few ashamed minutes, I told Willie, "When I first met Deke, I really did not want him along and told him I hoped that he had enough guts to stay and fight if we were attacked and not run like some yeller dog. I was dead wrong, and I hate that Deke died without me telling him so."

"What in the hell do you think was wrong with me? You're black, and damn Willie, I love you like family. Why did I hard ass this man? I guess it was just the damn redneck coming out in me!" I said.

Speaking softly, Willie said, "Mr. Bill, we alls' prejudiced 'bout sompin'. Red man don't like white man, and white man don't like black man, and the black man he done be suspicious of everybody. But the Bible say we all God's children, and someday gonna be peaceful toward everyone and I's searchin' fur dat day."

I laid back and contemplated what he'd said, before I drifted off to sleep. Willie checked the horses and then settled in his bedroll. The wind whistled down the creek and around the large rocks, scattering the coals of our fire before it.

The edge of the creek was covered by a thin layer of ice as Willie and I saddled our horses that next morning. My thoughts were running away. I had awakened thinking about Old Blue that morning, and couldn't help but worry about who had him and where.

Comanches were excellent horsemen and really liked good horses but the disappearing buffaloes were causing the Indians to resort to eating a lot of horses and dogs. I was confident that they weren't going to eat Old Blue, he was too valuable as a war horse, but if he got crippled or hurt, it might be a different story.

Making one last pass up the creek and across the top of the bluff, our breaths rose in steamy clouds, and I resigned myself to that fact that the cave had just disappeared.

Stopping quickly, I told Willie to change his saddle to the dun gelding and put the pack saddle on the big gray gelding he was riding. I had decided to drift awhile. Sending Willie back to the ranch, I swung north toward Fort Graham. I wanted to ride by and say thanks to Dr. Crawford for saving my leg and probably my life.

Comanche Peak lay north and west up the Brazos and I had decided to visit Bob Barnhart at his trading post near there. Bob had a good rapport with the Indians and he and his brother were old friends of mine. I had met the brothers when they had started out partners in a trading post near Waco. When Bob married a girl they had bought from the Comanches, he had moved up here and put in his own store. The Indians trusted him, and he was always fair with them. He was one of the few white men who gave them a fair price for their hides, a fair trade and wouldn't sell them whiskey. They brought hides and trade goods from as far as the Panhandle to trade with Bob.

Riding up to Fort Graham left me feeling hollow and empty in the pit of my stomach. For a minute all the hurt I had endured and the fear of dying and being crippled and one legged nearly overwhelmed me. I would always be beholden to Dr. Crawford. He had set with me day and night around the clock, checking the bandages every hour on the hour. My thoughts were interrupted by the soldier on patrol calling for me to halt and identify myself.

Private Joe Gear was on patrol at the fort's gate and was also the soldier that had driven me back to Waco. Shaking hands with Joe, I asked about Dr. Crawford and where he might be found. I rode through the compound and found the Doctor's quarters again. Mrs. Crawford soon was plying me with a huge bowl of stew and cornbread hot from the wood stove's oven. I expected their invitation to spend the night. They had sorta adopted me when I had been so sick and I nearly felt at home. The wind had been increasing all afternoon and sleet began to pepper down as I explained how much I appreciated all that Dr. Crawford had done for me. I also shared my regrets for the soldiers I had left in the cave. Describing their wounds and reactions to the doctor, he assured me that there was nothing he, nor I could have done to save them. Somehow this made me feel better and I shared my respect for Private Deke Williams and told him how Deke had covered us with his rifle fire while we entered the cave and him with a gaping hole in his back and a kidney blown away.

Dr. Crawford took notes as I talked, to forward to Washington for Deke's and Badger's military records. He also expressed his concern that it hadn't already been done. Sleet pounded on the roof as I slid into a deep sleep, the last night I'd spend in a bed for quite a while.

Chapter Seven

I bid Fort Graham goodbye and headed northwest for Glen Rose and Comanche Peak. Glen Rose was a small town about fifty miles from Fort Graham. Comanche Peak lay ten or twelve miles further west. I followed the Brazos to the Paluxy River and turned up the Puluxy toward Glen Rose. I reached Glen Rose in the middle of a cold, rain soaked night, found the livery stable but no one was around. A kerosene lantern had been left burning in the hall of the barn. Two stalls were empty so I stripped off the saddle and pack, dumped a heavy feeding of grain and hay and rubbed both horses' backs dry with hay as they ate. I was satisfied with the two geldings I'd raised. Fifty hard miles had been covered since dawn and they still had some left. They each showed a lot of the old stud's heart.

Going to the loft, I stripped off my wet clothes and boots, then wrapped my blanket around me, I burrowed up in my bedroll which I had placed on a soft stack of hay. I slept the night away as the winter storm howled. As usual, I awoke at dawn. The rain had stopped falling during the night, but dark clouds were rolling and the north wind cut like a knife. When I rolled out of my haystack, the horses nickered a greeting. After slipping on some dry clothes and pulling on my wet boots, I threw down some hay for the geldings and poured them another large measure of grain. The two grays looked hearty and strong after the hard ride last night and after checking their feet, I headed for the café. I wolfed down a steak and some eggs. A half a dozen cups of hot coffee was inhaled as I badgered the waitress for directions to Bob Barnhart's trading post.

God was stingy with the sun all day and the weather stayed cold and dreary. I stopped by the general store and did a little shopping. I bought another pair of boots, some socks and a couple pair of long handles. I also bought a couple extra blankets for my bedroll and a new tarp. A plan had been building in my mind and it looked like this might be a cold, hard winter for Bill Fowler. Stopping by the saloon, I played a few hands of poker and shopped for gossip about the Comanches, hoping someone might have seen one riding a gray stud. I just idled away the day and by late evening I folded my cards, bought a fifth of whiskey and headed for the stable. The cards hadn't been much more agreeable than the weather had been. I fed and watered the horses, rolled up in my new blankets, burrowed back in my hay bed and slept another cold winter night away.

Dawn broke cold but clear. The water in the buckets was frozen solid. After feeding and breaking the ice, I rubbed the gray geldings down then crossed the street to the café. Pulling out a chair at the first table, I greeted myself to the coffee pot and a big breakfast. I knew it might be a while before I got the chance again.

I stopped at the livery stable and paid my bill. The sun was just up and looked like it might work all day. I sure hoped so. My saddle and gear was still damp and could use some sun. Saddling my horses and readjusting my pack, I headed for Comanche Peak.

Shortly before noon I rode up to Barnhart's Trading Post. Stepping down and tying my geldings, I looked around and took note of what was going on. Spotting Barnhart, I went over and shook hands. Buffalo hides were stacked around in large stacks and a few Indians were present. To my disappointment none of them was riding the gray stud.

Our talk turned to Waco and when we'd first met. We talked about the trading post his brother had down there where the Tehuacana Creek ran into the Brazos. We remembered the big pow wows that were held there. Finally talk swung to the Comanches and I asked, "Bob, by chance have you seen a gray stud around these parts?"

I knew from the flickering in Bob's eyes he'd seen him. Bob knew and liked a good race horse, but he sorta skirted the question and after awhile, I asked it again.

"Damn Bill, you know I have a deep bond with the Indians and I don't meddle in their business," Bob said.

I agreed, but explained, "That gray stud was the one I was riding when attacked by the Comanches at White Rock Creek. Private Williams and Corporal Badger were escorting me and the Army's gold to Fort Graham. Both were killed by the Indians and our horses were stolen. The last I saw of him was one of the Indians riding him across the creek. I sure would like to get him back."

Bob got real quiet and didn't say anything for awhile. Finally he said, "Bill, I am going to do something I damn sure oughtn't to do. I for shore know the horse. They came through here with their hides the last two falls with him, and can this gray cuss run! They must have won a hundred horses each year off the other Indians, match racing him. I tried hard to buy him, but he can't be bought. Knowing you like I do, you're going after him and they'll kill you sure as hell you do!"

Bob ran out of breath and stopped talking, then finally said, "Running Bull, a Comanche, has him and you're a fool if you don't ride back to Waco and forget it. You ain't exactly afoot, from the looks of those two grays you rode in on."

I agreed, saying, "Yeah, those two are colts from the blue stud. Would really like to have some more by him, he's hard to beat as a stud."

With a pleading voice, Bob said, "Bill ride back to Waco, I like you. Running Bull is a powerful young chief with the Comanches and has led a lot of raids. His braves think the gray horse gives him a strong spirit and they will follow him through hell on that gray stud."

Never lowering my eyes, I asked him, "Where does Running Bull winter?"

This was the question Bob had been dreading. He knew then that when he answered, he was signing a death warrant for one of his friends. He knew I was going to have to kill Running Bull and probably others to get the gray back or I was going to be killed trying. Bob didn't know what to do. His white side won and turning away, said softly, "Palo Duro Canyon, the Copper Springs."

I knew the spot. I'd scouted for the Army up there and knew the canyon. Copper Springs was a great camp, nearly impossible to get into. There was one trail in and one trail out and a bottle basin with the best grass and water in the world. It was a horse heaven. The canyon walls protected from most of the weather and horses would stay fat all winter.

As I purchased some more supplies; salt, pepper, coffee, another skinning knife, and a couple of pairs of buckskin gloves and some wool scarves, I said, "Thanks for the information. Don't worry, but I aim to get my Old Blue stud back!" Mounting up, I headed due west and rode the afternoon away. Three hundred cold miles lay between me and there, and time was a'wastin'.

Snow flurries drifted across in front of me throughout the day. I'd switched horses that morning and was riding the larger gray. The ground was wet and sticky but the larger gray was making good time. I was riding real wary cause this was the heart of Comanche country, and by rotating the riding and packing, both horses stayed fresh in case I had to make a run for it. Riding the lower ridges, I was constantly scanning the country before me. I wasn't too worried unless I ran into a late hunting party because Indians were prone to winter camp until spring. Then the grass would get green and the horses fat and strong. Occasionally, you might run across a few braves making a late hunt and these were the one I was hoping to avoid.

The first night out of Glen Rose, I found an old dugout in a canyon that gave protection for the night. Cleaning out a rat's nest and one badly disturbed rattler, left me the sole proprietor. The rattler was about as cold and slow as I was and I killed him with a rock so as not to make any noise. I cautiously carried him outside and once again scanned the horizons.

After replacing the stove pipes, I built up a fire. Hobbling the horses and pouring a heaping measure of grain for both, I returned to the warmth of the dugout. For supper, I fried a little bacon and a potato, and was soon settled in for a quiet restful night.

When I woke, I could hear the prairie wind whistle over the dirt roof and down the old stovepipe. I checked my horses, making sure that all was well and fixed a quick breakfast. Switching to the smaller horse that day, we headed west. The sun had rose in a clear dry sky and the ground dried enough so the horses were hardly leaving a track. Again, I rode wary, keeping an eye peeled for any movement.

Seeing a movement off to my right, I pulled up short. Concealed by the thick brush that fanned out of the gully, I sat still and waited. The last thing I needed was to ride into a trap. The world seemed to stand still. Soon the shape of an old overloaded hide wagon came into view with buffalo hides stacked as high as you could stack them. The wagon was being escorted by three riders leading three over-burdened pack horses. The driver of the wagon whipped and cussed the four gaunt mules trying to get them moving faster. I was relieved it wasn't Indians, but wasn't thrilled to see any damn buffalo hunters. I was surprised that they had not stopped by Mobertie, the hide station for the plains, but decided they were eastbound for Comanche Peak and Bob Barnhart's Trading Post.

Thinking they might have seen Running Bull, I ambled out of the brush and rode toward the wagon. Easing my gun out of my holster and keeping it under my long coat was my first move. The closer I got the less I liked this deal. Four whiskered skinners made up the caravan and a scruffier bunch wouldn't be found.

Introducing myself, I learned Jed Blackwell and his sons Newt, Clem and Joe were heading for Barnhart's. They'd stayed out longer than usual trying to get a load. "Damn Indians have about killed them all," Jed complained.

I had to bite my tongue to keep from answering.

Trying to keep them all in my sights, I asked, "Have any of you seen Running Bull?"

They quickly agreed that he was at the springs. Newt stated, "We saw that stud and tried to get Running Bull drunk so we could steal him, but that damn Indian wouldn't fall fer it!"

"What I wouldn't do to get my hands on a hoss like that'n," said

Clem. All the while, they were eyeing my two gray horses and I couldn't wait to leave.

The stench from the hides and the hiders were too much for me and the two grays. I turned quickly and loped the horses till dark. I kept blowing my nose and the horses would snort trying to get the smell out of our nostrils.

I wished I'd stayed hidden because I didn't like the looks of this crew. Several times I stopped and listened, and twice I thought I could hear horses following me. I wished to hell I'd stayed hidden in the brush.

A ravine dropped off to my left and a thicket of mesquite trees covered the draw. Dry camping, I rolled out my tarp and blankets, pulled my rifle from my scabbard. With my extra blanket as a protection from the cold, I leaned back against a big mesquite. I knew Indians were not my biggest problem tonight. The Blackwells looked too long at my two gray horses for me to sleep much tonight. I dozed off as the full moon slowly moved across the sky.

The big gray's snort brought me full awake. Backed up against that big mesquite, I was invisible as something moved in the tall grass off to my left. The moon moved from behind the clouds illuminating the meadow. I squinted as the shadows moved and barely made out the form of a man about forty yards to the right. It looked like they were making for the horses. I knew I was a dead man if left afoot in Indian country in the dead of winter.

Slowly removing my blanket and looking around, I wished I had eyes in the back of my head. How many of these bastards had followed me? I knew two were here "a visitin," but what about the rest?

Trying to remember their looks, the two older boys were the ones that looked the most dangerous. Joe, the youngest, looked a little simple and Jed was too old to have ridden this hard. I knew either one would kill me for my horses. While still trying to pick up the movement to my left, I saw the smaller gelding's ears pick up. Making sure I could still see the one on my right, I slowly drew a bead on the one crawling up to Little Blue, as I'd taken to calling him.

The clouds moved as Newt Blackwell reached up to catch Little Blue and death came a 'callin'. My rifle roared in the still night and the side of Newt's head exploded. A scream split the night and Clem flattened out in the grass and began firing at the flash of my gun. As I fired I had rolled, knowing the flash would point to my hiding place. Taking shelter behind a large sandstone rock, the deadly game of wait began.

The geldings had lunged down the canyon a ways, when I fired at Newt. Now I was almost between Clem and the horses, but Clem had the higher advantage. Time stood still. I pulled my handkerchief over my nose so the frost from my breath didn't give me away. When the clouds moved, the moon was nearly like day. The wind started to blow and this made the tall grass sway and daylight seemed a long way off. The sky began to turn pink and my nerves were drawn tight. If a fight was going to happen, it would be soon.

If Clem was where I thought he was, it was going to be like shooting a duck in a rain barrel when the sun came up. If he'd been able to move when the wind came up, he could be behind me and this sandstone was too low to give me to cover to turn and look.

Studying the horses, I watched for any movement from them. If he didn't flush, I knew my number might be called. I'd seen what a buffalo hunter could do with those big guns from a mile away. I knew I had to kill Clem in the next few minutes or these gray geldings were fixin' to change owners.

Big Blue quivered and cocked his head ever so slightly and I followed the glance. My blood ran cold. The muzzle of that big buffalo gun was barely visible through the grass as Clem waited for a little more light to find his target in the shadows of the rock and trees.

Squinting down the barrel of my rifle, a cold sweat drenched me and the wind stilled, and dawn approached. Light glistened on the frosty ground around me. We both knew we had one chance. A checker game for life.

The horses grazing sounded like cannons booming. Time crawled. Suddenly Clem's rifle barrel wiggled as he reached to pull the trigger. My finger squeezed three times in rapid succession. Clem rose about two feet like a puppet as the first bullet caught him in the throat. Clutching his throat, he half raised himself, but the next shot hit him dead between the eyes and Hell's population was increased by two this night.

Daylight found Jed and Joe dry camped in the thicket, I had first spotted them from. After they had decided to steal my horses, they had hurriedly unhooked the mules and hobbled them loose to graze. Jed and Joe had jerked a tarp down from the side of the wagon and made a crude tent, then had talked most of the night about the two gray geldings. Jed was going to take his pick and the boys could fight over the other one. Newt and Clem had left almost immediately to follow me.

As time drug on, Jed began to worry. "Shore isn't like the boys to take this much time to kill one fella and steal two horses," he said to Joe, "but that Bill Fowler's a pretty cagey fella," as he recalled how I had kept all four of them in front of me at all times the day before.

He told Joe, "That fella had a pistol under his coat and had us covered the whole time. I should have shot him in the back as he turned and rode off, but he rode through the trees so fast, didn't have time to get my long gun ready. My eyes are too bad to see the sights on a little gun."

Jed had woke around four. He thought he heard the report of a shot, but when nothing else stirred, he drifted back to sleep. Around six, again he thought he heard another shot. He couldn't imagine the boys taking a second shot.

The sun had been up a couple of hours when Jed had started to pace back and forth. "What in the hell could take the boys this long to kill one cowboy and steal two horses? Maybe we ought to ride after them," he told Joe.

He hated to saddle up and ride. His rheumatism had been acting up something fierce since it had gotten cold, but Joe was so simple, he couldn't be trusted to go by himself. He might ride right into at trap by hisself. There was something in Joe's head that had never been right, probably from his birthin'.

His maw birthed him while Jed and the boys had been away on a hunt and both must have had a lot of trouble, because when they got back, she was dead. Joe was just a layin' there in all that mess, all bloody and dried and cold. Jed thought Joe was dead, but soaked him in warm water until he came around. Jed had ridden over to an Indian village and traded for a wet squaw to raise him. Joe had always been a little off. Why when he was twelve or thirteen had had got mad and killed that squaw that had mammied him. It didn't matter that she had cost two horses. Then he'd cut off her tits and made tobacco pouches out of them.

"Hell, I can't depend on Joe to finish this job," Jed thought, I'd better go myself or at least go with him."

Saddling their horses and a mule, they set out a following the tracks left by Clem and Newt the evening before. The tracks were fresh and last nights frost had filled them making it easy to follow.

That same sun rose over my camp a half a day's ride west. I studied the two corpses for a long time before rising and taking a closer look. I'd seen too many dead men "play possum" and shoot their attacker when he was careless. Satisfied they were both dead, I stood up slowly and scanned the scene. Clem was shot through the throat and between the eyes and Newt had died from one shot to the head. What about the other two? Should I go finish this or just ride on west? These shots were enough to draw every Indian in the country. If I left that old man and dim-witted boy alive, it would be like leaving a wounded snake. They might strike without warning.

Glancing at the sky, a "blue norther" was rolling in from the northwest. The sun that had come up right had started to back off and the temperature was already beginning to drop. Not taking time to bury these scabs, I saddled up and headed into the wind. I needed to cover as much ground as possible before the storm hit.

I rode hard and covered forty of fifty miles of tough cold prairie and feeling like a chunk of ice, I finally took cover as dark approached. A gully cut across my path about twenty feet wide. The banks were straight up and I decided this would give me some shelter from the wind. Riding down wind, the gully finally flattened out enough to enter. Entering the gully, I rode to the head of the draw where it dropped out of a cropping of rocks. It was a straight fall of six or seven feet from the top and eight or ten feet wide. This would give me plenty of protection and give room for the horses.

Unwinding my tarp and taking my shovel, I crawled back up to the prairie floor. The wind was cutting through me like a knife. I staked the tarp across the narrow gully, leaving enough room for a horse to get through. I weighed it down with large rocks and clods dug from the frozen prairie. Snow had started to fall as I finished packing the rock and the frozen dirt around the edge of the tarp.

A small spring flowed out of one corner of the rock dropoff and I was satisfied with my new storm shelter. Hurriedly I rode into the shelter of trees, fastened my rope around a dead tree the wind had blown down and drug it behind Big Blue, back up the draw to camp.

The temperature had been dropping all day and large snowflakes and heavy sleet had set in like it was here to stay. Night settled around me as I chopped wood and got a fire started. With hands stiff from the cold, I unsaddled and hobbled the geldings. Strangely, below ground level the storm seemed a long ways from here. The gully was out of the wind and camp was snug with the heat reflecting off the rocks. Unpacking my gear, I rolled out my other tarp. I spread my new blankets on top of my regular bedroll. Night was just beginning and I knew this was going to be a long cold spell. I'd laid in a good supply of food at Bob's Trading Post and Glen Rose, so food was no problem. Measuring out a couple of feedings of oats from my supply, I fed and took care of the horses as night set in.

The small spring pooled just below the crude shelter and the horses drank good and long before it froze. I made coffee and built up a good fire. With the tarp over the top and out of the wind, I felt blessed for this lodging tonight, as the storm set in with vengeance.

The cold woke me a couple of times as the fire burned down and the storm raged on. Snow was falling so thick I could barely see the horses. They had turned their tails to the snow and out of the wind, stood on three legs with the fourth cocked up and slept the winter night away.

Dawn broke begrudgingly. Like me, it didn't want to start the day. Cold dark clouds were rolling and the snow continued to fall. Snow had started to drift and I was more than thankful for my crude little camp. Given the weather I decided to remain in camp until it improved.

As night fell it got deathly quiet as the temperature plummeted. I doled out a feeding of oats and broke the ice on the little pond. I was again thankful for the little warm spring that kept bubbling out of the rocks.

The faraway howling of wolves woke me during the night. Rolling over quickly, I checked the horses and then dropped back off to sleep. I had nightmares and woke up thrashing with all the covers off. The Blackwells had been standing over me without their bullet wounds leering at me as the wolves were killing my geldings. I built up the fire and lay awake a long time trying to recall the dream, but shuddering at its reality.

Snow was still falling when I awoke shortly after dawn. It was barely light and the cold was overwhelming. My tree had about disappeared as I had kept the fire roaring. Saddling Big Blue, I started out toward the wooded creek again to lay in a supply of wood. Two feet of snow was frozen solid in the gully, but as I climbed out on the prairie, drifts lay horse high. Traveling was slow and time consuming, but I dragged up a couple of windblown trees and again broke the ice on my horses' pond. I rolled back into bed and the next couple of days where spent tending fire, feeding the horses and sleeping.

The morning was nearly gone when a flurry of wings startled the horses and a covey of prairie chicken flew in and landed where the horses had been eating grain.

Seeing a chance for a change in rations, I drew my pistol and killed two. I had them for lunch and supper. "Boy, you don't know how much fried prairie chicken beats fried salt pork!" I thought to myself. I fried them a golden brown and nearly forgot I was snowbound and a long way from home.

Night settled in once again and the quite darkness was shattered by the fighting of coyotes on the bank above my head. I had dressed the birds and just thrown the guts and feathers up on the bank. The snow drifts were making it hard for wildlife to travel and everything was getting hungry. The lobo wolves I'd heard for the last few nights were getting closer and I was glad I had my horses in the gully with me, close at hand.

Lobos were a dangerous situation when the snow got this deep. Cunning and smart, they would work horses or buffalo into a drift and when they mired down, would all attack at once. It always amazed me how they worked as a team. One would attack the head, another would cut the hamstring while another one would grab the throat, and maybe another would get the soft underbelly, ripping out the gut. I kinda shuttered as the mystery of the night was renewed by the howl of a wolf and not very far away.

Checking my rifle, I built up the fire and rolled back into my blankets. The horses moving restlessly about woke me up. The horses had backed up nearly under my tarp and knowing this to be unusual, I got up and threw more wood on the fire. As the firelight reflected off the snow, green eyes materialized out of the darkness.

Wolves had lined up on both sides of the gully and were waiting for a chance at the horses. I sat quietly studying the dilemma. I hated to start shooting, cause a rifle shot travels for miles in crisp cold air. Wolves weren't the only thing going to be looking for food, and I sure didn't want to arouse any Indians. The fire discouraged the wolves and they drifted back into the darkness.

The next day was pretty much like the others, except the snow had stopped falling and the world had frozen solid. I dragged up some more wood and led my horses out of the gully and hobbled them. I hobbled their back legs but left their front legs free to paw down through the snow to the prairie grass below. They were soon getting a bellyfull of grass that had cured like hay.

I took my shovel and climbed up the bank and began to shovel snow to help them get to the grass. I was grateful for the feed because my oats were running low. It felt good to be active after being "housebound" for four or five days.

The day stayed awfully cold, but no more snow fell and the wind had died down. I glanced up from shoveling to see the lobos off to the south a couple of hundred yards. I was surprised because what I thought was a large pack of wolves proved to be two smaller packs and one pack had drifted into the stand of trees where I'd been getting my wood. This explained why they had been lined up on both sides of the gully last night.

On closer inspection, the wolves were thin. The declining buffalo had taken its toll on them as well as the Indians. For several years, the lobo population had exploded on the plains feasting on the buffalo carcasses left by the buffalo hunters. Wolves got so fat and lazy they wouldn't even run when you rode upon them. With their advance in numbers and the dwindling supply of buffalo, they had started to switch to horses and cattle, the trail drivers were bringing into the Panhandle of Texas.

I had learned a lot about the wolves from the Indians while scouting for the Army. There was a pecking order. One wolf reigned supreme over the others and they all bowed down to him, then a number two, three and etc. Like people, after the first two or three, the others are mostly followers.

I figured tonight would be a blending of the two packs together and a lot of fighting would take place. I was worried about the horses as I moved them back down to the camp in the gully.

Knowing the ways of the wolves, I figured if they went together before assaulting the horses, it would be better, cause they'd kill each other fighting for positions in the new pack.

A wolf fight was vicious to watch. They would circle around the fighters and if one went down or was gutted or hurt, the wolf pack would jump on him and finish him off. No loyalty among wolves, thieves and buffalo hunters, I had often heard.

Just before dark the two wolf tribes stalked toward each other, eight in one bunch and ten in the other. Two in the last pack were just big old pups and didn't count for much. A big rawboned dog wolf from each pack walked stiffly toward the other and as their noses touched, the fight was on. Circling the action, the wolves cut off most of my view, but the fighting kept me awake most of the night.

The sun shone on five patches of bloody snow the next morning when I led my horses back to feed on the prairie grass. Bits of fur and bone were all that was left and about noon the integrated pack drifted out of the woods under a new leader. Thirteen now made up the new pack and with their appetites whetted by their own viciousness, I felt like this would be a long night.

The moon was full and the night was cloudless. A strange half-light fell over the prairie as I brought the horses back into the gully and tethered them to the downed tree. As Big Blue's snorts roused me from a half-sleep, I saw eyes in the darkness. This time the wolves were creeping up the gully for a surprise attack.

Shielded by the log I'd dragged up, I belly crawled to the log. Not wanting to be blinded by the fire, I kept my eyes on the same level as the wolves. I had the advantage. The fire was to my back and the wolves were looking into it, but as bright as the moon was reflecting off the snow, this wasn't much advantage. There was a grown wolf and a big pup on either bank that would attack from the top if the horses bunched against the bank. Nine grown wolves were positioned for the attack. I squinted as the lead wolf crept forward with two more close behind. Leveling my rifle, I squeezed the trigger and death leaped from the rifle barrel. Firing rapidly, I took out the first three wolves in succession. Wheeling and firing, I killed the wolf crouched to leap from the bank, then turning to my right, fired point blank as the grown wolf on the right bank leaped for Little Blue's throat. Collapsing in midair, the wolf gasped for air. The only sound in the stark clear night was the other wolves slinking back down the gully.

An uneasy day had began. I was afraid the rifle shots might have carried in the cold night air and draw unwanted attention. The snow had really begun to melt and I was a fixin' to get flooded out anyway so I began the task of breaking camp. I couldn't decide whether to leave my tarp or not, it would throw me a tarp short, but I had a ready made camp this way. Leaving the tarp intact, I packed everything else on my little horse and saddling Big Blue, rode off toward the west. I wasn't more than a two or three day ride from Palo Duro Canyon but I hated to leave this shelter. I would have probably frozen to death this week without it. This way I had a place to come back to if another blizzard struck. This one had 'bout played out.

I rode until dark, ever west and a little north toward Palo Duro Canyon. The snow had mostly melted and had been replaced by mud. I was leaving a lot of tracks, but rode the draws and breaks where they were less likely to be seen. A blow out in a sand hill loomed ahead in the gathering dusk. Nature made these when a wind current would flow around a sand hill a certain way. It was kinda like a sand cave with a shallow pocket three or four feet deep. I decided to den up in it.

The day had been clear but cold and as night approached the temperature fell rapidly. I unsaddled my horses and hobbled them to let them graze. I'd watered them a little before dark at the last creek I'd crossed. Gathering buffalo chips, I managed to get a small soggy fire going. The chips were damp from the snow but it didn't take much fire to heat the little cave and even though it was a dry camp, it wasn't too bad. I rolled out my bedroll in the back of the overhang and grabbed a piece of jerky. The little camp was protected from ol' man winter's wind as I snuggled in for a cold supper. I missed my little tarp house, but was glad to be riding again.

I rode the next two days kinda aimlessly looking for landmarks. You could ride off the bluff in the Palo Duro Canyon before you saw it. The bottom just dropped out of the world for two or three hundred feet and another world was down below. Palo Duro Canyon was a long time Comanche wintering ground, the buffalo and wild game wintered there too, but getting in or out was problem for everything else but eagles. Mentally reviewing all the details from my scouting trips though, I searched for a plan.

Chapter 8

Jed and Joe Blackwell followed the tracks from the boys' horses. About midmorning the roan horse Newt had been riding, was grazing off to thc wcst of my camp, with his reins a'draggin'. Old Jed got a real uneasy feeling, and said, "Thangs ain't good. Them boys ain't killed that bastard yet, and Newt's a foot."

Topping a small rise and leading Newt's horse, there was a lot more than Jed had imagined. His cold fury at the boys for taking so long, turned to disbelief when he rode upon Newt and Clem's corpses. "Damn," he wondered, "how did he kill hem both."

Cussing, Jeb told Joe to load Newt and Clem on their horses and they'd bury them when they stopped for supper. "We've already lost a half a day," he muttered to himself. Half to himself, Jed began to lament his situation. "Here I am an old tired man with an idiot son, who don't know how to do nothing but hunt buffaloes and shoot Indians and the damn world was running out of both of them."

Suddenly he started cussing, "If that damn cowboy hadn't been ridin' those two blue horses and acting so cocky, the boys would still be alive. It's all that cowboy's fault!" he concluded. He mumbled, "To hell with it! I had a powerful hankering for one of those blue horses myself." He'd wanted one ever since he'd seen that damn Indian win all those races on one, last fall.

Dusk fell as Joe finished burying his brothers in a joint grave. He hurried with the chore. He didn't dig the grave very deep and he knew Jed would raise hell if he saw how shallow it was. He wasn't sad about his brothers. They had made life miserable for him and gave him the dirty jobs. He was excited to know they would be at Barnhart's Trading Post tomorrow. He liked the trinkets Bob kept for the Indians and he liked whiskey when he could get it. "With the boys gone, maybe Paw will give me their share," he thought.

Jed was despondent over losing the boys. Both were excellent shots, skinners and strong as mules. He didn't know how he could get by without them. "Hell, I'm just barely getting by as it is," he concluded. "The next time I see that damn Bill Fowler, he's a dead man." He vowed then and there, "I'll kill that damn cocky cowboy, if it was the last thing I ever do. Dirty murdering bastard," he whined, "kill a man's son with no thought of their poor old daddy."

Copper Springs was the most prolific of the springs that flowed through the canyon. Situated in the middle of the canyon table, level grasslands stretched for miles and timber and game was abundant. The steep rocky walls protected the floor of the canyon from a lot of the snow and fury of the Panhandles blizzards.

A stand of brush overlooked the canyon and I nestled in the tangled branches with my spy glass extended its full length. Making sure the sun was full behind my back I scanned the canyon for Indian sign. The past three mornings were spent carefully scanning the area. I had tethered my horses in a grove of trees back away from the rim and I traveled afoot as I scouted the canyon. I could only use the looking glass from daylight to noon or the sun would reflect off the glass in the afternoon and signal every Indian for miles. Luckily, the moon had been full, so I had been sleeping in the afternoons and prowled all night. I usually went back and made camp about noon each day. I was nearly Indian myself and I painstakingly plotted my course.

Sleeping was nearly impossible in the bitter cold but I couldn't chance a fire. I lived on jerky for a week and one night after running out I ate cold, raw salt pork. Time was getting to be the key. I'd packed enough for two or three weeks but the blizzard had delayed me a week. My food was getting low and I was about out of grain. This weather was taking its toll on the horses. I was keeping them tied in the trees all day and just grazing a little on dark nights.

Moving cold camp every night was getting to be old hat, but the next morning's dawning brought results. I had located the Indian camp directly below me, but there was a granite bluff straight down as far as I could see with my binoculars. I studied the camp all morning through my glass. I spotted my Old Blue. He was tethered by a front leg in front of the largest conic in the compound. The gray stud was allowed to graze on about a thirty foot rawhide rope while the other horses grazed loose and mingled back and forth. I was afraid they might have gelded him but a mare walked by and he squalled and pranced up to her showing evidence they hadn't.

Breathing a sigh of relief, I sat back to think. My mind began to work overtime. There had to be an opening which they would be guarding it full time, twenty four hours a day. Carefully using the spy glass, I watched an Indian slowly ride up the ridge on a little paint horse. Just as he reached the rim, he turned and abruptly disappeared. Maybe I had found the opening. Suddenly an Indian on a black horse appeared at the rim and rode slowly down the grade. Just before dark the Indian on the black horse rode back up the trail and shortly the paint horse came back to camp with the other Indian. I had found the opening.

The dogs were going to be the problem. This camp, like all Indian camps, had a large pack of dogs. A great big pack hung around the village and roamed at will. Half wild, they roamed like wolves and hunted for most of their food. Taking mental notes, I saw them move off late that afternoon toward the south of the meadow and as I watched through the night, I heard them baying miles away as they jumped a deer and ran him until they killed it. After gorging, they returned to camp about midnight.

I watered the horses a little before dawn and crawled into a thicket of brush and holed up for a few hours sleep. Rising with the sun I noticed that the dogs were all laying around camp, tired from their hard night of hunting. Old Blue had been moved a short distance to fresh grass and the Indian guards once again changed shifts. I spent the next four or five days and nights watching the same behavior pattern. The guards changed at sunup and sundown. Dogs left to hunt about dark and came back at midnight. The

Indian fires burned down about nine o'clock and the village got quiet. It took about thirty minutes for the guards to get up and thirty minutes to get down from the guard station. About an hour before the dogs came back the chief would step outside his conic and check on the stud.

My timing had to be perfect. I couldn't go down before the fires burned down around nine, and if I gave them an hour to get to sleep, that made it ten. It would take about thirty minutes each way to make the trip. The Indian always appeared about eleven and checked the stud. The dogs came back about twelve. This only left a few minutes to do the job.

The next night I took a bedroll and some of the last of the jerky I'd been hoarding and set out afoot. Again the dogs left about dark in a pack and returned about midnight as if cue. Doubts began to assault my mind. What if I couldn't find my way up and down the trail in the dark? Or got cut off and couldn't get out of the canyon. Bob Barnhart's warning came creeping back in my mind, "that Running Bull or me one was going to die if I went after the stud. Damn, Running Bull looked like the safest bet," I thought.

I knew from past trips how narrow gorges cut through the floor of the canyon making crossing impossible. If I got cut off from the entrance, I was trapped in a Comanche camp. A personal insult was taken by just entering and no one knew more about cruel ways to die than I did after scouting where the Comanche had raided. "Hell, I'd come too far to back out now but, I had to make my move, I was about out of grub and horse feed," I decided.

Walking softly along the rim, I found the opening to the canyon. It was a game trail that led through a maze of large boulders. There was a narrow opening, one horse wide between the boulders. The boulders had formed a little nest in the jumble of rocks and nestled in the nest was the Indian guard. Only his head and shoulders were visible as I viewed the natural fort.

"How in the hell was I going to get the guard out of his nest without firing a shot or getting myself killed?" I asked myself.

I had a plan if I could get by the guard, but it meant sacrificing one of my gray horses. I had a few minutes from the time the camp went to sleep till the Indian chief came out to check the stud. If I could ride the big gelding up beside Old Blue without the stud squealing, I could change horses. I would have to untie the stud and tie Big Blue to the stake and ride out, and hopefully, no one should notice till morning. This would give me a five hour start and I knew they couldn't catch me on the stud. Getting back to the horses before dawn, I watered them and gave them a small feeding of precious grain. I was just about out. Shaving off some of the last of the frozen jerky and washing it down with cold water, I settled into a deep soggy sleep, as it began a cold drizzle rain.

I awoke that evening about five o'clock from the cold. The temperature was dropping and the rain turned to sleet. "Damn, I'd picked a bad night for my rendezvous," I swore.

I decided to sacrifice Big Blue. The little horse was a lot faster and escape was going to depend on speed. I sure hated to lose the big gelding, but I'd have given fifty like him for the stud. Packing everything on the little gray gelding, I led him back into the brush. Leaving my saddle and blankets, I jumped on Big Blue bareback and rode off into the cold sleet. I knew my big trouble would come from my white man's smell. The horses could smell me, the dogs would smell me and even the Indians could smell me.

I had slipped a piece of lye soap in my pocket and when we got to the little creek, I slipped off Big Blue and peeled off my clothes. Before I could change my mind I dove in the icy creek and started lathering my hair and whiskers. Bathing quickly and rinsing all the soap from my hair and beard, I rode naked back to camp. I scooped up the fresh horse manure where the horses had been tied and crushed it in my hair and beard, rubbing it all my body as the wind and sleet turned my skin blue.

I brought my lariat rope with me and if everything went as planned, I'd be riding Old Blue in an hour or so. If it didn't, this was my last ride. Life was a gamble everyday, but today, the pot was awfully big. I'd left my guns behind, stuck in the pack. I had a big skinning knife with the blade turned backwards in my teeth and was butt naked. Worried about the guard in his little fort, I tied Big Blue a ways back and started creeping along in the dark, watching for the opening. Stopping quickly, I smelled smoke. My body was craving heat and I nearly ran toward the smell. I'd been naked for nearly an hour by now and was soaking wet for part of that. Creeping up in the boulders, I stood for a few minutes to let my eyes adjust. It was a couple of hours after dark and the night was turning worse. A wind had gotten up and the sleet was turning to small ice pellets, nearly like hail. I spotted a small fire at the base of the boulder. The Indian had forsaken his eagle's nest and had built a small fire and had piled buffalo hides around him. With the boulder blocking the wind, the fire casting off heat, he had succumbed to sleep's charm and was snoring loudly.

Moving deftly, I pitched a loop of the rope around his neck and twisting it from behind slowly choked the guard to death. He never knew what caught him. Stripping off his clothes and wrapping him in a buffalo robe, I set him back up as if still on duty. I quickly pulled on the Indians clothes, moccasins and leggings. As "ripe" as they smelled, I've never had a suit of clothes that felt that good. I knew now I'd smell "horse and Indian." I had to fight myself to leave the fire, I was frozen. But striking a brisk walk, I headed back for Big Blue. He didn't like the Indians smell from my new wardrobe and was a little hard to mount. But after a few minutes he was all right.

After retrieving Big Blue, I stopped by the rock fort and traded my bridle for the war bridle on the Indian's little black horse. You could ride him with a string if you needed to. Remounting, I started gingerly down the trail in the dark for the blue stud or death.

The trail was slick but clear and easy to follow. The rocks were frozen to the ground, so none was rolling down the trail. As I approached the village, the night was shattered by a big brown gyp dog's growl. I froze and my heart nearly quit beating. "Damn, I thought I had the dogs figured out."

The clouds parted and I could see the gyp had pups under the base of a down tree, this was why she was in camp. Barely breathing I held my breath as she sniffed around the horse and stalked back to her pups. No more dogs showed. I had made better time than I thought. I was early and the Indian hadn't been to check on the stud yet.

Undecided, I sat there a minute and scanned the village. I got worried about the dogs coming back and decided to chance it. I had about two hundred yards of open field to cross and a dozen conics to ride by to get to the stud. He was standing with one foot cocked up with his butt to the wind and his head down in the storm.

I watched for a while and saw him shift his weight from one foot to the other. I was afraid he might be asleep and would lunge or squeal when I rode up on a strange horse. Riding "Indian" I rode slowly toward Old Blue, leaning under my horse's neck with just one leg over his back. At first glance I looked liked a loose horse and nothing unusual about this in an Indian camp. Riding slowly up to Old Blue, and barely breathing, I slipped off Big Blue and kneeling down, untied the foot tether on Old Blue. I quickly fastened it on the big gray gelding and changed the war bridle.

Old Blue never moved as I fastened the bridle and eased up on his back. I squeezed him with my knees and moved quietly for the trail up the canyon rim. I fought my impulse to run. Everything was picture perfect but I was out of time. The dogs would be back any minute and the Indian was overdue.

Big Blue began to graze as I looked back. My heart quit beating as I got back to the gyp and pups. She was watching me like a hawk but never moved. The flap on the chief conic swung open and Running Bull stepped out into the freezing rain. Big Blue was grazing not thirty feet from the conic while the Indian relieved himself. Satisfied the horse was okay, he disappeared back into the warmth of his conic. I froze while all of this transpired.

As Old Blue inched his way up the trail, I was tempted to hurry as the weather worsened and snow began to fall in huge flakes. But one rolling rock or a horse slipping would bring a whole village on the run. The trail was frozen slick, but Old Blue just tippy-toed along. As the trail would up, I could see the sleeping village in the valley below and felt like I was dreaming one of my nightmares again. The big blue gelding looked just like his sire from this height, as he grazed on the ice covered grass below.

In the moonlight I could see the dogs returning to the village and I began to tremble. I don't know if it was the cold or the narrow escape. I began to worry about the dead Indian and wondered if I had really killed him and what would happen if he had came to while I was gone. Everything had worked perfect up to now.

Riding by the dead Indian I untied the black horse and led him back to my camp. I didn't want him to break loose and set off an early alarm. Tying the black horse, I led Little Blue out of the thicket and tightened the pack. Grabbing my blankets and saddling Old Blue, I knew a long night was in store for me and the horses. Swinging aboard, we began our long ride.

According to the dogs it was about midnight. They had just returned, so if the sun came up by six-thirty or seven, I had me a six-and-a-half hour start, and if the dead Indian or blue gelding wasn't discovered for a while, I could use the extra time.

The weather began to worsen. Snow set in with earnest. Hitting a long trot, I headed southeast. The night rolled away as I held the horses to a ground eating trot. I was fighting my instinct to flee. I wanted to lope all night, but I knew how easy it was to burn their lungs. Sucking huge drafts of freezing air into the lungs can frostbite the lungs and kill a horse in a hurry. Pacing myself and the horses, miles rolled away.

Day came and the weather worsened again. Snow was falling thicker. I couldn't have planned it better. The snow was covering my tracks, and the gray horses blended into their winter landscape making them nearly invisible.

Morning gave way to evening and the horses were beginning to tire. Chilled through and through, I was heading for my little tarp house I'd left in the gully. I would be out of the wind, and out of sight in the gully. Me and the horses all needed to rest.

Night approached and I passed a boulder I recognized and knew we were about two hours from my little house. Pushing Old Blue we forged on. The snow was beginning to drift and Little Blue was beginning to lag on the lead rope. He'd been toting a big pack all day and Old Blue had set the pace.

I spotted the gully ahead and quickly rode down into it and up to the shelter. I stopped and surveyed the trail behind me and was satisfied that the snow had wiped out all our tracks. Unsaddling Old Blue and the gelding, I hobbled them and measured out a generous amount of oats from my dwindling supply. Rubbing snow into their steaming backs, I knew I'd asked a lot from my horses this last twenty hours. I had covered a hundred miles or more in freezing weather.

The storm was still raging when the day reluctantly began. I built a fire in the covered gully and walked off to the woods to check for smoke. The wind was blowing hard from the north and no smell could be detected. The snow hid the smoke, so feeling comfortable, I broke the small pool of ice and let the horses drink. Then doling out the shrinking sack of oats, I fed the horses and rolled back in my bedroll and slept the day away.

A huge full moon rose as the last snowdrops fell. Me and the horses were all rested and restless, so packing my little blue gelding and saddling the stud, I rode out of my camp, with red hair and blue eyes on my mind, and a long way to think about her. The snow had frozen hard and we hit that ground eating trot, and miles of frozen prairie flashed past in the moonlight. Old Blue hadn't changed in the last two years he'd been gone. Never before or since have I rode a horse that compared with him.

Chapter 9

Running Bull walked to the flap of his conic and stepped out into the frigid north wind. The sleet stung his face as he relieved his bladder. Windsong, his war horse, stood humped up against the wind. Running Bull thought fondly of the two summers he had been riding Windsong. He could nearly feel the wind in his face as he raced the other tribes for horses and he recalled the large herd he had won that was grazing in the canyon.

Many would foal this spring from Windsong's loins and thirty of his best mares had yearlings on them now and all of them silver. He had also killed many buffalo and stolen horses from the settlers on him. He had counted coup on his enemies the Cheyenne to the north and the Apache to the west and ran off and left them in the dust. He'd gotten him down on the Brazos in a storm when they had done battle with the dog soldiers. Many braves and white men had tried to buy him, but he was a gift from the Rain Spirit and had great medicine.

Crawling back into his buffalo robe, Running Bull went back to sleep and dreamed of buffalo that came for miles and Running Bull was leading them back to the plains on Windsong. Running Bull was awakened by his squaw building up the fire and frying corn patties. He decided to water Windsong and move his grazing stake. He was angry with the sun. It had been lazy and hadn't woke him up. It was dark and snowing and half the morning was gone.

Walking up to Windsong he noticed he seemed darker but he was wet and he reached out to touch him. Big Blue smelled the Indian and snorted, and turned to kick at him. Running Bull screamed in anger when he saw someone had switched horses and Windsong was gone.

A paint gelding was coming gingerly down the mountain as Running Bull was bellowing questions. Two Feathers was bringing great sorrow, for Dashing Horse, Running Bull's brother, was dead. Running Bull's horses were not strong because the grass was weak, but taking his best braves and fastest horses he set out to follow Windsong. But the bitter cold made travel nearly impossible.

By the time they reached the pass, snow was drifting. Ten hours had elapsed since the switch and a foot of snow had fallen. No one could see over a hundred yards and drifts were getting deep. Running Bull turned back for home as dark approached. His horses were weak and tired and his braves had nearly frozen in the storm.

Running Bull reflected that Windsong had gone like he came, in a storm. Much mourning and grieving was in progress as the Indians rode slowly into camp. Whoever had stolen Windsong had killed Dashing Horse and Running Bull swore to the Great Spirit to avenge both losses.

I rode long cold days as the weather cleared and spent lots of time looking back over my shoulder. I rode the draws and low places, constantly on the alert for Indian sign. I stayed off the ridges and high places, where I might be seen and steadily traveled southeast. The weather faired a little and the days weren't that bad, but the nights were still cold. Now knowing how far the Indians were behind me, I pushed hard.

Winding around like I did, a week crept by before I rode up into Comanche Peak and Bob Barnhart's Trading Post. Bob met me at the door and was genuinely glad to see me. Seeing the gray stud, he asked, "Where did you find him?"

I replied, "Exactly where you told me he would be."

"How is Running Bull?" he asked.

"Running Bull is alive and well, I was able to sneak in and switch Big Blue for my stud without anyone catching me," I told him.

Bob seemed relived to hear that I hadn't had to kill Running Bull. He was a favorite of Bob's.

Filling my plate for the third time, Bob relayed the story of the

Blackwell's and how they had vowed to kill me on sight. The food was the best I'd ever eaten as I had been living on jerky and salt pork for a month. I had even ran out of that five or six days back. Except for eating rabbit, there had been no meals. About the second day after my food ran out, I chanced a shot and killed a rabbit. I broiled half of the rabbit on a stick and ate the whole half at one setting. As cold as it had been, the other half had froze.

The next day, I killed another one and did this each day till I got to Bob's. I'd lost twenty-five pounds and the horses looked about the same. I'd rationed out the oats until the last few days they were just getting a double handful twice a day and grazing a little dry grass at night. I walked back to the stable after supper and checked on the stud. I gave them both another feeding of oats and curried their backs again, checking for galls. Both the horses had made the trip pretty good. The stud needed shod and the gelding needed his shoes reset, so I laid over a day and had it done.

Mrs. Barnhart's cooking was terrific and it was like a magnet, I couldn't get far from her stove. She was forever pulling a pie or cake from the oven and had a pot of chicken and dumplings stewing all day. Knowing me and the horses needed a rest, I spent the next few days at the trading post, feeding and rubbing on those blue horses, and eating and thinking about Ginny.

Ginny had kind of slipped up on me. I'd met her four or five years ago at the *Brazos Queen*. I'd known Bates for years and stopped by every once in a while to play a few hands of cards and have a drink. Not much of a card player or drinker either one, I mostly came to visit. I sure liked to hear her sing. I knew she entertained some men on the side, but wasn't interest in this part of her life.

Bates was sick in bed one winter and I was sitting at a table playing cards, I would have never became involved. A deck hand on one of the boats got drunk and decided he was in love with Ginny. She was trying to sing and was putting him off the best she could. Grabbing her arm and pulling a knife, he told her, "If you don't go with me, I'll cut your face to pieces then no one will have you!"

Ginny tried to refuse, but he continued, "If I can't have you, I'll make sure no one else will!"

As he started forward with the knife, I fired from my hip. A slug tore through his heart and I stood up quickly and disappeared out the door and into the night.

I thought back to that night, and recalled how I'd saddled my horse and rode to the ranch. After a night to think it over, I rode back to town the next morning, and went to the sheriff's office. An inquiry had been called for but when the witnesses were called, I'd been cleared of any charges. As I walked out of the courthouse, Ginny called, "Bill! Bill!"

I stopped when she called me by my name and when she walked over to where I was, she said, "Thank you for saving my life. Would you like to have dinner with me tonight?"

"She sure is a beauty." I thought to myself. Answering her question, I replied, "It would be my pleasure ma'am." Walking back to the *Brazos Queen*, I visited with Bates while waiting the appointed time for our dinner date. During and after dinner, well into the afternoon, we talked a lot about our lives, the war and how our life had played its sorry hand of cards.

Ginny took off from work the next day and I rented a buggy. We drove out to the ranch. Who seduced who? We just ended up in bed at the ranch and stayed a couple of days. We had just kinda been special for each other since. "Damn," I hated to admit it, "but I really miss her."

I'd been gone five or six weeks now and hadn't even told her goodbye. Hell, I hated goodbyes, they just seemed sad and final. I usually just rode off. It was more fun surprising them next time you showed up. I wondered what she'd been doing while I was gone and then got mad when I reckoned it! "Hell, she was grown. Let her do what she damn well pleased. I had plenty to worry about and besides," I reasoned. I had gotten Old Blue back, and was heading home.

I took my time going home. I hated to admit it, but thinking about Ginny had made me jealous and I wasn't really happy with that feeling. I rode by Fort Graham and spent the night with Dr. Crawford. I showed him the stud. I'd talked about Old Blue when I was out of my head, so he was familiar with him and I'd told him when I left I was going to find him. Now I was back with him! The doctor knew good horses. The Crawfords had a Thoroughbred mare for a buggy horse and I promised to come back in the spring and breed her for them.

As I turned down the river, my mind returned to the lost cave, the gold shipment and the two dead soldiers. Riding back up White Rock Creek, I once again searched the west bank of the creek for the cave. Again I rode through the brush looking for the hole I'd escaped through. The sun was setting as I rode off the bluff to the creek and I noticed a light in the meadow.

Making camp in the creek, my thoughts returned to the night I had escaped, the Indian raid on the horses and what a circle I had made since. I remembered how I'd lost Old Blue and now had him back. I remembered Deke Williams fighting with a huge hole in his back and never even saying he was hit. Once again, I remembered how I'd questioned Deke's courage in an insulting way and was sorry I hadn't made amends with Deke and Badger. "Dying was bad anytime, but hell, no one should have to die mad or insulted," I concluded. The stars blinked as I drifted off to sleep in the warmth of my bedroll and the Indians in my dreams had been replaced with red headed women without a lot of clothes on.

Saddling the stud the next morning and leading my gelding, I ambled through the meadow and checked on the light from the night before. A man was milking a cow tied to a wagon and a young woman was cooking on a camp fire, while two mares grazed in the lush meadow.

I stepped down from my stud and said, "Hello, I'm Bill Fowler. I have a ranch down by the Brazos."

The stranger replied, "I'm James Wagner and have homesteaded the bottom. My friends call me Jim."

He smiled as I said, "Looks like you're going to have to get a cabin ready mighty soon, seems like there's a little Jim on the way."

Mrs. Wagner poured coffee from a big pot and offered breakfast, but I'd already eaten and was ready to travel. While drinking my coffee, James Wagner and I talked about the lay of the land and Waco. Seeing Mrs. Wagner put me to thinking about Ginny again. Finishing my coffee, I said, "You've homesteaded a good piece of ground here, should make you a good living. This here creek is known as White Rock Creek, just be careful during the heavy rains."

With that, I mounted Old Blue and taking Little Blue's lead rope, I hit a soft lope down the river toward Waco.

I reined the horses to a walk when I reached the place where we had been attacked. I could nearly see the Indians again as they splashed into the shallow river. Riding out of the creek and crossing the river, I followed the buffalo trail out of the river bottom, and was once again reminded of the buffalo hunter's threat to kill me, relayed to me by Bob Barnhart. The unused buffalo trail was now growing over with weeds, which reminded me of my dislike for buffalo hunters and for a few minutes I could nearly smell the stench of the rotting hides they carried. Trotting Old Blue out of the Brazos bottom, I hit a slow lope for Waco and the prairie fell behind.

Coming in from the north, I rode through the tall pecan trees and once again I felt a surge of homecoming. The prairie grass was still tall and my cows and broodmares were slick and fat. A few January calves had been born and were laying sprawled in the sun, soaking up its last rays as darkness approached.

Chapter 10

When I rode up, Willie was sitting in a feed trough talking to a pen of steers he'd been pampering. Looking over his shoulder, Willie let out a whoop and holler when he saw me setting on the gray stud.

"Mr. Bill, where you dun come from?" he asked and "wher'd you find that old blue hoss? I dun figured you gone and got yo'self dead," he said.

As I stepped down he grabbed me and hugged me like he owned me. Tears filled his eyes and his voice choked up. I told him all about the trip, the rescue, and everything that had happened. I told him, "There's a new family named Wagner settling in the river valley."

The sun disappeared and a big moon came up as we sat and visited. Not wanting to worry Willie, I left out the buffalo hunter's threats. Willie didn't like buffalo hunters any better than I did. I knew he'd worry though, cause he knew how far those big buffalo guns would shoot and how accurate they were. You could buy murder from a mile away with one.

Willie heated water for me a bath and laid out my razor as I fed Old Blue. When I came in from the barn, he jokingly said, "Miz Ginny dun 'bout clean forgot who ya waz. You been gone so long and never evenn says goodbye. How come ya does that Mr. Bill?"

I never answered. Hell, I hate goodbyes!

Hating to leave Old Blue behind, I saddled him again and rode slowly to town. I knew he was tired. I'd rode him awful hard since I'd got him back, but I didn't want him out of my sight. I wanted to put him in a stall and baby him a little. Besides, I knew the Indian had set quite a store by this horse and would go to great lengths to get him back. Hell, I knew I'd lost them in the snow storm but damn their red hides, they could nearly smell a track and I didn't want to chance losing him again. I knew damn well they weren't going to ride into downtown Waco to steal him.

As I rode up to the livery stable on First Street, Jimmy the livery boy jumped up when he saw me riding Old Blue. He almost didn't let me dismount before grabbing the reins and stripping off my saddle. Then mixing hot water from the stove with Epsom salts, he added a little winter green and Witchhazel to it. Testing it with his finger he sponged old Blue's tired legs and back. Picking up an old towel he rubbed Old Blue down and taking a stable sheet from a pile, he fastened the blanket on him.

Jimmy got a large bucket and fixed supper for Old Blue. He started with two gallons of oats that he covered with scalding hot water, then he added two ears of shelled corn. To this he added three raw eggs and threw down a large fork of choice river bottom hay.

He assured me, "I'll have Old Blue fat in no time and no 'whumper jawed' fool Indians' gonna get this hoss no mo."

I grinned at his seriousness and flipped him a silver dollar. Jimmy always loved a silver dollar and still had everyone he'd ever earned, in a hole to buy him a hoss. I knew Old Blue was in good hands as I turned and headed for the *Brazos Queen.* Damn, it felt good to be back. The winter smells of the river and wood smoke had me whistling as I walked and I could hear Ginny's voice singing in the distance. It drew me like a magnet.

I pushed through the swinging doors then stopped to let my eyes adjust from the dark to the glow of the lamp. When Ginny saw me she squealed and stopped singing. Running to me, she kissed me hard on the mouth in front of everyone in the *Brazos Queen.* The crowd got real quiet.

Stepping to the bar, I ordered a round of drinks for everyone and Bates grinned slyly at me, as we shook hands. Bates said, "I was sure some Injun had scalped you and I didn't know what I'd do with Ginny when I had to tell her." From this moment on Bates and I both knew what Ginny meant to each of us.

After several rounds of drinks and details of the trip, I followed Ginny to her room and lying in her bed, watched her slowly undress. The dim lights reflected on the copper hair and porcelain skin that comprised her beauty. I'd seen naked women before but somehow this was different. I kinda got a catch in my throat, and had a little trouble breathing when she crossed the room to the bed. Maybe it was the liquor, but whatever it was I had, I liked it.

Turning out the lamp, I snuggled into the arms of someone who had missed me more than she had planned to. I have to admit, I'd missed her to.

After making love and talking till daylight, I drifted off to sleep knowing Old Blue was back and being cared for by the best of hands. My dreams turned to red headed women and gray horses, and somewhere mixed into the back of my mind was snow banks and barking dogs in Indian villages.

February blew in cold and wet and I just stayed in town, soaking up the lazy living and knew Willie was taking care of the ranch. I knew he was disappointed when I didn't leave Old Blue with him, but knowing me like he did, he understood why. I often thought and shuddered about what would have happened if the Indian hadn't seen a gray horse when he went outside.

The next time I went to the ranch, I left Old Blue. Breeding season was just around the corner and Willie wanted to get him used to the mares. I was paranoid about losing him again. Bring the mares to the trap pasture that bordered the stud pen, I told Willie, "Let him tease the mares through the bars until they are dead in heat, then let her in the corral to breed, then turn her back out." I was taking no chances of the gray stud being stolen again. Indians still drifted through the river bottom occasionally and I was afraid one might recognize Old Blue.

Bates was getting old. He'd lost his touch with the cards and had quit dealing. He'd even quit playing the piano for the other girls, but wouldn't let anyone but him play while Ginny sang.

The talk had kinda settled down around town about the soldiers and the gold. Mills hadn't been back to the *Brazos Queen* since I had humiliated him in front of Ginny and the whole town. Bates wasn't worried about the loss.

He said, "I've seen lots of Mills' kind in my life. Control freaks," he called them.

"They had to have everybody on a string like a puppet and jumping when the strings were pulled. The whole damn Army is like that," Bates muttered.

"I am contemplating making the *Queen* off limits to those damn blue coats," he said.

Ginny was happy for the first time since her parents' killing and gradually allowed her mind the luxury of thinking back to how things had been. The easy carefree life she had enjoyed and the luxurious life they had lived.

"You now fill the void left empty of love for so long," she said.

She thought back to all the sordid things she had done to get by and wondered if it bothered me. She asked, "Bill, the way my life has turned out and the things I've had to do, does it bother you and make a difference in how you feel about me?"

I said, "No." But to tell you the truth it always did.

Ginny swore, "I've been true to you since the day we first made love at the ranch." she said, "I knew from that moment that you were the man I'd been looking for in all the wrong places." Funny how a woman knows at once and it takes a man so long to decide.

I laid there at night and watched her soft innocent face sleeping and wondered how many men had done that same thing. Damn, sometimes I'd nearly choke on it. I set up on the side of the bed so I could breathe without choking and cussed the past. Pride is hard to get the right mixture on, without some you're a coward, and with too much you're a fool. I swapped ends with that see-saw in my mind a lot on those first nights back.

Hell, it really wasn't her fault, the war had done it. I even rectified it by thinking if it hadn't have happened, I'd never of met her. She would have been married to some rich planter. I guess you can justify murder if you debate it long enough.

Damn, I'd gone to thinking like a lawyer now. I needed to get back to the ranch where I could do some honest work and get my thinking straight. I always seemed to do my best thinking at the ranch.

Chapter 11

In the spring of '74 snow was falling the tenth of March and the next day it was seventy degrees. Old Man Winter gave way to robins and spring flowers. Large bunches of ducks and geese were wintering on the two rivers that bordered both sides of the ranch. Willie was watching them circle overhead and head north as I rode up to the corral.

He and the hands were sorting horses in the large corral. He was dividing the brood mares into two bunches. The larger draft bred and draft cross mares were put up on the north range with the big black Percheron stud I'd bought from an Amish farmer heading west from Pennsylvania. That stud was a bad tempered rascal but big draft horses were in demand and he was a prime specimen.

The thirty best mares were being sorted into the trap pasture that lay in the forks of the rivers. It was fenced and close to the headquarters and Willie and the hands could defend it from attack. Willie was a crack shot and many squirrels had lost their heads to his rifle.

These best mares were Old Blue's harem. I told Willie to keep Big Blue's mama in the trap. She was a little drafty but I owed that big gelding that much. If I hadn't of sacrificed him to the Indians, I would not have been here sorting horses. I sure wouldn't have gotten the blue stud back.

Breeding season was in full swing and baby colts and Shorthorn calves were everywhere. I rode the outside circle, checking pastures and let my mind wonder. I sure was needed at the ranch full time with all the work that needed done. Willie had his hands full with the breeding and ranch chores. Hell, Willie was getting old. He oversaw all the farming and haying, the roundup and sorting and selling. He had a lot of help, but hell, it's a job just overseeing the help. I don't know how I could have done it without Willie. It would have taken ten men to replace him. The hell of it was, the more he had to do, the happier he was.

I was riding along one minute planning all of the ranch activities and tending to business, then suddenly my mind took off and I was thinking of Ginny. How the lamplight danced in her big blue eyes and how good she smelled when she cuddled up to me at night. Grinning to myself, I reined Little Blue around and hit a lope back to town.

I played a few hands of cards after supper, but as the crowd began to gather I eased out of the back door and walked over to the livery stable. Stopping at Little Blue's stall, I rubbed his small head and tweaked his short ears. He sure looked like his old daddy, just not as big. His mammy was a little roan thoroughbred mare I'd bought off some Mexicans from Villa Cuna.

They said she came off of a famous ranch in Mexico that had pure Spanish blooded horses. She looked it to. Probably a cross of some kind but she sure could fly. They had won a lot of races with her but got drunk and landed in jail. I bought her so they could get out of jail and go home.

This was her first colt. I probably should have left him a stud. There were people who would have sure bred him. He was just a little small but oh so quick. He had developed into the best sorting horse I'd ever ridden. Dang, he was just now four-years-old, where most horses are first broke to ride, but he'd been through the mill. He would cut a cow out of the herd with the bridle off, working off instinct and leg pressure. Every cow outfit that came through tried to buy him.

As the noises quieted down I eased back over to the *Brazos Queen*. Several soldiers were coming out the door as I entered. As they passed, I heard one mutter something about the lost Army gold and the missing soldiers. Biting my tongue, I kept walking, but my mood grew black as the night.

Ginny sensed my mood as she turned out the lamp. I was already in bed and withdrawn. She lay down beside me and held me tight. Without saying a word, she started kissing me real soft. The black mood suddenly lifted and she led me further down lovers' lane than I'd ever thought of going before.

I lay in the dark as she drifted off to sleep. Damn, she could change my emotions so quick. I finally drifted off into a deep sleep. Once again my mind was plagued by Indians and nursing dying soldiers as I searched my mind for the disappearing cave and the Army's lost gold.

The sun broke blood red in the east as I loped Little Blue to the ranch. The soldiers' remarks were still smarting. I had dreamed all night of the two missing soldiers and the lost gold. I asked Willie to put my pack on his old dun gelding as I rolled up my bedroll and laid in a big supply of grub. I also loaded a big bolt of cloth I'd bought at the general store. I thought I'd ride up through the north range, check on the stock as I went through, then go by and see the Wagners. From there, I would ride on up to Fort Graham. On second thought, I told Willie, "Go ahead and saddle Old Blue, I might as well breed the doctor's mare on this trip."

Old Blue was fat and soft. After letting him lope a piece, I pulled him back to a ground eating trot and headed for White Rock Creek and the lost cave.

The prairie was green and plush. Wildlife was abundant and nursing young. The springs were running from all the snow and winter rains. Warm sunshine gently bathed me and I was at peace with the world. Riding leisurely along, my mind jumped from the tranquility of spring, to lost caves and horses and without knowing when, thoughts of Ginny had ran them all off. Breathing deeply and shutting my eyes, I could nearly smell how she smelled this morning when I left. I didn't tell her I was leaving. I hated to wake her up, but she'd know I was gone. I reckon she had a sixth sense about it or so it seemed. She had told me, every time I left, she knew as soon as she woke up.

The shadows were long and night was approaching as I rode into White Rock Creek and out into the meadow. Jim Wagner had gotten his house built. Sawed lumber and real split shingles. Dang, he meant to stay, I figured. A lot of work had been done since I left here last winter.

Hell-o-ing the house, I waited for a welcome before stepping down. A big yeller hound had been announcing my coming for the last ten minutes. Jim opened the door and glad to see company, asked me to spend the night.

Mrs. Wagner had supper ready and since I hadn't even eaten breakfast, I was more than willing to eat. Jim had sure done a cracker jack job on the house. It was plumb snug. I unsaddled Old Blue and hobbled him loose in the yard. The grass was green and lush and he was soon gathering it.

I unpacked and carried the bolt of cloth, along with needles and thread into the house. I'd made a friend for life with Mrs. Wagner that night. Jim and I sat out on the porch and talked till late. Mrs. Wagner got busy with scissors and patterns all over the kitchen table. I just spread my bedroll on the porch and slept out with Old Blue. As I lay there looking up at the clear night full of a million stars and hearing the river and creek gurgling in the night, it was hard to imagine the storm and violence that had taken place here the night of the attack. It seemed I was laying there counting my blessing one minute and Jim was asking the blessing at breakfast the next. It sure didn't take long to spend the night on this side of the Brazos.

Mrs. Wagner was all smiles. She had cut out three little outfits for the baby she was expecting any minute, a new table cloth and curtains and enough left over for her a new dress as soon as she got her figure back.

I rode the creek on my way out. No sign of a cave existed, although some of the debris had been washed off the mountain side and into the creek. Riding back across the top was no more fruitful than the lower search. I began to wonder if I had imagined that damn cave.

Riding back down the mountain, I knew I was about where we took shelter. I shut my eyes and tried to remember exactly how it had looked through the lightening flashes. It had gotten dark so fast when the storm struck and rain was falling in sheets, making visibility nearly zero. I could almost hear the wind blow and the sound of Deke's rapid rifle fire as he covered Badger and me while we stripped the pack of gold from the mule and dove for the mouth of the cave. I remembered a thick bushy cedar had nearly covered the opening, but it was gone. The whole world looked different today.

There was a rock overhang, but that to was missing. Any of the huge rocks lying on the creek bed could have been the overhang. When the side of the mountain sloughed off, it changed the looks of everything.

Heading back to the Wagners' cabin, I had dinner with them before riding on up to Fort Graham. Wagner had two mares he was plowing with and used to pull his wagon. Since one was in heat, he asked me about breeding her to Old Blue. He took a liking to that gray stud. He said he sure couldn't afford to buy a horse like him but maybe he could raise one.

I looked the mare over. They were both Belgium type sorrel mares, probably half bloods. They were about the same type of mares that had mammied Big Blue, the gelding I had left the Indians, but had a real pretty sorrel flax maned color. The colts would be a little thicker and more "pudden" footed than I liked to ride, but that Big Blue gelding had sure as hell been a good'n.

Leading the horses back behind the barn, I unsaddled Old Blue while Jim stripped the harness off of his mare and another foal was soon on the way. I promised to stop back by on the way home and with any luck, maybe we could catch the other mare in heat then.

I rode back up the mountain ridge as I left for Fort Graham and scoured the brush as I rode through it. Searching again for the little manhole I'd crawled out of three years before.

Mrs. Crawford had a mess of chicken and dumplings simmering on the back of her old wood stove when I rode up to Fort Graham about dark. They nearly made the ride worth while. Dr. Crawford was awful glad to see me. He was sure wanting a colt out of his buggy mare and Old Blue. She was strong in heat when I got there, or "horsing" as Dr. Crawford called it, so I just unsaddled Old Blue and turned them loose in the corral for the night, a "honeymooning."

The next day dawned hot and bright and I visited and lazed around the post. Soldiers were just back from a patrol out west. They said the prairie was really ripe after that wet snowy winter. All the moisture had brought lush grass and spring flowers. The springs were all running. It was a perfect prairie scene except - no buffalos. The soldiers reported seeing fewer than fifty the whole trip. The Indians would be starving by this time next year, they said. They mentioned running into an old man and his dimwitted son, a trying to "hide" again this year. They only had six hides all spring.

The soldiers felt sorry for them. The old man told them he was getting rich hiding till a damn murdering cowboy killed his two sons and those damn greedy Indians had eat all the buffaloes. Now he was left to starve and no one seemed to care. He was nursing a lot of hate and told them if he ever got that murdering bastard in the sites of that old Sharps buffalo gun, he'd be dead "a mile before God got the news."

I had pondered a trip on up to Comanche Peak to see Bob Barnhart, but after studying on it, I decided against it. Chances were good I might cross trails with the Blackwells or Running Bear and if I didn't there was still a big chance some Indian around the trading post would recognize the stud. Running Bull had won too many races with him and too many horses off of them for all of the Plains Indians to forget Old Blue anytime soon.

Suddenly I was tired of trouble. The last few years had taken its toll on me. I was sick of fighting, of killing and the fear of dying. I was homesick for Ginny and Waco. She kept cropping up in my mind without warning. Arguing with myself, I decided, hell, I was getting feeble minded. A whore was in control of my mind and my thoughts - and I'd risked my life, killed two men and an Indian over a damn stud horse. I must have been crazy! The world was full of horses and whores both, and as long as you had one under you, what in the hell made the difference which one it was. I had a mad on for Ginny and for a few minutes even Old Blue.

Walking over to the bar outside the fort, I bought a bottle of whiskey and decided I'd do my own thinking from now on. Damn when you let a redheaded whore and gray horses chart your destiny, life would always be a wreck.

After a few drinks my conscience got into the argument. The argument raged on between me and myself. Was she really a whore? Or had life just turned her that way. Why she couldn't no more help what had happened to her, than I could have helped killing those sorry assed Blackwell boys. I had to kill them to survive — this didn't make me a murderer and once again, I felt blue and was missing Ginny. Ginny was weighing heavy on my mind.

Paying for my drinks, I walked back over to the corral and Old Blue came ambling over to where I sat. I scratched his back and he turned his head so I could rub his head and ears. Grinning to myself, I thought so much for taking control of my life. It hadn't been but fifteen minutes and I was back thinking about Ginny and petting this sorry old blue horse. Hell, I guess, I'm just losing my mind.

I rose before daylight, as was my custom, and rode off without waking anybody or saying goodbye. I hated goodbyes, it seemed so final like you wasn't ever going to see them again and — aw — hell! I just hated goodbyes!

Riding up on the bank of White Rock Creek just before noon, I silently studied the terrain from the top, but no cave was visible. What puzzled me the most was what happened to the hole on top. It couldn't have caved in. I remember it was solid rock. Hell, I remember when I crawled out, thinking it was a hole in the rock and kinda sunken below the dirt and brush. Dammit, I was just missing it in this thick brush.

Dinner was on the table when I rode up to Wagners. This was getting to be a habit. As good a cook as Mrs. Wagner was, it was going to be a hard habit to break. Game was abundant in the valley and the river was full of catfish. An ample garden furnished the extra and they were just living off of the fat of the land. Fried cottontail rabbit with hot cornbread and milk gravy was topped by sliced tomatoes and onions from the garden. This was fit for a king. Washing all this down with fresh buttermilk from the spring house, I took on a fill before unloading my mind.

I pushed my plate back and told Wagner about the lost gold and the missing soldiers. Mrs. Wagner turned white when I told of the Indians using the crossing. Heavy with child, she walked to the door and looked out as if expecting them back. I told them of Deke's brave stand in the creek bed and how he held the Indians at bay while Badger and I got the gold off the mule and packed it into the cave. All the time this was taking place, his life was running out of him and he never even said he was hit. He had a hole in his back as big as your fist. Damn gutty even if he was a nigra and then biting my tongue I was ashamed again for my attitude toward Deke Williams.

Jim's other mare was in heat and we bred her after we finished dinner. I left in deep thought about the missing soldiers and the Army's lost gold. Jim said he'd poke around in his spare time. I hit a lope for Waco with Ginny on my mind. Riding into the ranch from the north always gave me a sense of contentment. I ran lots of country north of Childress Creek, but from Childress Creek, home was deeded land and it was mine. Cattle grazed in the meadows and mares and colts stood in the shade of the large pecan trees, twitching flies as the sun set slowly across the west bank of the Bosque River.

Willie was coming to the house with a large pail of milk and another full of eggs. Breakfast was guaranteed around this outfit and it wasn't even dark yet.

Chapter 12

Taking a quick bath, I saddled Little Blue and turning Old Blue loose in the corral, I watched as he rolled over and over in the soft river sand. Stepping upon the little gelding, I rode for town and the flickering lights reminded me how the lamplight flickered in Ginny's big blue eyes.

Jimmy was glad to see me and Little Blue. Flipping him his customary silver dollar, I headed for the *Brazos Queen* as Ginny's soft voice floated out on the cool spring night air.

Stopping to relieve my bladder behind the *Brazos Queen*, the world was shattered by the blast from a sawed-off shotgun and it came from the *Brazos Queen.* As I sprinted for the door, I figured Bates had killed someone.

Nothing prepared me for the scene that greeted me, and stopping in my tracks I couldn't believe my eyes.

Ginny was standing at the end of the bar, clutching Bates' sawed-off shotgun in both hands, and an Army officer with a shit-load of metals lay writhing on the floor. The lower part of his stomach was blown open and his whole groin area blown away from the blast of both barrels. Captain Mills was gasping for air and trying to not faint. The only Army general he had ever met had just been murdered while being entertained by him.

His whole army career was hanging on a thread. "This snotty redheaded whore shot the general for no apparent reason," he screamed. "All General McNight said, when they walked past," he whined, "Was that he used to own a little redheaded whore during the war that looked a lot like Ginny."

A strangled cry escaped Ginny's throat at the remark. She quit singing, and as Bates half raised from the piano stool, Ginny dashed for the bar. Quicker than lightning, she shouldered Bates' shotgun and squeezed both triggers.

In disbelief, General McNight looked down at his privates and saw they were shredded from the blast and nothing remained intact. Pain blacked out his next thoughts, and blood gushed from the hole in his lower abdomen. He bled to death before anyone could move.

Bedlam broke loose. Soldiers broke and ran as Mills began to shake and sob uncontrollably.

I rushed to Ginny and a strange glassy look had replaced the sparkle in her eyes. In a quiet small voice, she kept saying, “It’s him! It’s him!”

Deputies were there in short order with officials from the fort, and began restoring some semblance of authority. Bates whisked Ginny up the stairs to her room and guarded the door so no one could enter.

Shortly after the body was removed the sheriff himself walked in. Rudely awakened from his sleep, he was less than hospitable. Mills had regained his composure and began to scream at the sheriff to arrest this whore and turn her over to the army for a military trial at once. Sheriff Tate didn’t particularly like the military and their overbearing attitude.

Drawing up sharply and towering his big six foot three inch frame over Mills, he assured him that justice would be served, but this was not in a military jurisdiction. He informed Mills that he was the law and order in Waco, and for him to round up his men and get back to camp until further orders. Mills was fit to be tied and sulked as he called his men to attention and marched them toward the fort.

“Damned ingrates,” he cursed. “If it wasn’t for me and my soldiers, the Indians would still be living in this rednecked cracker town.”

Dispatching a report for Washington, he restlessly waited for instructions and his future as a commanding officer.

I followed Sheriff Tate as he walked stiffly up the stairs to Ginny’s room. Bates blocked the door, neither moved an inch.

Taking a deep breath Sheriff Tate said, “Bates there’s already been enough killing tonight. I’ve got to question her and take her in.”

Bates never moved a muscle, but from the bottom of his soul a flat defiant voice stated, “You can question her tonight, but you’re not going to lock her up. I’ll bring her over tomorrow after she settles down and cleans up.

Tate knew it was this way or hell to pay. He shrugged and said, “By noon, Bates, or I’ll come and get her.”

Sitting down softly beside Ginny, Sheriff Tate kindly patted her shoulder and asked questions pertaining to the shooting. Ginny was in shock and just sat ashen-faced saying over and over, “It’s him! It’s him!” Not a tear, not a whimper, no emotion other than those softly spoken words, “It’s him! It’s him!”

The sheriff finally left after getting no answers. He nodded to me as he left and said, “Have her at the jail by noon.”

Slowly moving forward, I turned out the light and undressed Ginny like a child. I stripped off her blood-splattered dress and bathed her with a pan of water and a wash rag. Lying down beside her, she drifted off to a troubled sleep.

Somewhere in the middle of the night, the dam of emotion broke and Ginny began crying rivers of tears for the night General McNight had killed her father. Once again, in her mind, she relived the rape of her mother, and saw her die as field hands and riffraff following McNight’s orders had raped her repeatedly. Again she was fourteen years old and felt the humiliation of being forced to strip and be raped by McNight and his officers. She recounted the years of captivity and the escape as the war ebbed slowly to an end.

Tears for her youth and womanhood, sorrow for her demented past, her future as she would have lived it, if not for the war, poured from her as she told me her story. Now she was facing murder, with no future and no past.

Pounding on the *Brazos Queen’s* door awakened me the next morning. Bates had slept leaning against Ginny’s door with his shotgun. I knew it would be the sheriff with a warrant. I stepped over Bates quickly and beat him to the door. Hell, there was fixing to be another killing if I didn’t think of something.

I told Sheriff Tate I'd bring her over after she had bathed and eaten breakfast. At first Tate said no, he'd take her now. He said he had company coming for lunch and didn't want to be late. Old Bates came gliding down the hall with that damn shotgun, about then and Sheriff Tate changed his mind, but said, "Be damn sure it's before noon." He stalked across the street to the courthouse and jail to wait impatiently.

My mind was in a quandary as I strode up the stairs two at a time. We had to have a lawyer and a good one. There were two in Waco, and I wouldn't trust either one of them "in a shit house with a muzzle on." They played checkers with their cases. "You win one, I win one."

Judge McCall was a fair and impartial man. He'd do, but I had to get a lawyer. Fort Worth was my best bet. Stephen T. Dill was the best available. Forty years-old and sharp. Old enough to appear mature with salt and pepper gray hair, worn short but still young and vibrant for justice. Raised in Philadelphia and educated at Harvard, he was the best.

Turning at the top of the stairs, I walked back to the jail. I needed some time. Knocking on the jail door, Tate quickly opened it. I told him I was going to Fort Worth for a lawyer and when the lawyer got here we'd bring Ginny to the jail. Cursing loudly, Sheriff Tate told me the warrant had to be served today. I asked him about just posting her a cash bond, but he told me Captain Mills had put a lot of pressure on the town. He had convinced them that Ginny was a threat to society and shouldn't be bonded.

Damn, I knew what happened next would shape destiny. If I led Ginny to jail and left her in her present condition, she might completely break down. If I didn't and let Tate go to the *Queen* and arrest her, Bates would kill the sheriff for handcuffing her. I thought about grabbing her and running, but then we'd both be fugitives from the law.

The country was getting too settled to hide in anymore. With a pretty red headed woman and a big blue Thoroughbred stud, I was going to stand out and I sure as hell wasn't going to lose either one again. The only place to hide was out West. With the Indians and the Blackwells out there, Ginny or the gray stud would get me killed, and God knows what would happen to her and the gray stud.

Ginny made the decision for me. As I turned slightly, she walked into the jail, perfectly groomed, every hair in place and Sheriff Tate quietly escorted her to a waiting cell. The cell was adjacent to the sheriff's office and afforded some scant privacy. It was around the corner from the male inmates.

Bates sat on the corner bar stool, the saloon was dark and empty. He cradled the sawed-off on his leg. He hadn't moved since the morning. He had figured Mills and the soldiers might come back for a little vigilante justice. Hell was awaiting that plan.

Kissing Ginny goodbye, I walked to the livery and saddled my good blue gelding. I didn't trust the mail or anyone going for me, I was heading for Fort Worth and the stage didn't run on Sundays. I stopped by the ranch and switched my saddle to Old Blue and leading the gelding I headed north. By changing horses every few hours, I could ride it in a hard day, and by riding all night it would be cooler. I didn't pack anything but a rifle and a water bag. I took a pocketfull of jerky to chew on as the ranch fell behind. I hit the Old Chisholm Trail and stopped at Bold Springs to water my horses and gave them a little grain. I passed West Station, a little railroad town about dark. Hillsboro slipped by in the night and I groggily remember seeing Itasca and Grandview slightly about dawn.

Stopping at daylight I ate breakfast at a stage station in Alvarado. I decided to leave Old Blue at the livery stable and let him rest. I had covered seventy five miles in the last fifteen hours and the stud was tired. I saddled the gelding again and washed my face at the windmill. Refilling my water bag, I swung up and hit the last leg to Fort Wroth. The gelding had lost a lot of his zip, but noon found us on the south side of Fort Worth. At two o'clock I walked into Stephen T. Dill's office, rum dumb but present.

Eyes burned from lack of sleep and wind as I answered Dill's questions. Like most lawyers he came right to the point. Did she kill him and how many people saw it? His fee would be a thousand dollars and expenses and he wanted half of it up front. What were the circumstances leading to the killing? Was she a whore and could she blackmail any of the towns fathers if things got tough?

Testifying grudgingly, I said hell yes she had been a whore, but not anymore. She didn't know it yet, but she was fixing to be my wife. Quickly explaining her life story, I was talking like a parrot and Dill was taking notes.

Booking a seat on the stage, Dill said he'd be in Waco Thursday. Told me he didn't like to ride horseback.

Leaning against the counter at the Cattleman's Hotel, I ordered a hot bath to my room. Wolfing a steak and a pitcher of beer, I headed for my room, a hot bath and a much deserved long night of sleep. I drifted off as dusk bathed the north side of Fort Worth, and the loud night began.

Rising at dawn I went to the livery stable and checked on Little Blue. I'd had new shoes put on him and as the farrier finished the job, I wrangled a waitress for some breakfast.

By eight I was heading south. I let the little gelding have his head and he did the rest. He had a little smooth trot, that could really cover some country. I rode through Burleson without stopping and ate lunch at Alvarado at the stage station. The first thing I did was check the blue stud over real good. He was fit and hardy and ready to travel. After polishing off a quick meal, I changed horses and hit the road for Waco.

Hillsboro was fading into the night as I stepped off of Old Blue at the livery stable and watered the horses. I eased my saddle off his back and dipped a bucket in the trough. I poured the cool water over his back real slow and washed the sweat from his steaming back.

Thirty five miles had been knocked off since lunch and I'd ridden him seventy-five the day before. I felt better now about Ginny. At least we had a chance now. Dim lights from the café across the street reminded me I was hungry and striding in the front door, I ordered whatever they could cook quick and lots of it. Eating hurriedly, I came back to the stable. Rolling up in a blanket in the hay stack, I slept the night away.

A rooster crowing from a tree by the livery stable brought me wide awake. Feeding my horses and washing my face in the water trough, I walked across the street to the little café again. The waitress smiled as I said, “more of the same.”

Saddling the gelding again, I led Old Blue west out of Hillsboro. I picked up Hackberry Creek and followed it until it ran into the Aquilla Creek. Riding steady in a southwest direction, I reached the Brazos.

The tiny settlement of Gholson lay off to my right as the Aquilla ran into the Brazos River. I crossed the river and riding out of the bottom, I hit the prairie that was the north end of my range. I began seeing Longhorn cows with red and white spotted calves. These calves were proof my Shorthorn bulls were working. The pastures were lush and green and Childress Creek was running clear and full as I crossed it. Hitting a lope, I was nearly home.

The next hours found me stripping my saddle from one tired little gelding and handing Old Blue back to Willie. It had been a long time since I had left Sunday. I took a quick bath and borrowed Willie’s old dun gelding to ride to the jail.

It was dark as I knocked on the door and a deputy cautiously opened it. A lot of talk about the Army lynching the red headed whore had been circulating. The deputy was jumpy as hell. He said she was too pretty to hang. Hell, him and the other deputies had thought of several things they’d rather do with her, he grinned. For a second I nearly killed him. Gritting my teeth I walked past.

The *Waco Press* was lying on the floor by the jailer’s chair. They had already had a press trial — Guilty! The headlines read, “*Prostitute Murders General in Rage*.”

The story went on the say that a group of concerned citizen were circulating a petition to shut the *Brazos Queen* down and a follow-up story concerning the trouble and open hostility to the Army that was displayed there. Another column went into great depth that she was assumed to be living with a renegade ex-army scout suspected of killing two soldiers and stealing a large shipment of Army payroll gold.

Blue flames leaped from my eyes as I looked for the editor's name. The paper was new here in town. The editor was none other than Captain Mills' fat wife's brother. This didn't surprise me. I remembered the lard ass when he was hanging around the fort. Old Mills and his wife had raised him. He must be twenty-five or so now, and Mills had set him up in the newspaper business, the weekly *Waco Press*.

With all the hullabaloo about the trial, J. Edgar Burns, the newspaper editor, had begun to print two papers a week. This had him busy. Thursday morning was especially busy as he ran off copies for today. The famous lawyer Stephen T. Dill was expected today on the stage, and he wanted pictures and an interview.

The editor was totally unprepared when I snatched him around by one arm and slapped him open handed. Blood flew out of his mouth, where he had nearly bitten his tongue into and his glasses that were sitting on the end of his fat nose landed in the cat box back of the wood stove. Stumbling, he nearly fell, and as he stepped forward to catch himself, I slapped him again. This time I turned him loose when I slapped him and his fat ass turned a backward flip. Violence was not part of J. Edgar Burns' world. He much preferred to assault with a poison pen and a printing press.

As I reached for him again, he began to blubber and cry. Snatching him to his feet again, he lost control of his bladder and pissed his britches. It ran down into his shoes. Gathering all the papers form today's printing, I opened the wood stove and started cramming papers into it. Striking a match, I fed the whole edition into its cherry red throat.

Ordering J. Edgar to get his pen, I told him to start writing. If he left out one word or deleted one paragraph, I promised I'd be back to finish what I started. I told him the whole sordid story, from the looting of Scarlet Oaks, the murder, the rape and Old

Mills' numerous attempts to seduce Ginny — her rebuffs and the insulting remarks made by McNight that led to the shooting.

Writing a new headline for the paper, I penned "*New Evidence for Waco's Battered Woman Proves McNight's Guilt.*"

J. Edgar's papers were always delivered by five o'clock and I told him that this edition had best not be late. A follow-up article told Ginny's story in full detail and when the trial opened Friday, the courthouse was surrounded by mad women.

Cookies and tea had been delivered to Ginny in jail by the wives of the Mayor and the Baptist preacher. Every woman was carrying a newspaper, and sitting on the front row was Captain Mills' fat wife.

Ginny heard my voice as I talked to the jailer and she knew I was back from Fort Worth. I talked through the bars to Ginny for a minute and she could tell something was wrong but didn't mention it. She said she didn't see the first paper but when Burns brought the Thursday one, she said he looked like he'd had a train wreck.

Shocked by the headlines, Ginny had just began to read it when Stephen T. Dill walked into her life and began asking questions.

Trial was set for the next morning at nine o'clock. The gossip was really circulating concerning the newest release of the paper.

Ginny was sitting on a jail bed in a white cotton sack dress, but still a pretty woman by my standards. I listened as Ginny talked and Dill took notes, I worried about tomorrow.

Chapter 13

The trial started at nine. By eight-thirty there was not an empty seat in the courthouse and chairs had been placed around the wall. Nearly all the seats were filled with women. J. Edgars' papers were serving two purposes. The courthouse began to heat up and they were folded and used for fans.

The prosecution presented its case first. The district attorney was assisted by an army of lawyers supplied by Captain Mills. Witnesses were paraded by and all the soldiers were called and testified to what they saw. Ginny was pictured as a low-rent whore that murdered a highly decorated war hero in a fit of rage.

Dill didn't cross-examine anyone. He just let the prosecution roll. With no halts to the prosecution, they wrapped up their case by noon, and the trial broke for lunch. All the women filed out and spread picnic lunches on the courthouse lawn. They reread their papers and began to talk about how this pretty little girl and been treated and abused.

The jury filed back into the courtroom and the wives followed. Nearly every wife had her husband's eye as the defense began.

Dill opened his defense. He called Captain Mills as his first witness. Mills reluctantly took the stand. He had avoided being a witness for the prosecution and wasn't happy about being called now.

Dill politely went to work. Graciously he asked Mills to state his name, rank, military authority and achievements. Mills puffed with pride as Dill complimented him on his desire to see justice served. Asking him if he had any children, and asking him to explain to the court how he and his lovely wife had sacrificed to raise her younger brother, Mills was fairly strutting.

"As a matter of fact," Dill said, "some folks consider you a shining example of a husband, family man, and community leader."

Mills' buttons were about to pop off his coat and Mrs. Mills was smiling and fanning herself.

Suddenly in the midst of the accolades, Dill asked Mills point blank if he had ever solicited a prostitute for pay. Mills nearly choked and mumbled something. Dill asked him to repeat his answer.

Turning purple, Mills half raised from the chair and began to curse Dill. Rapping for quiet, Judge McCall ordered him to answer the question. Sitting down abruptly Mills said "No" as he looked at his feet.

Dill quickly asked Captain Mills if he was aware of the penalty of perjury and he never answered him. Judge McCall asked if he was aware and he finally said "Yes sir," in barely whisper.

"No further questions your honor," Dill replied and Mills stepped down. All the color had left his face and his shoulders slumped. Mrs. Mills face was blood red and furious.

Dill called Ginny as his next witness. Ginny was dressed in a high necked white dress with long gloves. Her hair was perfect. Her makeup was softly done and she looked young and innocent.

Dill began by softly asking her name and place of employment. Turning up the heat he asked if she knew Captain Mills. Asking her abruptly if Mills had ever made advances or given her offers of monetary compensation, she answered yes to both and went into detail. Mills turned white and his wife was livid.

Dills asked for Ginny to step down with the right to recall later. Calling J. Edgar Burns as his next witness he again set the hook. He started by complimenting him on his fine paper and his patriotic duty in printing the facts. J. Edgar beamed and then Dill asked point blank if he had been pressured by his brother-in-law to print a shaded view of this trial.

Glancing nervously at his brother-in-law, Burns denied it. Dill then held up two editions of the paper and asked him why the flip flop from one edition to the next. Glancing furtively from Mills to me, he looked like a trapped cat. I stared straight at him, and he looked like he was gonna faint. Sweat popped out on his fat head. Burns didn't answer. In a loud authoritative voice, Judge McCall told him to answer the question. Again he stalled and McCall threatened him with contempt of court.

Breaking down on the witness stand, Burns confessed to Mills threatening to take the newspaper away from him, but not a word about the whippin' I'd given him.

Coolly dismissing Burns, Dill asked to recall Ginny to the stand. Assuring her she was still under oath, Judge McCall said, "Proceed."

Dill asked Ginny if she knew General McNight prior to the night of the murder. In a quiet clear voice, Ginny said, "Yes."

When Dill asked her in what way? She began. She started with the murder of her father by him, the rape of her mother by him, and the assault by the former slaves at his order. Then she related the kidnapping and rape of her own person. How she was traded among the officers for the remainder of the war. Of being broke and alone — a fifteen-year-old orphan and how her life had evolved.

Women were sobbing and grown men on the jury were blinking back the tears as the story unfolded. Finally she quoted McNight's last words to her and the boast he made with contempt. Dill asked softly, "Did you kill General McNight?"

She replied, "Yes," in a small, childlike voice.

Turning suddenly to the court, Dill shocked the court by resting his case with no further witnesses. The women were weeping and some of the jury were fumbling with handkerchiefs as the jury was asked to adjourn to its chambers.

The clock struck two o'clock. The defense had used only an hour. No one dared move as the clock slowly ticked past three o'clock. Only the squeaking of chairs and the rustle of fans broke the deathly silence of the courtroom.

As surprising as Dill's defense was, the timing of the jury foreman announcing "Your Honor, we the jury have reached our decision," caused a stir in the courtroom.

"Approach the bench," Judge McCall ordered. "Please read your decision he announced," and the jury foreman read, "We the jury find the defendant innocent due to justifiable homicide."

McCall said, "The defendant is dismissed."

Ginny sat in disbelief. Ginny rushed to me crying and we were both mobbed by well wishing women. Women who had changed sides of the street to keep from speaking to her, were hugging and congratulating Ginny now.

Judge McCall called Dill into his chambers and was visiting about cronies each knew from law school and rehashing the trial. J. Edgar Burns hung around hoping for an interview for his paper, and marveling at Dill's closing defense.

Ginny, Dill and I went to eat at a local restaurant up town, where Dill was staying. I furnished its beef. I told Dill this was Rafter F beef we were eating and I told him about the ranch, the missing gold, and showed him my old battle scars from the battle with the Indians. He took notes as we talked. He was the damndest man for taking notes.

I handed him his other five hundred and paid his expenses. He caught the night stage back to Fort Worth and I felt deep gratitude for the man as the stage rattled over the suspension bridge and disappeared into the dark.

We went directly to the stable and got Jimmy, the livery stable hand to hitch up a surrey. Leading Willie's old dun gelding, Ginny and I headed back to the ranch with Jimmy driving the rig. Jimmy was Willie's nephew by marriage. His mother was Willie's wife's sister and Willie had kinda raised him. Willie didn't have any kids and sure set quite a store by Jimmy.

I asked Jimmy how he'd like to go to work for his Uncle Willie and you could see that grin in the dark.

"Jimmy shore like that plenty fine," he said. "Uncle Willie 'nos a heap about hosses, I'd be much obliged to work wid him!"

As we drove into the ranch yard the moon had rose full and bright and we stopped and drank in the peace and tranquility of the ranch. Suddenly Ginny gasped and said, "Bill what about Bates?"

Quickly taking the reins of the surrey, as Jimmy led Willie's old dun to the barn, we turned and galloped the surrey horse all the way to town.

Bates had watched the trial from the balcony. Fear and hate for the Army had nearly consumed him. He was afraid Ginny was going to be convicted. He had looked at himself in the mirror that morning and realized that Ginny and I were all the family he had. Thinking this was about to be taken away, he laid out this plan.

He slipped a new Army Colt into his boot. Mills had been bragging around town that he'd turned up the heat on that uppity whore, and she was fixing to boil. Bates had decided that when the verdict was announced he was going to kill Mills first, then J. Edgar Burns, the sheriff and the district attorney in that order. He knew death couldn't cheat him out of much time and he'd decided to take a handful to hell with him.

As the jury foreman had made his entry, Bates had eased his pistol out and had started to raise his gun up, when the verdict came in "Innocent," Bates was shocked. Easing his gun back in his boot, he solemnly slipped out of the courthouse and into the back door of the *Brazos Queen.*

Bates slipped through the backdoor feeling defeated, and sat down in the dark. He decided to never open the *Queen* again. Hell, Ginny was the *Brazos Queen* and when she wasn't singing it was just another riverbank whore house full of drunk soldiers and cowboys. Bates knew he was alone and old. The two together was nearly more than he could handle. He had been alone since he had turned his back on God so many years before, but this "old" was going to take some getting "used to," he thought.

Bates did something in the dark that he hadn't done in years. He got down on his knees and began to pray. Haltingly at first and barely audible, he poured out his heart. Without knowing when, Bates began to softly cry. It was as if the tears were cleansing his soul and his old, cold, hard eyes seemed to melt as the tears continued to flow.

The *Brazos Queen* was dark and forbidding as we drove around to the back. The back door was slightly ajar, and as I stepped cautiously inside, I waited for my eyes to adjust to the dimness. I looked empty and dead. The girls had left after the killing and only the tinkling of glasses and the hollow laughter from the *Cotton Palace* next door broke the haunting silence.

As Bates raised up from his knees where he'd been kneeling, I was startled. I stepped back and grabbed for my gun. Seeing it was Bates, I explained that Ginny and I had come to get him. Bates turned and walked up the stairs without a word. I walked back to the surrey and waited, not knowing what to expect. Shortly Bates appeared with a suitcase. Not a word was exchanged as we drove to the ranch.

Bates was a changed man. When we got out of the surrey at the ranch, he finally spoke. With his voice low and controlled, he patted Ginny's arm and said, "Honey, I thought it was all over."

When he picked up his suitcase and followed us to the house, he had an old Bible under his arm that was stiff from disuse and had been covered with dust.

Chapter 14

The ranch settled into a flurry of activity. Willie and I, with Jimmy helping, began to gather everything from the north range and moved it to the meadows. All the calves had to be marked and branded and the bulls castrated. We would bring in a bunch one day, work them the next day, then the third day we'd take them back and bring in a new bunch. We'd gather up a bunch on the way back to the ranch.

The work continued until we had branded five hundred and forty-four calves. Checking my tally books, I was elated. I had been keeping all my heifers and the herd had ballooned. All the Shorthorn bulls I had invested in were paying dividends now. My herd was nearly all red and roans. The grass was abundant, and the future looked good. Nearly all of this crop of calves was three quarters Shorthorn, and the calves were weaning nearly twice the size the Longhorns were originally.

Riding slowly back to the ranch, the sun was setting in the west over the Bosque River. Ginny had settled into the house and her role as mistress of the ranch. I was nearly content. Ginny had brought a couple of young girls up from the quarters and they had cleaned the old house till it shone and shimmered like a new silver dollar. She had stolen a yard boy from Willie's crop of field hands and the yard and house took on a charm of the Southern plantation she grew up in.

She had also commandeered a cook and the house was always steeped in the smell of Southern cooking. Hell, I was contemplating marriage, but couldn't figure out how to address it.

Bates had gotten old overnight. He just shuffled back and forth from his bedroom to the kitchen and out to the front porch. He'd spend the day reading his old Bible, that he'd neglected for so many years and shooting the heads off the squirrels that were raiding the huge pecan trees that shaded the house and barns. His eyes were still good and he was a dead shot with that pistol he'd brought to kill Mills with.

Muffin, the cook, Ginny had selected, was always glad to get fresh meat. If it wasn't needed at the big house, she would tote it home for her family. Bates was a favorite with the help and they would spend a few minutes a day visiting with him. They loved for him to read the Bible to them. None of them could read and it was like God himself speaking as Bates would read. Well educated, he could cast a spell. Every evening after quitting time, the hands would gather in the yard to hear Master Bates read and they were spellbound.

Raising up from the windmill pipe, I watched the mares and colts come into the corral single file for grain. Willie grained them every evening and they knew when it was time for it. Sweat poured off my brow as I stopped to get a drink and cool off a little. It was hot for November. Nearly like July. Winter was lazy about coming this year.

We'd been breaking the colts that were born when Old Blue had been stolen. This sure was a good set of three-year-olds. The babies following their mammies were the next crop from the gray stud. That damn Indian had the two crops in between. He had cost me a bundle of money those years. Willie had bred everything to a Percheron those two years and all we had coming along for a while were draft horses. With Willie farming more grain every year, we could use the best ones and the others would bring top dollar. The west was in need of good big draft horses for the settlers.

I loved to watch the baby colts, fat, slick hided and everyone a blue or roan. I just loved horses. All of Old Blue's fillies were being kept for brood mares, and they were getting old enough to breed. Another stud was needed to cross on them. I had better mares than the studs that were available. I didn't want to in-breed them and hated to cross a draft horse on them. They were a choice set of gray and red roan mares.

I had been thinking of going to Kentucky to get me a real class stud. There were more good horses in Kentucky in ten square miles than the rest of America put together. I walked over to the filly pasture and looked them over. Again I was proud of these fillies. Short backs and long hips, straight legs and long necks with little heads. These were a cowboy's dream. I knew if I crossed the right horse on these mares you could outrun a train that left yesterday. I raised cattle but I loved horses. Stopping to pet one I headed for the house.

Bates was on the front porch holding court. Listening to Bates read the Bible, I had a hard time believing this was the Bates of old. The Bates who could kill as easy as a bird could fly. A card shark, a pimp, a cold hard killer, but something had changed in Bates. He now idolized Ginny. His affection was for the daughter he never fathered and he couldn't remember any other feeling he'd ever felt for her as he looked at her now.

Chapter 15

The winter finally came and time at the ranch was mostly spent feeding and tending to stock. Willie and I weaned all the foals and it was bedlam for a few days as mares were nickering all night and the foals squalling till daylight.

Same was true with the cattle. I had left them on the cows as long as the weather was good and the grass was growing. When frost hit the roundup started. Again we brought everything to the home ranch. We stripped the calves and colts off and drove the older stock back to the outer ranges. The prairie grass was tall and cured like hay. Most of the brood stock was glad to be relieved of its burdens but a few would hang around bawling their heads off. Every morning Jimmy would push them back across Childress Creek until they finally quit coming back. They were through baby sitting till spring and then it would begin all anew.

The crew and its work had just started. Large cottonwood logs had been hollowed and burnt out on the inside to make huge troughs. We would drag these to the meadows with the teams we used for farming. Every morning Willie and the farm crew would haul corn and cotton seed we bought from the Waco Gin Company and fill the crude troughs. My Shorthorn steers were turning feed to fat and it in turn was turning fat beef into cold cash.

It sure beat driving them to Kansas City or Dodge. After weaning we drove the heifers into the bottom pasture that joined the Brazos River. This pasture lay idle all summer and fall and was just used to winter the heifers in. Little supplemental feeding was needed to bring the heifers through the winter in ideal breeding condition.

Next spring a bull would be placed with them, and then they would be kept around close till they calved as two-year-olds. After their first calf they would be moved out on the north range with the main cow herd. This care and careful breeding had played a major role in the developing my Shorthorn herd and keeping the heifers is how I'd expanded so quick.

The spring of '75 came early in February with warm soaking rains and March was like summer. Grass got knee high in the river bottoms. Wild rye grew thick and lush. Spring flowers exploded, and Ginny's yard was a picture. She and Shine, the yard boy, had been working on the yard and garden since the trial. The lawn was thick and green and the flower beds were well manicured and ablaze with color. The garden was a criss-cross of reds, yellows, blues and pinks. Rows of flowers rotated with the vegetables while the fruit trees were living bouquets.

A new crop of foals was born in the mare pasture and once again, true to their breeding, they were nearly all blues or roans.

Coming back to the ranch house after a long ride, I'd been checking cows on the north range. I had never seen the range more prolific. Rye grass was already bedding down and loaded with seed nearly mature. Burr clover was thicker than fleas on a hound's back and the cattle were hard fat. Little supplemental feeding had been done that winter and cattle prices were strong. With the hold over of last years calves and a good crop being born now, the future looked good.

I had those two hundred and fifty heifers I'd kept last fall and they were ready to breed. Dang when you kept all your heifers a cow head really swelled in size. I thought back to that first hundred cows and how long it took me to get them. How I'd took the scouting job to pay for the last of them and now they were all replaced with better cattle. Mentally calculating and making room for hard dry years, I figured I could run about a thousand cows on my range with the mares. Even in a bad dry year, I'd be ok. Hell this year I could run a thousand in the meadows and put up hay.

The field hands were putting up hay in the meadows around the headquarters as I rode in. Huge stacks twenty feet wide were being piled up for next winter's feed. Willie was busy overseeing the haying.

Willie's hair had turned nearly snow white, but he was still robust and strong. Worked from morning to night, every day, mostly overseeing, but would jump on a buck rake or grab a pitchfork at a moment's notice. I was recounting these past few years of prosperity and realized I owed a lot of it to Willie. Willie was kinda family or as close to family as I had.

Coming from my rednecked cracker background, this took a minute to soak into my mind. I'd never really thought about our relationship, just took it for granted. It dawned on me that Willie had never had a regular salary. I had bought him before the war and after emancipation I just took care of him. I'd freed him before we left the south and he was free to do what he pleased. I had always furnished his house and food, clothes, medicine and when he needed or wanted money he asked for it and he always got it.

Money was never discussed. He handled most of it. Willie ran the ranch, and paid the hands from a cash drawer in the big house if I wasn't there. He bought and sold like he owned it all. He bought the feed and sold the cattle when I was gone, even supplies for the big house. He could draft on my bank for whatever. I had taught him to read and write when it was against the law to do it, but hell, I'd always kinda done things my own way.

Suddenly it dawned on me that slavery hadn't changed that much for Willie. Riding back to where Willie was sitting horseback, I motioned for him to follow me. Riding into the heifer pasture I cut out twenty-five of those red shorthorn heifers and Willie and I pushed them to the house without a word. Loping into the corral, I opened the gate as Willie pushed the heifers through the corral wings.

Running them in the branding chute, I explained as Willie built a fire. I told him to put a big W on their side. I told him these were his cows for all the work he'd done for me through the years. I also cut out a half a dozen big draft mares and colts for Willie to brand. Willie's life had taken a dramatic turn. From a slave to ranch foreman to rancher and he just stood speechless. Big tears sprang into his big brown eyes and grabbing me, he nearly squeezed me to death.

"Mister Bill, you have dun gone and made a plum fool of yourself. You can't go giffin' ever 'nigger' field hand you got yore cows or you'll be broke." he said.

But there was pride in his steps as he turned his cows and horses out, with that big W fresh branded on their right side. His life's ambition had been fulfilled. Willie had always longed for something of his own.

Chapter 16

Bates was playing the piano as I walked up the steps, and Ginny's velvet voice sang along. I was surprised when Bates chimed in with a deep bass voice. Damn, I didn't know he could sing, but a lot had unfolded about Bates since the killing. He had started to preach again to the hands every evening about dark. Several had been baptized in the river. He was as concerned for their souls as he had been at cheating with dice and cards before. I had always heard two things usually got a man before he died - it was either whiskey or religion and I had seen Bates make the choice.

Sitting down to a huge Southern style meal, I rolled out my plans. Willie and the hands had all the crops in the ground. The cows were all about calved out. The range was in excellent shape, and other than salting and checking periodically it would be fine. The mares had all foaled and were about bred back. I had decided not to brand or castrate this year till fall.

Lots of ranchers were wanting to buy my yearling Shorthorns for bulls. My cattle were becoming the envy of the range and I'd sold twenty, three year-old geldings to a ranch south of San Antonio for a hundred dollars apiece. This was good money, but they looked like peas in a pod, all blues and roans. I broke the news that as soon as haying was done I was going to Kentucky and buy a stud or two. I'd also been hearing about Hereford cattle that had been brought over from England. Big red cattle with white faces and legs, perfect beef cattle, built close to the ground.

A far cry from the old Longhorns I'd started with. I had heard they were even better than Shorthorns, but I'd have to see for myself. Knowing how the Shorthorns had improved my herd, I was open for new advances in breeding.

I asked Ginny to go, and was disappointed when she said no. She said she had the house to run and who would take care of Bates.

"Damn the house and Bates both," I muttered, as I stomped off to the barn. Who took care of Bates and the damn house the last hundred years, I fumed to myself.

Hating to go alone, I decided to take Jimmy. Jimmy was an expert horseman, young and eager. He was elated with the idea of the trip.

Jimmy was puttin' on the dog as he relayed the plans for the trip. Kentucky, he bragged to the other hands, as they gathered around for Bates' preaching. Texarkana, Little Rock, Memphis, Louisville and Lexington rolled off his tongue like he knew them all and he didn't have a clue about any of them. Hell, he'd never been to Marlin or Hillsboro yet, but he was ready and willing.

I decided to take a spring wagon for the trip. The roads were traveled and I could take a lot more bedding and clothes back east. Jimmy and I spent a lot of time picking the right horses to take. I would have liked to take Old Blue but breeding season wasn't finished. Plus I was going after another stud or two and didn't intend to referee a stud fight for twelve hundred miles.

Jimmy picked a pair of black geldings for the buggy. Full brothers, one four and one five, both were by Old Blue and a black Percheron crossed mare that I'd gave Willie. She was old Ellie and a favorite of all the field hands. Her colts were just like her, steady and dependable.

Satisfied with Jimmy's decision, I roped a big blue roan gelding, a four-year-old named Spooks. He had been the only colt out of Old Blue that was hard to break. He was snorty and would still buck when you first saddled him. He was tough and could take a lot of riding.

Little Blue had been my top horse since I'd kinda retired the stud, and he was a crackerjack. Whether cutting cattle, running horses or just crossing country, he was outstanding. He was my other pick.

Packing a trunk for me, Ginny was having second thoughts about not going. She wondered if we might go by Vicksburg and maybe go see *Scarlet Oak.* All day she had thought about the tranquil beauty of the South and the picture perfect life she'd lived before the war. Elegant parties and leisure days in the tree shaded plantation home that she could nearly see again in her mind.

Her mind wondered back to the huge pillars that crossed the veranda, shading the house from the sub-tropic heat. Field hands would be working in the fields as her father oversaw the plantation activity from the back of one of his famous "Wanecloth" Tennessee Walkers. They were the best walking saddle horses in the whole South. Treasured among the Southern planters for comfort and speed in traveling, no hunt was complete without one under you.

Shutting her eyes, Ginny could hear Mammy Lou, their cook, whistling in her mind as she went about her work. She oversaw the big house and did the cooking. Nobody had more clout at *Scarlet Oaks* than Mammy Lou. It was God, Master Wanecloth and Mammy Lou when authority was handed out and sometimes she forgot the order in which it lay.

Ginny smiled, and remembered how her mother would even ask Mammy Lou if an important decision needed to be made. And cook, lord how she could cook. Every meal was a feast and her ample body showed she tasted every dish personally.

It seemed she could still hear the young'ns playing out back beneath the honeysuckle vines that grew around the house. It was their job to bring the eggs to Mammy Lou. She culled the biggest and best for the big house and mustered out the others to the hands, according to how many was in each family. If one was dropped or cracked in transit she was quick to crack her knuckles on a head in a minute, and likewise the milking. Woe to the milk hand that didn't wash and dry his cows' udder before milking. Mammy Lou inspected each pail before accepting it into her ultra clean kitchen. It better not have any dirt flecks or flies in it, and they had rather face "God's Judgment," than face Mammy Lou with dirty milk.

Homesickness nearly overwhelmed her as she continued to pack my trunk. Suddenly she stiffened as she heard the shot again in her mind that killed her father. Once again she had a mental vision of the assault on her beautiful mother. Things she had mentally blocked from her consciousness came thundering back. Mammy Lou attacking the soldiers with a meat clever and was beheaded with an officer's saber.

Choking on memories she had best left forgotten, she closed the lid on the trunk and on that tragic part of her past. She changed her mind and decided not to go with me after all.

We made love as a full moon beamed through the open window. Moonlight gleamed on her naked beauty, but I felt a coolness between us I couldn't explain. Sometimes old memories are best forgotten. I guess it was the tragedy she'd been remembering, but I wondered if maybe my hurt feelings had been showing, or was she just getting tired of the ranch. Maybe she was missing the *Brazos Queen*. My heart shuddered as I thought about her past. This had always bothered me and now half doubts assaulted my mind and I wondered if maybe she was wanting to leave. I'd always heard once a whore always a whore. Maybe it was true, time would tell.

As dawn broke, Jimmy had his team hitched and the buggy packed. He was ready to go. Yesterday had been spent shoeing horses and oiling my saddle and the harness. Willie oversaw it all and gave Jimmy shoeing tips like he was a beginner. Jimmy just grinned. Willie had taught him to shoe when he was twelve-years-old, but still would give him a few tips as he watched.

Saddling Old Spooks, Jimmy cussed him for humping up and wanting to buck. "You shame yore daddy, yo,' bronkie bastard," he muttered as he cinched up the saddle.

Kicking at Jimmy as he reached for the back girth, Spooks was gonna buck and they both knew it. Leaving Spooks tied, Jimmy caught Little Blue and tied him to the back of the buggy. After loading oats and hay, along with the shoeing tools and clothes he drove to the house to load my trunk.

Just enough room was left for my trunk and Jimmy slid my double barreled shotgun and my new Winchester '73 under the seat. This was a powerful repeating rifle. Jimmy loved to shoot it, and felt pretty secure as he mounted the buggy seat. He was setting on go.

Ginny rose earlier than usual to see me off. She knew my aversion to goodbyes, but didn't want last night's mood to prevail. She too had felt something missing from our love making, but couldn't put a handle on it. A coolness still lingered this morning. Her mind was questioning.

She wondered if may be I was tired of her. I'd been a loner for thirty four years. Was I bored with her? For the first time since the war began, she felt at home. At peace with the world and as Bates preached every evening, she had found peace with God. The only thing lacking was marriage.

This was as close to God as her life had been since the attack on *Scarlet Oaks*. Big tears filled her eyes as she kissed me goodbye and watched as that roan horse bucked and bawled out of sight. Jimmy was clattering along behind shouting encouragement to me.

Chapter 17

Riding north I decided to ride by Wagner's and see if his mares had their colts. Hell, I thought, I'd check for the cave and the lost gold as I went by. The colts were just an excuse for coming again.

Jim Wagner was plowing corn in the field by the creek when we drove up. His big sorrel mares were sweating and hot. He'd stopped in the shade to let them cool and a red roan colt was nursing at both their flanks. Jim was awful proud of those colts, and had hoped I was riding the stud so I could breed them back. But that wasn't to be this year.

As we talked I told Jim the black Percheron stallion was running with a set of mares across the river and along Childress Creek. I told him when he caught them in heat just ride them down the river till he could see the stud and tie them up over night. The stud would come to the mares. I told him to be careful because that black stud was pretty ornery and he agreed.

The colts weren't the only babies in the bottom. Mary Wagner was nursing a big ol' boy, nearly a year old when we rode up to the house for lunch. Catfish were cooling on the back of the stove and green beans and new taters from the garden made a king's banquet. Mrs. Wagner loved to fish and she and "Little Jim" would fish in the creek and river while Jim farmed nearby. Along with the rabbits and squirrels and ducks and geese, they had a key to God's meat market. Hams and bacon were hanging in the new smoke house, along with smoked jerky and sausage was proof the Wagners had came to stay.

After a long meal and visit, Jimmy and I headed up the creek toward Hillsboro and Wagner returned to his plowing. I sure felt blessed by his friendship.

Riding slowly up the creek looking for the lost cave, I quickly told Jimmy the whole story about Deke Williams' bravery. I deleted the part about doubting his bravery. Hell, after all he'd done, I was ashamed for doubting his guts. He was a damned hero, even if he was a nigra and catching myself I said a"black. Skin may be different color, but courage is all the same tone.

Jimmy rode up the floor of the creek as I climbed to the top of the bluff and searched for the hole in the rock. Neither discovered anything new as we met at the spring where the White Rock heads. The mystery remained, where in the hell could the cave and the lost gold have gone? Did it slough off when the canyon did, and if so what about the hole in the top?

We had to be missing it. These thoughts rambled through my mind as we approached the livery stable at Hillsboro. Night was approaching as Jimmy took care of the horses. I went across the street to the little café. The waitress remembered me and fixed us a half a dozen fried ham sandwiches, an apple pie and two quarts of fresh milk. She was just closing so we ate our supper off the tailgate of the buggy.

We slept in the wagonyard. I awoke when the little rooster went to crowing. Sore from riding Old Spooks through his little fit yesterday, I arose gingerly. I was about mad at that damn rooster. I could have slept till daylight. Since I was awake, I might as well stay up. I never could go back to sleep once I awoke.

Picking up a handful of rocks, I knocked the old rooster out of his tree. Damn his hide, if I couldn't sleep, he sure as hell wasn't going to get to. I hope a fox caught him, I grinned and headed for the café as pink tinged the east.

With a setting of eggs and a big piece of pie under my belt, I brought Jimmy some breakfast. He had just finished feeding and harnessing the team. I told him to catch Old Spooks again. I'd decided to ride him till he gave it up.

Saddling him cautiously, I reached to pick up the girth and was ready when he kicked at me. Stepping nimbly forward to elude the flashing hoof, I grabbed Spooks by the mane and stepped back toward his withers. I kicked him in the soft part of his stomach as hard as my long legs could kick. Not expecting this, all the air was driven out of him. Grunting and farting like a pack mule, Old Spooks got him a lesson. I kicked him three or four times before he recovered and then finished saddling him.

Mounting quickly, I was ready for him. He was mad about being kicked and really came unwound. I was about as mad as he was and this wasn't a kid he'd picked on. I'd ridden lots of horses that were ranker than he was and as his bucking began to lessen I was ready with my rawhide quirt. Every time he bucked I whipped him down his flanks and belly and raked his shoulders and side with my spurs. Suddenly Spooks decided being an outlaw had some disadvantages.

Hitting a long lope, Hillsboro disappeared as Spooks began to tire. About five miles out of town, I pulled the roan gelding up and let him blow. He was lathered and hot, but his mind was beginning to make some changes. This fighting was taking its toll on his body. Sweat dripped down off his hocks, mingled with the blood from the fresh gouges my spurs had made. Long red streaks rose from his shoulders to his flanks from my spurs and quirt.

While letting him blow, I rubbed his neck and patted his shoulders. When Spooks realized his temper fit brought on this pain, he might think different. He sure could be a good horse if he decided to be. Jimmy caught up with me as we rode toward Waxahachie. We camped on the creek close to Ennis that night. Watering the horses and pouring them some grain, we just cold camped with no fire. We ate jerky and dry bread for breakfast the next morning.

Travel was settling into a hard grind as we passed through the eastern outskirts of Dallas late that evening. We grabbed a bite to eat but traveled a while to get out of town. Along about midnight we camped at a spring about half way to Greenville. We ate lunch in Greenville and bought some food and grain. Next was Texarkana. The little towns of Mount Vernon and Mount Pleasant flashed by as we traveled to Texarkana. We bathed at every clear creek and river but didn't tarry to visit. I was Lexington, Kentucky bound and hell wasn't going to stop me.

I rode Spooks ten days straight without resting him, before he quit trying to buck and would let me mount without moving. He had that same smooth running walk his sire possessed and he could really cover some ground. The buggy horses were gaited the same and we were grinding out forty to fifty miles a day.

I decided to get a hotel room and a hot bath at Little Rock. The room was clean and the sheets cool and fresh. A hot bath was a luxury I'd been dreaming about. The bath and a shave, along with a haircut had given me a new lease on life.

We hit town Friday night about dark and it was raining. After cleaning up I settled in a soft booth at a new café and destroyed a huge steak and a mountain of potatoes. A big jug of coffee and most of a pie finished off my meal.

Feeling restless I drifted over to the saloon and played a few hands of winning poker. I wasn't much of a gambler. If the cards were falling, I'd bet them but if they were cold, it didn't bother me to leave. I won about a thousand dollars and drank a pitcher of beer before the cards got fickle. I mostly visited and traded trail stories. It was early May and the spring rains were falling. It was muddy all the way to Memphis they said. I turned in pretty early and enjoyed the rain on the roof.

I'd left Jimmy at the livery stables to take care of the horses. Jimmy was ready to see the big town. Bathing in the horse trough, he put on his best trousers and new shoes he'd bought before leaving Waco. These shoes were patent leather and shined like new money. Willie's wife had made him a shirt for a going away present. It was snow white and she'd found some old brass buttons that she sewed down the front on each side.

Jimmy was a "Yankee Doodle Dandy" as he stepped out down the street. He could hear the wail of a "jews harp" and the blues of an old trumpet coming from the quarters and it led him home. The music made you want to dance, and dancing Jimmy did.

Quickly catching the eyes of the local fancies, Jimmy became the center of attention. Girls were flashing him white tooth grins, and presently Jimmy was family and let the good times roll. Good times wasn't all that was rolling. A dice game attracted Jimmy nearly as fast as the half-naked high yellow girls had. Jimmy had his life saving in his pocket. He'd saved his tips from the livery stable over the years and his salary. All those silver dollars I'd flipped him for caring for my horses. He was toting a pretty good roll for a black man traveling through strange country.

Jimmy quickly cleaned out the other players as lady luck smiles on him. As the game broke up, his good luck charm had attached herself to a winner. Slipping out into the night, Jimmy was in love. Love at first sight.

Nothing prepared Jimmy for the night ahead. No stranger to sex, he had been getting "a poke" in a cotton wagon or hay barn since he was ten or eleven years old. What Clara brought to her bed was more than Jimmy could fathom. She wore a green dress that clung to her shapely body and had excited his imagination all night. Her yellow complexion was flawless and the white blood that flowed through her veins was evident.

Her mother's owner before the war had been her father, a Frenchman from a plantation in Louisiana. Clara was experienced in the art of making love and turned her experience into the greatest night of Jimmy's life.

Rising early he ran through the rain to the livery stable to feed the horses. He hated to leave her bed. He was afraid he'd never see her again if he left, or someone else would have her when he came back.

He was feeding the horses when I came in the livery stable and suggested we lay over till Monday to leave. I thought he was going to kiss me and turning, he ran back to Clara's house in the rain. He was so afraid she would be gone or someone else would be there, he literally flew.

Clara cooked him catfish and corn pone and they spent the afternoon making love and talking. They ran to the livery barn in the rain and she watched Jimmy feed and brush the horses. He checked their feet and shoes. She was impressed with a man from Texas going all the way to Kentucky for a race horse. As she strolled down the street with her arm in his, she was some proud of this fancy horseman from Texas. With his real shinny shoes, brass buttoned white shirt and the red bowler hat he'd won last night in that dice game.

He had a pocket full of money and didn't have no woman at home 'ceptin two or three he just "poked" and no chil'en's to finish rais'en. After being someone else's poke for years, Clara had found her man.

The juke joints were jumping again and Jimmy's luck stayed strong through the weekend. When the joints closed Sunday night, Clara hated to see this race horse man leave town — Kentucky or no Kentucky.

Chapter 18

It rained a lot on the way to Memphis. Just sort of a drizzle, the buggy was cutting deep ruts in the road as we approached the Mississippi River. Jimmy had kinda diddled along behind since we left Little Rock. His mind was on that high yeller wench. A ferry was waiting as we pulled down to the river. Jimmy's eyes were big as saucers, the river was running strong and a mile wide. He had never seen this much water in his life. Jimmy was still lovesick and I'd been thinking of home all day.

Ginny and the ranch had been steady on my mind. I was missing them both as the ferry boat ground into the dock on the opposite bank. Memphis loomed in the distance as night fell on the river.

Memphis was a hot bed of activity as cotton brokers and mule traders were everywhere. Goods were being shipped and received at the river docks, and Jimmy found out about bananas that came up the river on a boat. I bought a stalk and he ate most of them before we got to Kentucky.

We began to see horse high cotton and tobacco growing along the roads. The river bottoms were lush and fertile. Blue black field hands tilled the fields and Jimmy was proud to be my horse boy. His red hat was cocked at a jaunty angle that caught all the other blacks' attention and none of them had ever had new shinny store bought shoes. Jimmy was toting more money in his pockets than most blacks had ever made in their entire lives.

I asked Jimmy if he wanted me to carry his money for him. He was insulted. He had saved, done without, scraped and clawed for that money. Be damned if anybody, black or white, was gonna tote it for him. He'd made it, he'd tote it, he said. He just might buy him a real race horse, he said. He had dreamed of owning a race horse since he was a little boy. He had saved all his tips from the livery stable in a can he kept under his bed. Just to buy him a race horse.

Not having enough money, he had saved all of the wages from

the ranch to add to it. When he got the chance to come to Kentucky with me, it was a dream come true. He still didn't have enough to buy a real race horse, but with his gambling winnings, he had enough to dream and at least he was going to see some real honest to goodness race horses.

We stopped and ate lunch and spread a blanket out on the ground. We decided to count Jimmy's money. Lady Luck "had come a-courting." After the dice games at Little Rock and his savings, he kinda had him a race horse stake. He had eight hundred dollars in his pocket, a fortune for a young dapper dressed black man.

"Enough to get you killed," I told him, but Jimmy answered "That's the only way they'll get it. I's agoin' to buy me a race horse be damned! What I really want is a race mare, that way when I get thru racing her, I can raise race horses from her."

He said, "That way I's always have a race horse. God just made me for race horses," he smiled, "Even my size."

He was small and light, but strong as a bull. He could shoe and break one as good as anyone. He grinned and said he knew as much as anyone about hosses 'cepten Uncle Willie and Mr. Bill. I kinda agreed with him.

Kentucky kinda came a-creepin' up on Jimmy and I and suddenly we were there. Blue grass meadows and rolling hills, tobacco fields and huge barns with tobacco hanging upside down, their leaves were curing and new crops were growing. We made our way to Lexington and enjoyed the scenery.

While I was in Little Rock and Memphis and as we traveled, I'd shopped for breeders from everyone I talked to. The one that kept turning up was Willard E. Brooks. He was supposed to have the best Thoroughbred horses in America and probably the most.

When we reached Lexington there was a Brooks Feed and Grain so we stopped and made some purchases. Asking directions we found out we were too late. Willard E. Brooks had died last winter from pneumonia and his estate was undecided. He had owned the feed store as part of his horse operation. He also owned the bank and substantial land holdings.

Getting directions I rode toward the horse farm. The man at the feed store said his widow lived out there along with just the hired help. I learned that he had indeed owned the best horse farm in Kentucky, that he had left a rich widow a good bit younger than he and no children. He had been seventy-five years old at his death and up until two weeks before his demise he was hail and healthy. The feed store operator said she was going to disperse part of the horse herd.

Armed with new information and prepared for dealing with a bitter old woman, we set out for the farm with the directions I had acquired. I was unprepared for what met my eyes as I rounded the last turn in the road.

I was awed by the splendor of the place, glistening white fences, green fields and red shinny stables. I turned around and rode back to town to spend the night. Hell! I needed to do some thinking. I was afraid I was jumping on too big a dog to fight. Why, I figured they'd want more for one horse than I'd want to spend total. There was a lot of things you could say about me, but short of guts wasn't one of them.

At nine o'clock sharp the next morning I was knocking on the front door of the largest white columned brick house I'd ever seen. The lawn was larger than my mare trap. I had already seen more black stable hands than Willie and I farmed with. A butler opened the door, and asked me in and asked to take my hat.

I just smiled and said, "I guess I'd just rather keep it."

This butler was dressed in a starched white shirt and coat, creased black pants that would cut your finger and a bow tie! "Pretty nattie," I concluded. Every worker in the house was dressed the same.

Standing awkwardly awaiting the old widow, I was shocked to see an angel appear at the head of the stairs, and this angel was a-wearin' britches. My mouth flew open and I just gawked as she smiled graciously and descended the stairs. She was dressed in a starched white blouse that opened daringly at the throat and fawn colored jodhpurs tucked into rich sorrel riding boots and a flat leather hat was hanging down her back. It was secured by a leather thong around her neck, kinda like a stampede string the Vaqueros from Mexico wore.

I was speechless as I answered her smile and introduced myself. She was warm and hospitable, offering coffee or breakfast or a drink if I preferred. It was barely nine and I wondered how in the hell could anyone look so cool and lovely this early.

Eve Brooks was easy to look at and just as easy to get to know. She shook hands like a man, wore pants like a man, but was the most feminine person I'd ever met. I had never seen a woman wear pants, but if an election was ever held, I'd damn sure vote for them. Her body looked like it was carved out of soft white soap, and her hair pulled back in a ponytail with soft curls framing her face.

I felt like a new colt, I wasn't sure if I could walk or breathe. I had never had anyone have this effect on me. Finally turning the conversation to horses, I at least felt I was on firmer ground.

I could hardly tell you what happened next, but it was over, it seemed, in about fifteen minutes. She had gotten a surrey and a driver by snapping her fingers. I vaguely remember eating lunch at her table. We drove for miles looking at mares and foals and suddenly it was night. She insisted that I stay at the big house. This house was larger than any hotel I'd ever stopped in. I was escorted by the dandy butler to my room, which was as big as my ranch house.

After I had soaked for an hour in a tub bigger than my stock trough, I was escorted to a banquet table full of the finest food I'd ever tasted. Squabs in a milk sauce, braised quail, friend chicken and more. I had never seen so much food and only myself. Mrs. Brooks and a Mr. Sinclair and his wife were present.

Mrs. Brooks explained that Mr. Sinclair ran the bank and soon after supper, that they kept calling dinner, they retired to the drawing room to sign some papers.

The houseboy poured me a glass of brandy and brought me a

black cheroot cigar. I didn't smoke but stuck it in my pocket for Jimmy.

Meanwhile, Jimmy was making the rounds with the stable help. He was shown the stables, horses and horses and horses. Jimmy's mouth drooled as he looked at horse after horse. Mose, the senior groom and trainer, took Jimmy under his wing, and was Jimmy's mentor. He knew a race horse man when he saw one, cause he had been the best. Taking Jimmy home with him, he'd bedded him with his sixteen year-old daughter. She sure wasn't no Clara, Jimmy decided as he drifted off to sleep.

After the Sinclair's left, a houseboy appeared with a fiddle, that he kept calling a violin. He began to play softly. Mrs. Brooks asked me to dance. The candles were turned down and as we began to waltz, I pinched myself to see if I was dreaming. Here I was a riff-raff Texas cowboy being entertained by a queen like I was royalty.

As the night wound down, Mrs. Brooks, became just Eve and we talked until the wee hours. Never had so much pleasure been crammed into one day as this one has, I thought as I drifted off to sleep.

Eve lay awake tossing restlessly in her huge four poster bed. She said, she kept feeling my arms around her as we danced and was ashamed for the way she was feeling. William was hardly buried, and here she was thinking about another man. She knew she seemed bold, but bold was what had attracted William to her. She was twenty when she met William, and was the belle of every ball and Kentucky courted her.

From the Governor's Palace to the Race Track Ball, she was pursued. The daughter of a large tobacco farmer, her beauty left men her age stammering and left old men wishing they were her age.

William E. Brooks was a dashing widower, approaching sixty and hoping to hold old age at bay with young beautiful women. He had pursued and won her body and soul. They had a grand but childless marriage. As she looked back, she knew she had loved him, but as a father figure.

He had loved her with all his heart and soul. Never had he told her no. Her every whim was of major importance to him. She felt fortunate to have married him and had enjoyed the fifteen year they had spent together. But no one had ever stirred her soul or emotion like this cowboy from Texas with his good manners and Texas drawl, she confessed.

The day began late as gray clouds hung over the meadows. After a large leisure breakfast, we decided to ride horseback to do our looking today. Eve had the groom saddle her horse and Jimmy saddled Little Blue for me.

She took me through several pastures of brood mares and we stopped for lunch on Shady Brook Creek. She had left instructions for a driver to meet us there with a picnic lunch and a bottle of chilled wine.

The driver was waiting when we reached Shady Brook Creek. Spreading a table cloth on the creek bank like it was a fine piece of furniture, Eve was a gracious hostess. Fried chicken and deviled eggs, sliced tomatoes and thick cheese sandwiches were washed down with the wine. Dinner or lunch as they called it, was a treasure of taste.

Soon after, the driver left with the remains of our lunch, and we had just started in another mare paddock when it began to rain. A large hay barn lay ahead of us along the creek. Eve motioned for me to follow and we raced for the shelter.

Thunder rolled and lightening flashed as we slid our horses to a stop in the large barn. Rain had started to fall in earnest as I tied our horses and lay back in the soft warm hay to wait out the storm.

Sitting softly beside me, she began to trace patterns across my chest with her finger and reaching up to catch her hand, I knew this rain was a divine blessing. As I grasped her hand, she melted and rolled on top of me. Murmuring my name, she kissed me like I'd never been kissed as thunder and lightening flashed across the meadows.

I pulled her to me and kissed her softly, stroking her back and long blonde hair that had escaped its clasp during the race for the barn. Her emotions, long buried, were dangerously close to the top as Eve basked in the touch of my rough work calloused hands. Tortured breathing expressed the torment her conscious was experiencing. Was it too soon, or would it be too late if she held back. She knew this cowboy wasn't one of the toy tin soldiers she had used and thrown away in her youth. I was no boy, but, neither was I an old man and her body craved hard masculine maleness.

Slowly I unbuttoned the starched white blouse she wore. It was much like the one she wore yesterday and as I did, her soft warm, milk white breast seemed to rise with her passion. Turning from me, she removed the clasp from her hair and quickly pulled off her boots. Without blushing, she swiftly dropped her blouse and standing, slowly removed her pants.

Nothing in my imagination equaled her naked beauty. Long golden hair spread out on the soft warm hay as she lay down beside me. Soft white breast with big dark nipples nestled in the palm of my hands and I feasted on their abundance.

Soft rain fell as we made love throughout the afternoon. Peaks of ecstasy were reached that had escaped us both before. Had there ever been two people so ripe for each other or more in tune?

Slowly dressing, Eve stopped and kissed me as I pulled on my boots. No remorse showed on her face as she tucked her pants leg into her boots. Contentment flooded her soul and body, and she felt like she had reached the crest of a long hill she'd been climbing forever. Never had she been so fulfilled or felt more like a real woman, she whispered.

We raced like kids for the stable at the big house, and she squalled when Little Blue slung mud in her face. He outran her gelding for three or four hundred yards to the gate. I pulled up before the big bay she was riding could hit his stride and left her thinking I was riding a race horse.

Night was falling as we made our way to the house. Dinner

would be late, she told the help, as we hurried up the stairs.

The same fancy butler escorted me to my room and drew my bath. No emotion played on his solemn black face as I watched him. He filled the tub brimming full of steaming hot water and I soaked in luxury. Washing my hair and shaving, I felt like I had taken a trip to fairyland. I had found the princess and was just waiting for her shoe to fall off.

Donning my new clothes I'd bought in Memphis, I looked the part of a Southern gentleman, except for my fancy new calf skin boots and new black hat, I'd bought on my last trip to Fort Worth.

A feast was once again spread and the violin was playing softly in the background. When the meal was over, Eve and I began to dance slowly. The night was lost in the passion that lay simmering between us. As the clock struck midnight, I retired from the parlor and the maid began to tidy up the room and cleared the table.

My bed had fresh clean sheets and was turned down. This had to be the softest feather bed I'd ever seen, a far cry from my bedroll on the freezing Texas plains. The large house got quiet. A full moon was standing at half mast, illuminating the room in a glow of splendor. Hearing my door open quietly, I was startled to see Eve standing just inside. As she dropped the gown she wore to the floor, the moon bathed her soft, pale features with a dusky gold. My breath caught in my throat and I thought for a minute I would choke. More of the magic that had transpired this afternoon was in store as passion took control of the night.

I smelled her fragrance as she snuggled up to me in the damp chill of early morning. I hated to awaken her from her peaceful sleep, but I didn't want the servants to catch her in my bed. Her beauty radiated from her thin nose and ivory complexion to her big blue eyes that were closed softly in sleep. Her hair was flung casually across my pillow. Kissing her eyelids softly as I rose, she opened her eyes slowly as if seeing life for the first time. I knew I had gotten in over my head, but couldn't and didn't want to do a damn thing about it.

The next two weeks were spent in Utopia. Neither of us had

ever imagined such perfection. We had looked at hundreds of horses and neither of us had the heart to make a deal. Both of us feared when the trading started the magic would end, and neither of us could stand the thought.

I told Eve about wanting to buy some Hereford bulls and she knew a breeder. Both anxious to delay the end, we spent a week in her carriage, just driving and looking at bulls. I finally bought ten bulls and had them shipped down the Ohio to the Mississippi and then on to Galveston. They could ship them to Waco on a paddle wheel steamer, on the first high water rise.

I was excited about the new cattle. Herefords were the breed I decided. They were bigger, longer and deeper than Shorthorns. The cattle also seemed to grow faster. I looked at some Shorthorns while I was back here, but decided to go with the Herefords. I also looked at a new breed of black cattle they called Angus. They were from Scotland. They were naturally polled. They were pretty cattle, but hell, turning one of those loose on my range would be like going to a knife fight without a knife or buying a wagon without a tongue in it.

As we drove back to the farm, I knew the bubble had to burst. I needed to get back to Texas and I knew Eve would never leave Kentucky. If ever a queen reigned, Eve was queen of Kentucky. Everyone knew her and rolled out the red carpet when we came by. Men were mesmerized by her charm and beauty and the women were appalled by it.

Riding along in her carriage, she rested her head on my shoulder and sighed contentedly. Raising up quickly, as if the thought had just entered her pretty head, she said, "Bill, if you sold your ranch and I sold the bank, we would have all our time to spend with the horses."

I had pondered the same solution many times in the past few weeks. This jolted me back to reality, and suddenly I was homesick for Texas and thoughts of Ginny again rushed through my mind. Feeling guilty, I assayed my feeling and couldn't decide if I felt guilty about loving Ginny or for loving Eve.

Damn, I hated it when life got complicated. Why did I have to choose between them. Hell, I was in love with both of them, I just loved them in different ways. This was possible. I had two good horses and I liked both of them. They were as different as daylight and dark, but each great in their own way. One was gentle and solid, the other a bronc but tough and resilient. I liked them both for what they were and accepted it. By God, was it any different with women, I wondered, as I continued to mentally justify my feelings. I felt torn between my thoughts.

I grew quiet as darkness settled in and the carriage rocked along. Feeling she was losing me, Eve turned and kissed me passionately. Torn between loves, my body took the easy route out and shucking clothes like newly weds, fresh love ruled the coach. The driver drove through the darkness toward the farm in the early night, unmindful of all that was going on beneath his seat.

We continued the night of love in my big four poster feather bed. Both of us knew it was coming to an end, but not knowing how to end it. As day broke, I was awake and restless. I knew I was out of my class. No way could cows ever pay for the life she was accustomed to. I couldn't imagine Eve at the ranch and when I thought of the ranch and Ginny, I knew where I belonged. Aw! I could have stayed right here, but I had too much pride to stay here and live off of Eve. She would have liked nothing better. Pride is a tough mixture. Too little and you're worthless and too much and you're a damn fool!

Eve knew she was losing and knew no way to combat it. She'd played her hole card and saw it hadn't worked. She lay there in the bed and smelled the maleness of the bed. Opening her eyes she watched my bare torso as I stood and looked soberly out the window. Tears welled up in her eyes. Never had she been loved, or been in love like these last few weeks. She wasn't sure she could go on living without me, yet she knew she couldn't leave Kentucky. This was her world. I was bound for Texas and she knew I felt the same way about it. Crying softly she watched from the window as I made my way to the barn.

Chapter 19

Mose and Jimmy had been inseparable since the first day. Mose the teacher and Jimmy the student. Jimmy had been galloping horses everyday and Mose was teaching the art of race training. Mose had raced and trained at all the big tracks, Lexington, Louisville, Cincinnati, New York, you name them. He was the one who made Willard E. Brooks famous. He was no stranger to the winner's circle, first as a jockey, but much more as a trainer.

He was thrilled to have Jimmy to teach. Mose had shown him how to wrap, what to do for and to keep from getting splints, pulled tendons and bows. Feet, legs, back, lungs, nothing was left out of Jimmy's crash course and he had passed with flying colors. Jimmy was a racehorse man - except he didn't have a racehorse. Mose was hoping his daughter, Lucinda, would have Jimmy to stay in Kentucky, but Jimmy's affections seemed far away. They rattled the bed every night, but not with any enthusiasm, Mose thought.

I walked into the cool fragrant horse barn, bluestem hay and horses. They had a smell of their own. I was nearly drunk on it. Damn, this was the best horse country in the world, and I was nearly persuaded to stay.

I walked to the stall of Domino Duke. Of all the horses I had looked at, this was my choice, a bright red roan. I guess he was really a sorrel but he had roan hair in his flanks and around the root of his tail. A big blaze ran down his face and he had four stocking legs.

"Too much white for a Thoroughbred," Mose complained. "Ain't no good fur nuttin'," he mumbled. "He ain't nuttin' like the old Domino horse. This hoss got tremendous speed early but he can't finish. Da first half he win, but the last half you catch 'em on a pig. Too much muscle in dis hoss. He too heavy and thick to go da mile," Mose kept repeating. He did have a lot of muscle and bone, but this was what attracted me to him.

Eve walked into the hall of the barn. She was framed by the

morning sun, behind her back, shining thru the open doors of the barn. She looked like a mirage. Damn, leaving ain't going to be easy, I decided.

The horse trading began. Eve told me heads up, this horse couldn't go the distance. She said she would have had him gelded or sold him, but he was the last son of the famous Domino horse that had built her late husband's fortune. She never priced him.

She asked me how many mares I was looking for, and we picked out ten. They were greys mostly and a lot of them with the same bloodlines as the stallion. A few nice sorrel mares, and a roan mare that was a full sister to the stud.

Mose and Jimmy came along before we could establish a price. I had decided what ever it took I was willing to pay it. Never had I seen this good a set of mares and stud. Jimmy had his red hat in his hands and was bad needing to talk to Mrs. Brooks.

Mose had shown Jimmy a little old stunted filly that was down in the bottom. She was an orphan. She was sired by the roan stallion and out of Old Cricket. This was an old mare that Mr. Brooks had won a lot of money with. She had quit breeding and when the stud had gotten back from the track he was bad to stall. He would walk and fidget, so Mose had put her in his stall to babysit him.

Not thinking she'd still breed, Mose was surprised when he went to the stall and found the foal. She was too old to nurse, so Mose raised the filly on a goat. The filly was a two year-old, but about the size of a good yearling.

Jimmy had never bought or sold anything in his life, but Mose said this would be a short race horse deluxe and Jimmy was going to own her somehow. Mose told him she wouldn't ever go a mile but should run good at short distances.

Jimmy had her on a lead shank and was ready to do business. Rolling up that red hat and shuffling his feet, he said, "Mrs. Brooks, I sure would be beholdin' to ya to sell me this here mare." and pulling out his whole roll, he handed it to Eve.

Taken back, she didn't know what to say. She didn't even know the filly existed. Asking Mose the particulars, he told her that this was Old Cricket's last foal by the Domino Duke hoss and putting in a plug for Jimmy, he said she ain't never goin' be much of a miler, but this boy might make a right passible short hoss outa' her.

He explained how Jimmy had been workin' every day, a gallopin' hosses and was a tolerable good race-hoss man. Eve looked at Jimmy's pleading eyes and his whole roll of money held out to her, crumpled bills and silver dollars and change. She knew he wanted this filly bad.

Smiling at Jimmy she said, "Jimmy since you've been working for me every day since you've been here, I owe you. Why don't I just give you the filly for your labor and we'll be even."

Jimmy was so excited he dropped his money and his red hat both. Bending down quickly he just scooped the money, hay and all up and put it in his hat. Big tears sprang to his eyes. Nobody had ever gave him anything, he said, 'ceptin Willie and Mr. Bill.

His dreams had just come true. He had him a race hoss mare, and he's sure 'nough a race hoss man. Life was goin' to be different for Jimmy from now on, he thought as he turned to hug the filly and Mose. Hardly able to control himself, Jimmy grabbed a brush and began to brush her like it was going to make her grow.

Mose took the ten mares that we had selected and put them in a trap. He was sad, cause he knew they were leaving for Texas and Jimmy was going to be leavin' too. Jimmy was the son he never sired and he was mad at Lucinda for not sweet talking him or getting with child or something to hold him. Texas was a long way, and he knew Jimmy ain't never coming back.

Eve's mind was running parallel with Mose's. She knew the end was nearing and for a person who was in control of her own world, thirty days ago, her world had gone to hell. She said she was having trouble remembering life before we met and sure as hell couldn't imagine it after I left. She told me she hadn't hurt like this when William died.

Why had she let herself fall so hard, she questioned. She loved the way I smiled, the way I talked, my slow drawl, my wisdom and way with horses, she said. Hell! She just loved me! It was like loving the wind she knew she couldn't hold it and when restrained or blocked, it always did a lot of damage.

Dressing for dinner, Eve knew this was our last night together. She dreaded closing the horse deal. Without being told, she knew this was goodbye. Hell, she would have given the whole horse herd, she thought, to keep this feeling, but some things are not meant to be. Knowing something doesn't make it hurt any less, she thought, as she slipped a string of pearls around her neck. A low necked, black dress that clung to her like a second skin really set off her pale skin and dark blue eyes that looked violet when she became intense.

I dressed slowly, dreading this night. Though I knew I needed to leave, I hated the thought. I knew this goodbye was going to be forever. Damn goodbyes! Anyway, I knew that with her charm, grace and beauty, she would be married the next time I came to Kentucky, if there was a next time. Hell, she had enough money to buy a husband, any kind she wanted, except me, I grimaced. Why in the hell couldn't I bend a little. This was the chance of my life to have the horses of my dreams. This lady has more good horses than I had ever seen in my lifetime, but homesickness is a strong emotion and I was homesick for Texas and Ginny. Hell, I was even homesick for Bates and Willie. I was even looking forward to fall round-up and all the work I had to do when we got home. June had turned hot and July was just ahead. We had thirty hot hard days travel to get home.

The meal was one you could never forget, yet I could hardly remember eating it. Conversation was forced and neither of us was saying what we were thinking. As dinner came to a close there was more food on the plates than we had eaten. As the violin began to play, the mood was somber. Slow waltzes were the musical menu. As Eve melted into my arms, I wished I could stop the world.

This was as close to heaven as I'd ever been and with the thought spinning in my head, I wasn't going to get any closer.

Neither of us said a word as we danced. Taking my hand, she led me into her office. A string was tied around a bundle of registered pedigrees and bloodline sheets. There were twelve head in all, the ten mares, the roan stud, and Jimmy's filly.

A note was wrapped around the papers. A lump formed in my throat as I read the note. "To Bill, with all my love. You made dreams into reality and I will never forget you. Love Eve!"

No money could buy these horses she said, and she wouldn't take any money for them. Nothing I could say or do, would change her mind. My mind did not want to accept them as a gift — but it either this or go back to Texas empty handed.

Leading me by the hand, she took me into her room which made my room look like a closet in comparison. Hers was really a three-room apartment with plush velvet furniture with matching drapes and thick carpet. The bed was the largest I'd ever seen. The night slipped away as Eve and I became one in the night. One thought, one emotion, but two heartaches as the sun rose on the sad day.

Spooks couldn't stand prosperity. Standing in a stall a month on good grain and bluestem hay made him really try my ring on that morning. He really bucked! After the first five or six jumps, I took down my quirt and raking Spooks from his shoulders to his flank with my spurs, we put on a show for Kentucky. As Spooks began to weaken, I took my quirt to him and really punished him. Spooks was about to see the light.

Jimmy tied the filly behind the wagon beside Little Blue. Haltering ten mares, I tied the lead rope of one mare to the tail of another, with a knot Mose taught me. Head and tailing Mose called it. An old trick that traders and race horse men used. Tying the lead mare to the wagon beside Little Blue and the filly, we set out for Texas.

With my roan bronc and leading the stud I set the pace. Jimmy with the wagon and the mares strung out behind, bringing up the rear. We took our time passing through Kentucky and didn't push very hard till we got the horses used to traveling. We soon left the bluestem country behind and drifted into Tennessee.

Jimmy had chopped up tobacco real fine and mixed with oats to worm his filly. Mose had shown him how to mix oats, corn and a dollop of black strap molasses and three raw eggs to really fatten a hoss up. The regular exercise behind the wagon along with the new feeding program and all of Jimmy's brushing, really changed the looks of Moonshine. Mose had named her after the hillbilly liquor. Jimmy had been saddling Moonshine and leading her with just the saddle. He would tie the reins up to the wagon seat and just let the team follow me while he'd ease on her back. Lot of times he'd just ride her bareback as she led behind the wagon. By the time we reached the Mississippi at Memphis, Jimmy had her broke and was galloping by the time we crossed on the ferry boat. He really had her broke by the time we got to Little Rock.

Little Rock has been calling Jimmy. Clara was waiting at Little Rock. We laid over again for the weekend to restock and lay in supplies and rest up a while.

I could hardly find Jimmy. As soon as he tended to the horses, he'd run back to Clara's, or be training his mare. Jimmy wouldn't go to the juke joints or shoot dice this time. He had two things on his mind, that yeller skinned girl and his race mare.

Jimmy rode her over to the fairgrounds every day and worked her. She was green as a gourd but she could fly. Too little for anyone but Jimmy to ride, but for three or four hundred yards, she made the ground smoke.

Jimmy wanted me to stay an extra day. There was a gambler who had been making fun of Jimmy's hat everyday. He also had a Steel Dust race horse and seeing Jimmy leading his little filly along on a rope, he asked him if he had a collar for that dog. This was the catalyst for the whole deal. The gambler knew he had Jimmy mad about his hat and then he really hit a nerve about his mare.

Jimmy was proud of that red hat, but when he called his race mare a dog, that was the final blow. Without thinking Jimmy told him that's all a fish eyed fool like you knows, you can't tell a genuine Kentucky race mare from a dog.

Being white had a lot of advantages and having money gave him some more. Showing out before his friends, he asked Jimmy if he had a couple of quarters he'd like to bet on a horse race.

Fully insulted now Jimmy said, if he thought he would run this mare for two quarters, he was a bigger fool than he looked and he looked like a fool. Fully riled and full of pride Jimmy told the man he'd race him for eight hundred dollars.

The gambler kind'a joking said, "Okay, put up your money," and Jimmy unloaded his pockets. He had exactly eight hundred dollars. The gambler laughing at his good fortune peeled off eight hundred dollar bills and the race was on.

Jimmy ran to the stable in a panic. Crying, "Mr. Bill, come quick!"

Telling me the story, Jimmy was scared and about to cry. He kept saying, "Mr. Bill, what I gonna do? This here filly ain't ready to race and they done got all my money."

They had let the saloon keeper hold the money and the news was all over town. I went to the saloon, thinking I could get the bet forfeited when they knew the circumstances, but the bartender was holding the money and a bet was a bet. Jimmy had let his temper write a draft his ass might not could cash.

Coming back to the barn, I was mad through and through. Damn gambler, taking advantage of my nigra boy. I oiled my guns just in case. The race was set for the next morning at ten o'clock. The sheriff would flag the starting line and the judge would call the finish. They would just walk the horses to a line and when the sheriff dropped his flag the race was on.

Jimmy was up early brushing and washing his mare. He had shod her the day before with some little light shoes he'd had the blacksmith make him. He had told him to put toe grabs on the shoes and to calk the back shoes. Mose had showed him this trick. It helped a horse get a hold of the ground and gave them a lot more grab.

At nine-thirty the gambler showed up with his Steel Dust horse.

A big powerful gelding, with a grulla strip down his back. Fifteen and a half hands and weighing twelve fifty. He was a powerful horse. He had a colored jockey on him that was a local favorite and the crowd was a wanting to bet. At nine-forty-five Jimmy came leading Moonshine up on a rope. She had really slicked off and gotten in shape on the trip. Everyone was giggling as Jimmy hopped on her bareback. She looked like a kid pony and Jimmy looked like a kid.

Moonshine walked down the track like a plow mule, just ambling along. The gambler was doing a lot of talking and when he finally got around to Texas, I'd had about enough. He was really enjoying the attention and started giving long odds trying to get a little more money bet. When the odds got to four to one, the gambler had finally gotten me mad, and peeling off a couple of hundred, I called his bet. Handing the bartender my money I watched as the gambler counted out eight hundred and laughed. I decided I wasn't any smarter than Jimmy. We had both let our pride do our betting.

Walking to the line was nearly comical. It looked like a mare and a colt instead of a horse race. The big gelding had ran a lot of races and was real hyper. He was rearing and lunging trying to unseat the jockey. Frothing at the mouth he reared and lunged just as the sheriff dropped his flag. Moonshine had never raced against another horse and she was paying him no mind. She was just waiting for the cue from Jimmy, they had been practicing. As the flag dropped, Jimmy squeezed with his knees and Moonshine broke Little Rock's heart.

She just sprinted off that line and hit flying. She broke on top by two lengths and was ahead by six when they crossed the finish line.

I was in shock. I thought I had bought a two hundred dollar ticket to a mismatch, and here I had won eight hundred dollars. Jimmy could not believe it. He kept pinching himself. He actually had him a sure enough race mare and a good one. Cooling her down, he was about to choke on his pride.

I walked quickly to the bartender and collected our money. The crowd was beginning to mummer and the gambler was wanting a rematch for tomorrow. I just kept walking. Taking the filly, I told Jimmy to hook up the team, halter the mares and get moving. I went to the hotel and got my trunk and clothes. Quickly saddling Old Spooks, and haltering the roan stud, I was ready to get out of Little Rock.

Picking up my rifle, I stuck it in my saddle scabbard. Might need this before the day's over I said as we headed west. I motioned for Jimmy to lead out and that's when I saw Clara sitting on the wagon seat holding that double barrel gun across her lap. Jimmy was going to Texas, a genuine race horse man with a new wife. Jimmy had struck gold, and was a fixing to mine it.

We traveled hard till dark. We kept watching our back tracks. Too many people saw that little mare run and all that money change hands, not to have company a comin'. Dark came slowly and Jimmy was a settin' the pace. We had changed places, Jimmy was leading the filly and Little Blue behind the wagon with the mares strung out behind. I led the stud and rode drag. We had pushed hard since we had left Little Rock at noon. We'd probably covered twenty or twenty-five miles, but a man traveling horseback could catch us in a hurry.

The brush was thick along the road and I was real nervous. I sure as hell wasn't going to camp in these woods. Midnight came and went as we trudged on west. I hated to punish the horses, especially the little filly, after the way she had run, but his filly would be the talk of the country tomorrow and someone was sure to be after her.

I could feel someone a comin,' but no one was in sight. About daylight we came out of the woods into a pretty good clearing. An old cabin and a big deserted old barn sat out in the opening. A windmill was pumping clear cold water into a big rock trough. A fenced garden had grown up in grass nearby.

Pulling up in the hall of the barn, Jimmy jumped down and

unhooked the wagon. I led the mares to the rock trough and watered them. After they drank, I turned them into the garden to fill up on the lush grass that had taken it over.

Six stalls were in the old barn and by tying up a couple of gates we stalled the team, the filly, the stud and the riding horses. I was worried. The mares would give us away if someone rode up. Taking my rifle I climbed up in the loft and stretched out on the hay that was left. Jimmy and Clara lay down in the wagon. Clara was holding on to that shotgun and I gave Jimmy my pistol.

We slept lightly till noon. The stud squalled and I knew company was a comin.' Quickly grabbing my rifle, I moved silently to that end of the barn. Four heavy armed drifters were watering their horses and taking stock of the ten blooded mares. You could see the greed in their faces.

Dismounting quickly, two headed for the barn while one started toward the mares. The leader rode off to the side of the barn to cover all their bets. As they approached the barn, I coldly told them to keep riding or die. Quickly drawing their guns, the two ran for the barn door. I quickly swung my rifle site to the leader out to the side as the two ran out of my sights under the loft. As the leader jerked out his rifle, my bullet hit him behind his right ear.

The other two thugs jerked open the barn door, but nothing had prepared them for the welcome. Clara had stood up in the wagon bed as they raced for the barn. She shot them both point blank in the face, at close range. The lone survivor broke and ran for his horse and Jimmy fired wildly with his pistol. The bullet ricocheted off the windmill tower and the lone bandit had enough. Dropping his gun and begging for mercy, he abandoned the plan. I questioned him as Jimmy hooked up the team and caught the mares.

Jimmy headed west as I saddled my horse and caught the stud. Turning the thieves' horses loose, we strung the dead men up in the hall of the barn where everyone coming by could see them. I tied my lariat rope around the coward's neck and made him pull off his boots. I led him all evening headed west. Just before dark, I found out the gambler had set the thieves on us. He had offered them a thousand for the filly and market price for the other horses. They were to get a hundred apiece for killing us. This crook had walked all afternoon barefooted and could barely walk. Pulling my rifle from its scabbard, I told him I was fixing to get down and piss. If he was in my sights when I quit shaking it, I was going to kill him.

If ever a tired thief ran, this one did. I fired a couple of shots after him for good measure. I figured I'd made my point. We traveled till we hit a town and turned in for a much deserved rest, for horses and folks alike.

I took the rifle and Clara kept the shotgun. We spent the night in the livery stable and slept in the wagon again. After a hurried breakfast, we struck out for Texarkana. Jimmy was spending about as much time feeding and petting the filly as he was a petting on Clara.

Chapter 20

Stopping in Texarkana to restock our supplies, Jimmy matched his filly in another race. I could have killed him. "Dammit Jimmy! You're going to get us killed," I cussed him. "And you're going to get our horses stole if you don't keep your damn mouth shut. This little mare draws too much attention to be ignored."

Jimmy and Moonshine ran at it the same way. Walking to the line, Moonshine was quiet and docile till Jimmy squeezed her and dropped down over her neck. No one could believe the little filly could run so fast. She won by ten lengths going four hundred yards against a big sorrel gelding from Hot Springs that had won a lot of races.

Word had spread about the Little Rock hijacking and we were pretty much left alone. We had each bet two hundred on the filly when the odds got three to one. This netted us twelve hundred dollars, thirteen Clara said as she held up a fist full of dollars. Jimmy had given her a twenty dollar gold piece to bet and she had cleaned out the colored section. "Old Big Red" was a local favorite and they gave her five to one odds. Clara broke the bank.

As surely as Jimmy said it, we had a "shore 'nough" Kentucky race mare on our hands and I wasn't sure how to handle it. Jimmy was a walking dead man if he didn't change his style. Jimmy's fortune had skyrocketed since we had left Waco. He had left Waco with two hundred dollars in nickels and dimes and silver dollars. Mostly tips he'd earned at the livery stable, a lucky dice game on his lucky night and his race winnings, had made it eight hundred.

It was a fortune for a former slave. Jimmy had popped off and doubled his fortune. That's sixteen hundred I figured and I'd given him half my winnings. That made two thousand. Again I'd split my winnings at Texarkana and we'd both won six hundred. That made him twenty-nine hundred and Clara's hundred made a smooth three thousand he was totin'. Jimmy had it all in his pocket and would pull it out to show it. I was plenty worried as we pulled away from the fair grounds and headed for Texas.

As the day wore on Jimmy was a walking and pampering the mare while Clara drove. Thinking it was time to talk to Jimmy about his money, I dropped back to the wagon and just let the mares travel. As I started to discuss Jimmy's money, Clara patted her bosom.

"He dun went and put dat money in da bank, Mr. Bill," she said. "Cocky fool nigra gonna get hisself kilt, I done told him. I take care da money from now on," and cradling the shotgun in her lap, I knew it was in good hands.

We made Waco by the fifteenth of August and Jimmy became a hero to the hired help. He came home rich and with the race mare. Willie had to raise hell with the other hands, they were trying to race the work teams.

Bates had died before we got back. Ginny had gone in to wake him the last day of July, but Bates had died in his sleep. He looked at peace, Ginny said, as tears filled her eyes. They had gotten awful close.

She buried him under the pecan trees in the corner of the yard. He loved to set out there in the shade and read. Bates had made peace with God this last year and finished the job God had given him. He had baptized all of the farm help big enough to make a decision. Funny how someone who had taken so many lives without blinking an eye, could become so concerned about the hired hands souls. God just works in mysterious ways, I'd always heard.

Ginny was thrilled to have me back, and as night fell she acted like a new bride. She laid out a new lace gown she had ordered from a mail order catalog. It was beautiful with little lace eyelets. A champagne color and as she slipped it on, it really complimented her red hair and blue eyes. I was already in bed, and as she turned down the lamp, I saw her as if for the first time. I was glad to be home.

I realized I'd made the right decision and Kentucky and Eve

seemed far away. As Ginny nestled in beside me, I stroked her hair and as we began to make love, she trembled. It had been such a long time.

Morning came early this time of the year and I was way behind in my work. The crops were all laid by and the fall round up wasn't far away. I needed to go to Galveston to check on my bulls. I needed them home if I was going to get a calf crop out of them next year. I wanted to get them here and get them acclimated to this country before I put them to work. I made the rounds with Jimmy driving the wagon putting out salt. We checked all the north range and salted the water holes and shady places.

Jimmy and Clara set up shop in a little house over on the Brazos side of the ranch, close to Willie's place. He wanted some deep sand to make him a race track. He had taken the roan stud and the full sister to him along with the filly. He spent his mornings galloping these three and training. He still helped out if Willie needed him but he was pretty well on his own.

Willie was awful proud of Jimmy, but when Jimmy talked about Mose and what he had taught him, Willie was a little jealous. He'd huff up and say, "Kentucky "nigra" don't know everything 'bout hosses," as if he did.

Rain began falling in late August and it rained intermittently for two weeks. The Brazos was running bank full. I had gone to town for a load of lumber. The field hands were idle and Willie had them building corrals and building Jimmy a race barn for his horses.

The blast of a steamship ripped the quiet morning air. A boat had made a run while the river was full and my bulls were aboard. I had to hurry back to the ranch and get some hands to help drive them home. The Bosque could be forded at Rock Creek. It was out of the way but it was down enough I could cross without floating the wagon and soon we were back for the bulls.

Hereford bulls were an attraction for Waco. Thousands of Longhorns had crossed here but big red and white Herefords were a new deal. People lined the streets to stare at the big white faced cattle as we made our way to the ranch.

I didn't like summer calves but I was anxious to get some calves on the ground out of my new stock. I had those two hundred and fifty Shorthorn crossed heifers in the river pasture above Jimmy's house. Seventy of these were nearly pure Shorthorn. I decided to sort them and put purebred Shorthorns back with the seventy and turn the Herefords with the rest of them.

As soon as the sorting and reshuffling was over, the rain ended and we began to gather the ranch for the fall work. Fall was approaching and the work looked like it would never end. There were colts to wean and halter break. Calves to wean and work. Corn to pull, cotton to pick and after all this rain the meadows would yield another crop of hay. My life was awful busy but I was happy. Ginny and I had captured some of the magic of before, but the storm was about to strike.

Chapter 21

I came in from the first day's gather and was really tired. The calves were bigger than usual and we had a real good crop. I had filled a tub with hot water and was bathing when Ginny came into the room. Sitting down on the bed she began to read, "To Bill with all my love, you have made my dreams reality, and I will never forget you! Love Eve."

I knew I'd heard this song before — Ginny had found Eve's note wrapped around the pedigrees when she unpacked my trunk. What could I say? Hell, Stephen T. Dill couldn't defend this. If all else fails, try the truth, I had always heard.

Drying off with a thick towel, I sat down on the bed and told my story. Not lying about it, but skirting some of the more intimate details. Hell, you couldn't sketch it thin enough to hide the fact that there had been a serious love affair.

Ginny began to cry, silently at first and then louder, then letting anger into it, she had a cussing fit. Finally, getting herself together and settling down, she faced me.

Taking a deep breath, she said, "Bill, I've had my body used and abused, I've had my soul stole and sold, but I had never given my heart away before. You're the first man I have ever loved, and coming from a whore, maybe that don't mean a lot to you, but it meant a hell of a lot to this whore. It's all I had, and this part of me, I kept pure and innocent all these years. You have trampled my heart with muddy boots. But you nor any other bastard will ever have the chance again!"

Turning from my guilty eyes, she began to pack her things in the same trunk I'd taken to Kentucky. She had Jimmy bring the wagon to the house and she disappeared into the gathering dusk.

Jimmy rushed back to the house, sick with disappointment. Running to the house, he jerked off his red hat and knocked rapidly. As I opened the door, Jimmy blurted out, "Mr. Bill, I ain't said 'nuttin to nobody 'bout what I seen in Kentucky. I plum deef, blind and dumb. Nobody heer'd it from me. I don't e'en tell Clara."

Afraid I'd think he'd blabbed it to the hands and the hands had told the maids and they had told Ginny. Jimmy was half sick with worry. Looking dejected, I told Jimmy about the note and he sighed with relief.

I told Jimmy not to worry about that, Ginny would cool off in a few days and come back home. But Jimmy said, "Naw Sir, Mr. Bill, she gone. That old river boat fixing to leave and I dun carried her trunk on da ship."

I ran to the barn and grabbed my bridle. Just as I caught my horse the sound of the steamer backing away from the dock and the scream of its whistle as it shifted down stream rent the night air. I knew it was headed down stream faster than I could travel horseback and that a big part of my life was gone forever.

Chapter 22

I tried to lose myself in the ranch. So much to do and time was slipping away. Winter was approaching as we drove the brood cows to the north range. The brood mares were lounging along Childress Creek as we rode by and the Percheron stallion came to meet us. He was a mean ornery cuss, and I wondered if Wagner had gotten his mares bred.

I got to thinking about the cave, the missing gold, and the lost soldiers. Swinging back toward the Brazos, I set out for the Wagner's. Hell, I thought, anywhere but home. The house was a tomb without Bates and Ginny. A man's a fool to mess up something that good, decided, but in a few minutes my fickle mind was thinking about Eve and the magic of my Kentucky romance.

Damn, life is a fickle old dame, I chuckled. From two lovers to no lovers, and I couldn't decide which was the most unsettling! For a man that had always been alone, I was suddenly lonely.

Jim Wagner was putting his mares in the barn as the early norther blew in. The wind was gusting and sleet began to fall. The ice pellets were singing on the roof when he heard me call. He was pleased to see me.

Unsaddling Old Spooks, I began to tell Jim about my trip, the horses, the roan stallion and the race horses. He listened intently. He liked good horses and questioned me about the roan stud. Jim told me about taking his mares to the black stallion, their colts tagging along.

He had planned to leave one and ride the other one back. Then in a couple of weeks go back and switch the mares. The black stud took them both away from him and ran him up a tree. He stayed treed until after dark before the stud left, then had had to walk home.

Mrs. Wagner was scared to death when he got home the next morning. A few weeks later the mares showed up at the barn with the colts behind. One old mare was still wearing the blind bridle

Jim had been riding her with. He had weaned the colts and had them in the barn on full feed. They sure were two nice colts, red roans with plenty of size, just as I had predicted. They were a little course, but just right if you wanted to work and ride them.

Returning to the house, I spent the night. We talked and played dominoes till late, as the winter howled around the snug little cabin. I asked about the cave but nothing had changed. The next morning dawned cold and bright but the north wind had lain during the night.

Mrs. Wagner with Little Jimmy toddling along, were going to pick up pecans along the creek. Obsessed by the disappearing cave and the missing gold, I retraced the old route again. I had ridden it so many times I knew it by heart. Again, I was baffled by the disappearance.

Jim went with me and riding back down the creek we climbed to the top of the bluff and scoured the brush till noon. Dropping off the rim, my heart sank. Mrs. Wagner and Little Jim were off in the bottom of a cove about a hundred yards away busy gathering pecans.

As I looked across the river, ten Comanche braves were silently crossing the Brazos. The woman and child were between me and the Indians about halfway. The Indians hadn't seen them yet. The Indians were below the river bank and she was out of their sight. I recognized the big blue gelding and knew it was Running Bull. I knew Running Bull was retracing his route to where he'd stolen Old Blue and was on his trail.

Someone recognized him and the only way I was going to keep him now was kill this Indian. Bob Barnhart's prediction rang true. He told me he was signing one of our death certificates when he told me where the gray horse was.

Telling Jim to run for his wife and kid, I spurred Old Spooks for the river bank. I made for a big dead tree that lay where the creek ran into the river. The Indians couldn't hear my horse running as their horses splashed across the Brazos.

I slid my horse to a stop and fell behind the big dead log. I was thirty feet above the braves as they entered the creek. Laying behind this log, I knew I had the advantage but I was bad outnumbered. I was afraid to look back and see if Jim had got Mrs. Wagner and Little Jim to safety.

Drawing a bead on Running Bull, all the frustration I had suffered because of his arrows came back. I saw Deke dying, remembered the bitter cold and the death defying rescue of Old Blue. I recalled the colt crops I'd lost, the tarnish on my name because of the missing gold and the lost cave. I coldly pulled the trigger and Running Bull crossed over to the Happy Hunting Ground.

My '73 repeater got the first four warriors. Six to two, now I thought. Not expecting an attack, the Indians, although in full war paint, withdrew to the west bank of the river to regroup. I quickly mounted Old Spooks and raced to the house.

The dead Indians' horses had run up the creek and out into the meadow. They had been ridden hard, were hungry and had already started to graze. I wished I could catch Big Blue. Risking my life, I made a dash for the loose horses as I glanced back to see if the Indians had regrouped.

The Indians were milling in the river. They were without a leader. I had taken out their war chief, their medicine man, their bravest warrior and another brave in that first volley.

Circling the loose horses, I drove them toward the barn. Jim saw what I was doing and ran from the house and opened the corral gate. The horses poured into the corral as I made a mad dash for the barn. Shouting for Jim to get back to the house, I covered the barn.

Just as I reached the barn and Jim got back to the house, the Indians regrouped and came hell for shelter. I scrambled for the loft. Indians were circling the house and barn screaming and firing burning arrows. I was sitting in a tinder box. Jim had the barn crammed full of hay and feed. One arrow and I would roast in the loft.

Jim took dead aim and knocked the new leader from his horse.

Shot through the thigh, his leg was broke. He was lying about forty yards from the house and his horse circled back to the horses in the corral.

A young buck came charging from the river and scooped up the crippled brave. As they turned and raced back to the river bank, Jim started shooting from a hole in the front door. The young buck and the crippled Indian didn't get far. Jim killed them both. Now it was four to two. I liked the odds better but I was sure afraid of a fire.

The Indians regrouped again and it was beginning to get late. An Indian is awful superstitious; he won't hardly fight at night. They think if they die at night, their souls will get lost. I knew if they were going to get us, it would be in the next few minutes. It got deathly silent in the sharp cold evening.

Suddenly they decided to burn us out. They raced from the river bank with arrows lit and ready. Taking aim I decided to shoot the last ones first and leave the closest till last. I sure as hell didn't want any to get away. They ran hard at the barn first. They set Jim's outside hay stack afire, and a flaming arrow bedded in the eve of the house and began to burn. I fired point blank as one ran in the hall of the barn and fired a burning arrow in the loft with me. One more down.

While I was kicking the burning hay out of the loft, an arrow buried into a rafter. From my right eye I caught a glimpse of the shooter. Turning quickly, I shot the Indian clear through his neck. Two left now. Even steven!

Jim's rifle barked and another brave hit the ground. Just one left now and I'd lost sight of him. I counted their horses and there were ten. They had come back to the horses in the corral. One was afoot and dangerous. I looked around cautiously. I knew this was a dangerous situation. A wounded snake was a better neighbor. I knew if this Indian got away, the Indians would come back and burn Jim out. They were hell to retaliate for their own mistakes.

Crawling out of the loft, I ran for the house. Mrs. Wagner was white and Little Jim was real quiet. Jim was worried, he knew he had to put out the burning arrow or his house was going up in flames. He also was afraid the Indian was waiting in the tall grass. Grabbing a bucket of water, he shouted for me to cover him. He ran out and sloshed water on the smoldering house. The eve of the house was scorched. Running to the well he drew another bucket and extinguished the smoldering wood.

Nothing moved in the grass as night approached. The waiting began. I counted the bodies and the horses. Ten horses - nine dead Indians. Finally mounting my horse I rode cautiously to the river. My hunch was right. A body was floating in the river. This made the count right. Grabbing two shovels, we dug a single grave. We buried dead Indians, saddles, bridles, bows and all their belongins. No trace of the attack was left.

Jim kept their rifles and I told him to keep the horses. These weren't Comanche horses. These horses had been stolen from across the Comanche hunting ground. Most were taken from dead settlers and looted wagon trains. Jim was wanting to raise horses and he would use these for a start. He could trade these geldings for mares or cows. This was a blessing he hadn't counted on.

Chapter 23

I rode back to the ranch relieved. Running Bull was dead, along with his best warriors. The Indians were like the buffalo. Their great days were over. I was sad in a way, but it was hard to feel sorry for them if you had buried the dead and mutilated where they had ravaged settlers' homes and burned his buildings. Hell, I thought, I'd have done the same thing if I'd been an Indian. But I was born on the other side. You weren't allowed to change sides. Color prevented that.

I spent a lot of time thinking about people's color and why God had made them different. Funny how color blinded a man to the other's way of life, I thought as the sun sank in the west and darkness deepened in the river bottom.

The house was dark and forbidding and I just kept on riding, crossing the river and made for the bright lights of Waco. I went to the *Cotton Palace*. The *Brazos Queen* was open again under new management. Too many memories haunted me, to enter. I found out that when Bates had died, he'd left the *Queen* to Ginny and Ginny had sold it. That's what she left town on. She never took a quarter of my money, I learned.

I got a room and after cleaning up, I came down stairs and got a bottle of whiskey. I really tied one on. I never was much of one to drink but lonely had taken over. I kept seeing Indians attacking, horses racing and women leaving in the bottom of each glass. I was wasted when I finally headed to my room. Stopping and pulling a little red headed whore to her feet, I took her with me. I really didn't need her in the shape I was in but I paid her just to sleep with me. Lonesome is a hell of a disease and I wasn't sure I was going to survive it. Thinking of Ginny I drifted off into a drunken stupor.

I awoke groggy and hung over. At first I didn't remember where I was, not recognizing the girl, I was lost for a minute. Quickly rising and leaving money on the table for the sleeping whore, I made a hasty retreat. Passing through the bar, the stale smoke and liquor was almost too much for my queasy stomach. Feeling nauseous, I made for the door and fresh air.

Waco was bathed in clear, cold sunshine. Regaining my composure, I walked to the livery stable where I had left Old Spooks. Spooks had really made a good horse. The hard riding had taken the buck out of him, but he'd still roll his nose when you caught him every morning.

Loping back to the ranch, I felt a restlessness. I should be on top of the world. I had a good ranch, friends, top livestock, the good horses I'd always admired, but something was haunting me. Maybe it was Ginny leaving. Hell, I was happy before I got her, I thought, but seeing the *Brazos Queen* again had rattled me. I couldn't make myself go in. Getting drunk last night and hiring a whore to sleep with me was out of character for me. I'd never had to pay a woman to sleep with me before. The last problem I had was too many to sleep with. Damn, I hated it when life got complicated.

Riding up to the house, I knew something was wrong. The field hands were all gathered in the yard and the house was strangely quiet. Stepping off Old Spooks, I was confronted by a weeping Jimmy. "Uncle Willie is daid," he cried.

A nester farmer had settled up on Childress Creek, and had started stringing barbed wire along the little bottoms by the creek. The nester had intended to farm both sides of the creek. This was the range that the brood mares inhabited. Concerned for the safety of the horses, Willie had ridden up there to talk to the farmer.

This pure redneck took offense to a nigra calling on him. Taking down his rifle, he was going to humble Willie a little and make him crawl. Willie was a rancher, and had ran my outfit for years. Hell, Willie didn't crawl even when he was a slave. Willie respected every man he ever met, but most of all, Willie respected Willie.

Turning his team around, Willie turned his back on the cracker and started to leave without another word. Taking this as a personal insult, the nester shot Willie in the back. Willie made it back to the big house, but he had lost too much blood. Willie had been asking for me, over and over, before he slipped away to another land.

No more cotton to pick, no mules to harness and the color of your skin won't make any difference now.

I went insane! Saddling Old Blue and grabbing my rifle, I left the house on a dead run. Hell was going to be seasoned with a rednecked bastard before dark if I had my way. Old Blue was lathered and winded when I reined him to a stop on Childress Creek.

All the barbed wire was taken down and the lean-to was empty. Wagon tracks led away, traveling west. I spurred Old Blue after the wagon. Just before dark, I saw a wagon dry camped on the prairie. My anger had boiled all day. Willie had never harmed a soul - black or white, and was all the family I had.

I cocked my rifle as I rode to the wagon. The trial was already over. Six scrawny little kids, from diapers to ten years old, were huddled around a fire in the cold, as night approached. A hollow cheeked woman in the last stages of pregnancy was struggling to unhitch two old, poor mules that had seen better days.

Answering questions reservedly, she informed me that her man had gone on to Amarillo and instructed her to follow him. He had been attacked by a gang of nigra while trying to fence his farm. He told her he feared for his life and had to run.

My disgust for this cowardly bastard nearly choked me. This woman didn't have as much chance as a "one legged man at an ass kicking." I remembered the frigid cold from my winter up there, and these mules would never make it through the snow. I contemplated following this "slime" to Amarillo, just to kill him. But, looking out across that sea of grass, I knew it would be like looking for a "rat turd in a river."

Turning and heading for home, tears began to flow as I mourned for Willie. Sobbing loudly, I decided, hell, while I was crying, I might as well cry for Ginny, and Eve, and Bates. My whole damn world was coming apart, and there wasn't a thing I could do about it.

Approaching the ranch about daylight, the hands were still in the yard. A cold, lonely vigil was awaiting the return of Mr. Bill 'fore they buried Willie.

Bitter wailing and sobbing filled the river bottom as we buried Willie. I wished Bates had been there to say a few words. I wasn't much for preaching, but I just couldn't bury him without a service. I found Bates' old Bible and read a passage he'd marked from Ecclesiastes in the Old Testament, about a time to live and a time to die — I guess it was just Willie's time to die. The blacks sang and this was probably the saddest moment I'd ever experienced. Damn, I couldn't hardly remember not having Willie.

We buried him beside Bates. They were my two best friends and as close to family as I had. From the corner of the yard, Willie could sorta keep an eye on the house and barn like he always had.

The fight had gone out of me and the fatigue from the hard ride and hangover set in. I crashed across the bed and slept the day and night away. First light greeted me, as I heard the cook rattling around getting breakfast.

Bathing and shaving gave me time to think. I made some hurried plans. Eating and quickly washing it down with a pot of black coffee, I formulated my plan. Riding over to Jimmy's, I saw Willie's wife sitting on the porch in the early dawn. A look of blankness covered her face. For the first time in all these years, she didn't have Willie to get up and cook breakfast for. The most important person in her life was gone, and it hadn't really hit her, that he wasn't coming back. The finality of it hadn't soaked in and she kept looking down the road like she expected him to ride up. They had never had any children and Jimmy had taken her in.

Jimmy came to the door as I called. "Let's go to town," I told him and headed for the barn.

Jimmy saddled the roan stallion. He needed some riding and

this way "he could kill two birds with the same stone," he thought.

Riding along in the cold frosty morning, I laid out my plans. I was going to sell off my main brood mare herd and most of the brood cows. I was just going to keep the best ones that the three thousand acres in the bottom could run. Homesteaders were crowding in on the north range and I didn't want to risk anybody else's life. I would just pull back to Childress Creek and ranch my deeded acres. I wanted Jimmy to take over for me while I was gone. I told him to cut back on the farming, just raise feed, to hell with cotton. Jimmy quickly agreed to that. As a kid, Jimmy had picked cotton to feed him and his mammy, and he had no love for cotton.

I told him I would sell the whole north herd. We would keep the pure bred Shorthorns and the Hereford bulls. We'd just keep those two hundred and fifty youngest Shorthorn cows, and Willie's twenty-five cows. I wanted to keep the Kentucky Thoroughbreds, and the best fifteen gray daughters of Old Blue.

For Willie's memory, I told him to keep Willie's brood mares and the best twenty-five draft mares we had to raise teams with.

Keep Willie's wife enough heifers to replace anything that was sold or died. I told Jimmy and take care of her till she dies. Don't let her want for nothing as long as I have a dime, I told him. What she wants — get it. That's the last thing I could do for Willie. When she dies you get her cows, I advised him, and if I don't come back, you get everything here. We rode to the lawyer's office and made this all official in a will.

We went to the bank and fixed it to where Jimmy could draft on my account, like Willie had for years. Jimmy was well educated for his time, cause Willie had taught him everything I had taught him. While at the bank, I opened Jimmy an account. His race winnings had continued to multiply this last year. Moonshine was yet to be out ran, and the two roans from Kentucky were hard to outrun for four hundred yards. The stud could fly and Jimmy secretly wondered if he might could outrun Moonshine, but he really didn't want to know. Race horse people were already bringing mares to breed to him and spring was still six weeks away.

I headed up to see Jim Wagner. I led a two-year-old red roan stud along with me. He was a full brother to my Little Blue gelding. They were both out of the little roan match race mare from Mexico. He'd come a red roan like his mammy but was sired by Old Blue. I wanted to give him to Jim Wagner. I really liked Jim and he needed a good stud to get started in the horse business. He had traded the Indian geldings for a handful of brood mares and this would fix him up. I thought back to the story he told about the old black Percheron stud stealing his two mares, and had to laugh.

I reached White Rock Creek about dark. I had ridden across the north range and lights were shining in places they had never been. Homesteaders were coming in and taking that range. Hell! I didn't blame them, I got it the same way. I knew now I should have bought it all from the state when I bought the river bottom. A dollar an acre, but hell, I didn't have twenty thousand dollars. I barely had the three thousand, and the first cows had been a struggle. Now they had really multiplied. I had over a thousand head and had decided to drive them to Fort Worth to sell them. A good demand for brood stock had developed as more ranches were being deeded. I guess I just lost my desire when Ginny had left and Willie died.

Chapter 24

Jim's cabin seemed to be getting crowded. Mrs. Wagner was nursing another little Wagner boy. Jim was really proud. "Raise me some farm help," he laughed, "or a couple of cowboys."

I gave Jim the stud colt and he was thrilled. He showed me the mares he'd got for the Indian horses. He's traded with someone up at Glen Rose. He got fifteen mares for the nine geldings that we had commandeered. He had kept Big Blue for me. He knew I'd hated like hell to give him to the Indians and figured I'd want him back.

I thought about it a minute and said, "Jim you just keep him for a riding horse. That old black stud can't catch him," I grinned, and then told him, "besides, I want you to help me drive my cows to Fort Worth and you need to be mounted on a cow horse."

Then I laid out my plans.

Rising early the next morning, I rode up the creek and looked for the cave. I took Jim's oldest son with me and told his eager little ears the story. Spring rains had been falling through February and the spring grass was coming early. I knew we could gather pretty quick and I was ready to get it over with.

Jimmy had his farming done early, and taking this break in farming, we began to gather and sort stock. We gathered the horses first. Catching that old Percheron stud and separated him before someone got hurt.

Cutting out the biggest and best draft mares, we drove them in the trap with the riding mares. I explained to Jimmy, that these would give him draft teams from the black stud. All of Blue's fillies would give him plenty of ranch horses to work the cattle with, and the ten Kentucky mares would cross on the roan stud to keep him in the race horse business.

Readying a chuck wagon, I took eight of my best cowboy field hands and gathered the north range. These were the ones Willie had used to work stock, and did tolerable well at it. Jim Wagner came over and helped with the gather. It took us a week to gather, sort and keep what we wanted. The herd was impressive as we strung out for Cowtown.

We had about seven hundred and fifty cows, and nearly all had big full grown calves a following them. Most of the bulls were good blooded Shorthorns. Lots of bellowing and fighting was taking place the first day but they kinda found their niche after that. There was still a hundred or so Longhorn and half Longhorn cows mixed in, but most were red or roans, showing the Shorthorn influence. Most of the cows were half to three quarter Shorthorn and a ready market awaited us at Fort Worth.

Jimmy followed the chuck wagon with the remuda. Each rider had brought a couple of spare horses to swap off and keep fresh. Behind all of this came three hands with a hundred and fifty mares and colts. I had kept eight gray and roan studs out of Old Blue through the years. So nearly all of this bunch were grays. I cut the studs off and left them at the ranch. Hell, ain't anything hotter than eight or ten studs on a drive. The mares and colts had thrown together and were just kinda following the leader.

Not really pushing very hard, the herd took eight days to make the trip. The trip was real smooth and after the second day the mixed herd would string out behind the chuck wagon and just kinda grazed along. We crossed the Brazos at Kimbell Bend, and throwing the herd out west of Cleburne, we just let them drift into Fort Worth.

A wet norther broke just as we were hitting town, and ice was making the trail slippery and the gate hinges were icing up, when the last mare trailed in. I turned the horse herd over to Jones Horse and Mule Commission Company and the cattle over to John Clay Commission Company to sell.

They were busy sorting riding colts from draft colts as I turned up my collar and hunted a pot bellied stove. The mares were sorted the same way and night fell on a cold, tired set of field hands with saddle sores on their butts. They quickly made their way to “nigra town” for a hot meal and a warm place to sleep. The cold ground had taken its toll on them. I knew March was too early to drive but I was in a hurry to leave.

Calling on Stephen T. Dill, I brought him up to date on all I’d done. I gave him the power of attorney to settle up on the cattle and horses. I gave him my account number in Waco and told him to take care of the transactions. The next morning dawned cold and bright, as a sheet of ice lay over Fort Worth.

Rousting out my hands and saddling one horse apiece, we headed south to Waco. Setting the course with the chuck wagon, the hands just kinda straggled along behind till we reached Hillsboro. With no spare horses to worry about, we made good time and by not stopping for lunch we were in Hillsboro before dark. As they all crowded into the wagon yard at the livery stable, I went across to the café and ordered us some food. They sent over a huge kettle of beans and skillets of corn bread and a mountain of fried ham. We washed it down with steaming coffee and sweet milk. After a week of chapped legs, campfire cooking and sleeping on the ground, the boys were ready for home and home was just a day away.

I shook hands with Jim Wagner when we left Hillsboro and something told me it would be a long time before we shook again. We left in different directions. Always before we’d traveled together until we crossed the Brazos and we’d ride back through the north range. It felt funny not riding back that way, but the north range as we knew it, was gone. Fences were everywhere and you could hardly get through it anymore.

Jim headed down Hackberry Creek. He’d follow it to Aquilla and out across to the river. He’d be home in no time. The hands and I headed south to Waco. I sure hated not to ride back through my old range, I was feeling nostalgia, but I was afraid we might have a run in with a nester and the mood I was in, this might not have been good.

Chapter 25

I spent the night in the cold lonely house by myself. Rising before the sun came up, I packed a trunk and was waiting out on the front porch for Jimmy to take me to town. I'd walked over to Bates' and Willie's graves to sorta say goodbye, but the words stuck in my throat. Saying goodbye to them was saying goodbye to a big part of my life, and the way I felt probably the best part of it. The damn world was changing and I wasn't ready for anymore changes.

Jimmy arrived shortly, driving the two black geldings we'd taken to Kentucky. This sure was a flashy team. Not really big enough for heavy pulling, but sure could make the wheels on a buggy turn.

He helped me load my trunk and then drove across the Bosque crossing and headed for Waco. Jimmy was awful quiet. He hated to see me leave. He was a good boy, but he just wanted to be a "race hoss" man. I think the will, where it said, if I didn't come back, scared him.

The dock was crowded when we reached the river. The water had been up for a week but was going down and the Captain was in a hurry to leave. This old river was treacherous and could run down awful quick, leaving you stranded for months at a time. A river boat captain had to have nerves of steel and the guts of a pirate to master his trade. I was early but I couldn't stand the thought of staying any longer.

Saying goodbye had never been my long suits, so I just turned and walked aboard without a wave or a word. I walked down in the boat and glancing out a porthole as the ship headed south, Jimmy was still standing where I left him.

Suddenly the enormity of the situation descended on Jimmy. Three months ago he had two hundred dollars and a red hat and nothing to do but keep his shoes shined. Suddenly he was responsible for a wife, an auntie, and dozens of families. All the hands to oversee and a large farm and ranch to run. All of Mr. Bill's cows and horses to see after and plus his money. Suddenly racing horses seemed far away.

Jimmy sighed as he drove back to the ranch. He'd always had Uncle Willie and Mr. Bill to make decisions for him, and suddenly he'd been thrust into that position. All he ever wanted to be was a "race hoss man," and thoughts of Mose and Kentucky were strong on his mind.

The river boat backed slowly to the middle of the muddy Brazos. Shifting forward, it let out a shrill blast from the steam boiler and headed south for Galveston and to the Gulf of Mexico. The weather warmed considerable as the boat rushed south.

Galveston was a loud and colorful city, with gambling houses and honky tonks everywhere. I made my way from the dock to the best hotel in town. After securing a corner room on the top floor, I made my way to the dining room. This was my first encounter with seafood. We'd eaten a ton of fried catfish from the rivers, but for the first time I ate crabs, shrimp and oysters. I couldn't get enough. I ate till I bulged. As a cowman, I thought nothing could beat beef, but I was a quick convert. I was soon a lifetime member of the seafood cuisine.

I drifted back to the bar as a band played the latest tunes. Coming from a one piano saloon, this was all new to me. After the hangover I had from my last drunk, I decided I'd just gamble instead. I wasn't much of a gambler, but I guess from my years of sorting cattle and horses, I had developed an uncanny ability to remember the cards and where they were. As usual, when you don't need to win, you usually do and I was lucky with the cards.

My luck held strong for the next three days, and playing aggressively, I won a pretty good stake. I never was a compulsive gambler. If the cards were falling, I'd bet big, but if they got cold, it didn't bother me to go to bed. I didn't need the money and the wilder the betting the luckier I got. Three thousand dollars was a lot of money in Galveston and everybody was talking about the lucky cowboy in town. They changed dealers and cards and back again, but my luck was on a roll.

I was anxious to get the night behind me. I'd booked passage on the *Bayou Belle* from New Orleans the next morning. I'd been gathering information as I gambled. I knew Ginny had came down the river and I was trying to pick up her trail. A pretty redhead that could sing like she could, was going to be hard to hide.

The river boat captain remembered her for her startling beauty, the bartender remembered how she could sing and a gambler from New Orleans, I played poker with, said he just remembered her from New Orleans and smiled. He didn't say what he remembered about her, but the way the fire burned in my gut, when the bastard smiled, I kinda figured it out.

Not sleeping very sound, I was lulled from a restless sleep by the squeaking of a hinge on my hotel door. A body had stepped just inside my door as if waiting for it to get quiet. A silhouette of a person was framed by the door entrance.

I was suspicious after winning so much. I had just lain down with my clothes on, had unholstered my gun and laid it on my chest. Pulling the cover over me, I had dozed off to sleep. The gun was resting across on my stomach as I squinted to make out the shape of my visitor. Seeing a man in the shadows, I drew the hammer back to a cocked position. That hammer cocking sounded like a cannon going off in the still of the night.

Whoever came a calling left a running and by the time I could get to the door, my robber to be, had ran down the hall and jumped from the back porch. Running foot steps were disappearing in the night as I fired six rounds into the alley. All hell broke loose for a few minutes. Women were screaming and police were running as I quickly slipped back into my room as if nothing had happened.

Chapter 26

I stayed awake the rest of the night and when daylight came a creeping, I was boarding the *Bayou Belle* for New Orleans. The wind was calm and the bay was peaceful and quiet. The water captivated me. So much of the success or failure of farming and ranching depended on water and down here it seemed to rain everyday. There were acres of water. The ship moved out into the gulf and I was hypnotized by the ocean. Drawing the ship's captain, into a long conversation, prepared me for New Orleans.

The Gulf was rolling as we steamed into the mouth of the Mississippi. A squall line lay off to the southeast and the wind was really kicking up. Rain had been falling since we left Houston and we had snaked along the shoreline from town to town, picking up and delivering freight. The weather was getting rough and it started to rain in earnest. Ships large and small were docked along the Mississippi.

Suddenly, New Orleans appeared out of the night. A jumble of lights and sounds, that seemed to leap with joy and music. The music made you want to dance as it floated down to the docks. I just thought I'd heard music before. Loud accordions were playing in the distance and fiddles and Jew's harps filled in, and somewhere, there was the blues of a saxophone and the rattling of a trumpet. Whatever it was, they were proud of it, and as loud as it was, there was enough to go around for everybody.

I collected my trunk and checked my money belt and pistol. I hired me a carriage per instructions from the Captain, and made my way to the *Orleans* the best hotel in New Orleans and maybe the whole southeast. Doormen were waiting and opened the doors of the carriage and ushered me in.

I had never stayed in anything this elegant before, except Eve's plantation home. Brass rails and crystal chandeliers were everywhere. Tales had traveled fast about my winnings and I was taken to the plushest of plush rooms. They already knew my name and an usher was waiting to escort me to my room. The Captain of the ship had been right, this was the best New Orleans had to offer. It was an expensive son-of-a-gun, but I was on a roll, and didn't care.

A bath was prepared for me at once and a new suit and shirt, compliments of the house. An usher came for me shortly after I finished dressing and escorted me to the dangest seafood setting I could imagine. We started with raw oysters and graduated to shrimp, fixed every way you could do it. We got to the main entrée after a bit. They brought me a crab as big as our old soft shelled turtles get at home. I wrestled this sucker till I was tired and full both, and then retired to the bar and gaming room.

The gaming room was large and brightly lit. Dice tables and card tables lined the wall. Lots of money was changing hands over games, I didn't know or understand. Not understanding or wanting to learn, I just eased along until I found a game of seven card stud. They say real gamblers like five card but I kinda always liked those two extra changes. Every eye followed me as I milled around the room. Gossip travels fast and I heard murmurs about that lucky cowboy from Galveston. Hell, I guess I did kinda stick out like a sore thumb with my new black hat and soft calfskin boots I'd picked up before leaving Fort Worth.

One player pushed back his chair and I was asked to sit in, seven card stud. I must have played a couple of hours, just sorta trading money. I'd won a few pretty good hands, but had folded a lot of maybes. You could tell the dealer was getting pissed off by my style of play. I just bet the good hands and folded the rest.

Cards were dealt, and I had a pair of queens down with an ace and a jack and a ten showing. The dealer bet a hundred on every card. The players began to fold. The dealer had a pair of aces showing, my card was a queen, then the dealer hit another ace up. The dealer had a pair of tens down in the hole. This gave him a full boat, aces over tens pat.

Looking at my hand, it looked to him like a possible straight, no more. I looked at the triple aces and figured I was in trouble. I was pretty far ahead of the game, with my winnings. I was kinda figuring on folding, but the gambler seeing my indecision, decided to buy the pot, and bet one thousand dollars.

Something about the way he sneered, kinda ticked me off. Nobody in their right mind would try to beat a full boat with a straight. I called his thousand and it got awful quiet. The cards were dealt. The dealer checked his hole card, he had a three and no help, but he didn't need any. He was setting on a full boat.

I looked casually at my last card, taking my time. Nothing showed on my face. This was no test of courage for a man who had gone into a Comanche war camp unarmed and stole the chief's favorite war horse.

The gambler studied my face a minute and saw nothing that gave him a clue. Reaching for his chips, he coolly bet another thousand dollars. The "sweatees" were gathered around the table and the crowd had gotten real quiet. The murmur was making the rounds. That damn fool cowboy was calling thousand dollar bets with a possible straight, when the house dealer was setting on a pat full boat, with three aces up. Glancing at my last down card again, lady luck was a grinning at me, in the form of the fourth queen.

No expression changed on my face, as I coolly called the thousand and raised him two thousand. You could have heard an ant's heart beat it got so quiet. This was a big gamble in a big gambling town.

A hush fell on the crowd. Now the heat was on the house. Carlos Belyere was the house's top dealer. He had nerves of steel. He could read people like people can read books. He saw nothing in Bill Fowler's eyes. Like looking in the eyes of a dead man, Carlos thought. Damn fool should know he's beat, Belyere reckoned. Hell, I can't let him buy this pot for two thousand, he thought, it's time to put this smart assed cowboy in his place.

Reaching for house chips, Carlos called the two thousand and raised the house limit — five thousand dollars. I never quibbled.

Reaching in my back pocket I counted out ten thousand dollars. I'd seen an instant moment of doubt in Carlos Belyere's eyes, and I knew where his other ace was.

Looking him coolly in the eyes I said, "I'm calling your five thousand and raising you five thousand. That is the house limits isn't it," I asked.

Carlos Belyere got gray around his mouth. Grimacing to himself he thought, this damn fool knows something or he is a straight idiot. Looking at my cards again, all Carlos could figure was an ace high straight. Does this dumb bastard know what order wins in cards, he wondered.

To deep to quit now, he again reached for house chips as the casino owner walked up behind him, "Call the bet."

Carlos looked at me again and saw nothing. Carlos had played lots of gamblers, but none could he remember being this stone cold. Turning up his pair of down cards, he said, "Full boat, aces over tens," and smiled.

The crowd started to chatter. I flipped over my last queen and said, "Two pair." Flipping over my two down cards, I declared, "Both queens."

Four queens were starring at Carlos Belyere, and cold fury consumed him. This bastard has made him look like a fool, he thought. Smiling thinly he picked up the cards and began to shuffle. Never taking his eyes off mine, he coolly stacked the deck, four aces for him and four kings for me. He reached up and pulled his visor down with his card hand. This was a signal for the other two players, who were house stooges to fold on the first bet.

I was no stranger to the poker table, the war had taught me a lot. Gambling was just a way to pass the time for me, but I had a mind for remembering cards and who had what. Seeing him stack the deck I knew what to expect. My first card up was a king. The dealer had a nine of clubs. One stooge had a queen and the other a jack.

I was high and the dealer softly said, "King high bets."

I'd seen him stick two aces on the bottom and knew he had the other two turned down in front of him. This was an old Army trick. I'd seen Bates bust up a many a game the same way. Carlos was fixing to get back the house money and more. I checked my king to the dealer. The dealer bet five hundred on his nine. The two stooges folded and without moving an eye, so did I.

I picked up my chips and excused myself from the game. Casually looking down at Carlos Belyere, I said, "I think I'll turn in, it's been a long day."

Carlos Belyere was furious. He knew he had misread this cowboy, and he knew I had caught him stacking the deck and he'd never been caught before. Carlos was livid with rage as I walked off and I knew I'd made a bitter enemy in New Orleans.

This casino wasn't going to mug me tonight, but I knew they would be waiting for me at the gaming tables for the rest of my stay.

Counting my winnings and cashing my chips, I'd won fifteen thousand, mostly from the house. The dealers and the stooges were all playing house money, and this was a big hit for any table to absorb.

For a guy who didn't care a lot about gambling, I sure was on a roll. With what I had won in Galveston and my winnings tonight, I had a lot of cash on me.

Maybe I'd find Ginny tomorrow, I thought, and I'd decided if I could talk her into it, we'd go to New York or maybe Europe. Maybe we could start over, I thought. Money would be no problem.

Ignoring the poker table each night, I made the rounds of all the taverns. Subtly picking up leads, I discovered that Ginny was in town. The *Flamingo Club* was the ritziest place in town where the cities most elite wined and dined. No longer a whore, Ginny was singing to the town's best.

Ginny had a great voice, I thought as I sat in the crowd. The place was dark and she didn't see me. I attended three nights before I decided how to handle it. Thinking money might do the trick, I gave the waiter a twenty dollar gold piece. This was a fortune for a singer in most clubs. I told him to give it to the singer and tell her a client would like to have a drink with her.

She sent back a message, "Tell him I'm not for sale anymore. If I'd wanted to drink with the bastard, I wouldn't have left Texas!"

I left the *Flamingo* with mixed emotions. I think I just wanted her back because she had done the leaving, my pride was wanting her back. As I sifted through my thoughts, I tried to remember when it had happened. I always liked being with her, but then I'd get tired of her and just leave without a goodbye. I think back and maybe I was afraid of commitment. I'd stay gone for months and then just drift back in and pick up where we had left off.

It must have been the winter I spent up in the Panhandle, looking for Old Blue. Loneliness does things to a man. As I thought back, maybe it was the trial. She seemed so forlorn and vulnerable in jail, totally dependent on me. Hell, I couldn't decide just when, but I had fallen in love with her, but damn, I'd also fallen in love with Eve. Maybe I was just in love with love. I guess I just liked the feeling a new love brings, but I sure as hell could do without the pain of its leaving. Damn, it was a lot like childbirth. It starts with a great sensation to begin with, but the end sure brings a lot of pain. Satisfied with my summation, I drifted back to the *Orleans*.

A new dealer was shuffling cards waiting for a fourth player as I walked in. Sitting down, I thought I'd kill some time and do some visiting. I sure missed the visiting. I missed the hands stopping by and asking questions and Jimmy or Willie filling me in on what's happening.

Making conversation with the other players, I played a dozen hands or more. Just kinda floating, win some, lose some. I'd gotten to be an intense poker player, always on the edge. The dealer was wary, they had seen me fold four kings, and buy a couple of pots with a pair of deuces. Damn, his stony looks, they thought. I believed luck ran in streaks and I never forced it. If the cards were falling, I'd bet them, if not I'd go to bed and try again tomorrow.

I'd won a lot of money from the house, and they were wanting it back. They had tried to cheat and got caught, had tried to outplay me and got burnt. They weren't sure what to do next, but had to keep trying. I stole a pretty good pot. I didn't have anything. A pair of tens, but it looked like I might have a straight flush. I had just played a hell of a game of bluff and had enough money on me to make it work.

Carlos Belyere had let me get under his skin. This was dangerous for a gambler, it clouds his wisdom. Watching the game, he decided to break in. Tapping the house dealer on the shoulder, Carlos relieved him. Opening a new deck of cards, he began to shuffle and I cut the new cards twice. Just kinda letting him know I thought he was a cheat.

The stakes were getting higher. I had been studying Carlos and had picked up on something. When Carlos hit a good hand, he had a nervous tick that would make his right cheek tremble ever so slightly. I played through a few hands to check him out. Carlos was under a lot of pressure, he was the pit boss, the master of the game, and he had lost a lot of house money.

Big money bets were the house limits. These were only to be used when you had a drunk or a big time loser. This place made its money off of hundred dollar bets and less and a large percentage of wins, blackjack and games that favor the house. It made a lot of money off of drinks and food, and from the hotel rooms.

It took a lot of service to cover the money Carlos had lost and the boss was on him. Serious poker was in now in process. I was just sparring, waiting for the right hand. I cut the cards and Carlos began to deal. My first two cards were the ace of hearts and the king of hearts. Carlos had a pair of sevens down. As Carlos dealt the third card, he dealt me a jack of hearts. I saw Carlos's cheek move ever so much. I looked at the cards on the table and saw a seven of diamonds. My jack was high and I bet a hundred. Carlos called and raised five hundred, as he reached for company chips.

I called. I figured him for triple sevens. Hell, nobody got

excited about a pair of sevens. The next card he dealt me was a ten of hearts and I began to get hopeful. Four hearts but split. Carlos hit an ace of clubs. He again bet five hundred, I just called. Carlos dealt another round. I caught a three of hearts. Three hearts showing, but I had a heart flush.

When Carlos dealt, he caught another ace. Pair of aces bet. Carlos saw his chance, he coolly bet one thousand, reaching for company chips again. I knew from the quiver in his cheek, he had a full house. I thought I should get out, this flush wasn't about to beat a full boat, but all those big hearts had me thinking the impossible.

Calling his thousand, on an impulse I raised him a thousand. Carlos turned pale. His mind was churning. This bastard is bluffing again, Carlos thought, as he looked over the cards. All he could see was maybe a flush with those hearts.

Carlos called my bluff, but his fingers felt clammy. This son of a bitch has taken the fun out of gambling, Carlos stewed as he got ready to deal the last cards. Now was the time, Carlos decided but his fingers felt stiff and cold. He hunched over the table and tilting the cards ever so slightly, dealt me a black nine of clubs and no help.

As I glanced down at this card, Carlos dealt his card from the bottom of the deck, another ace. He had seeded something bigger than sevens for a lead. Carlos was sitting on three sevens and three aces. I was pretty damn sure those last two aces had come off the bottom, but I'll say one thing about him, he was the best I'd ever seen at it. There were fifty people watching the game, and no one else had suspected anything. My flush was in a lot of trouble with his three aces and three sevens behind them, and I knew this greasy headed bastard was about to bet them.

Carlos knew if he bet it all, I'd fold. Hell, he knew I was just bluffing with this flush anyway. Carlos deftly bet another thousand. The hotel owner had drifted over to watch the game. I could see him studying me out of the corner of his eye, and he was puzzled. I wasn't a marked gambler, one who the casinos all knew or had heard about. I didn't play with any passion, and they couldn't find any weakness, but I was wrecking their gambling hall.

I nearly didn't call that last raise. Hell, longshots wasn't how I gambled, but I guess I'd let Carlos Belyere get under my skin too. I should have called his hand when he palmed that last ace, but I knew I'd have to kill him.

Waiting for that last card, I knew I had that fourth ace, so Carlos was as stout as he was going to be. Carlos made a show of dealing the last cards off the top with a flourish, as if he knew what I was thinking. Carlos glanced at his hole card and his cheek twitched. He had hit the fourth seven. Carlos was sweating, damn he thought, he'd took a hell of a chance dealing those two aces off the bottom and now he was going to have to discard three aces.

Never in his career could he remember having to discard three aces. Hell, he'd seen the time he would have killed and had been nearly killed for three aces.

I saw that cheek twitch and I knew something had changed, as Carlos reached for the chips. Slowly looking at my last card, I was shocked to see the queen of hearts. I had nothing showing and the best hand in poker before me.

Carlos reached for the company chips and coolly counted out the limit, five thousand. My expression never changed. I had always wondered what it would be like to have this hand, but from my manner you'd have thought I had a pair of deuces.

Calmly I counted out the five thousand. I called his five thousand and raised him five thousand. You could have heard a "rat piss on a bale of cotton." The casino got deathly quiet.

Carlos licked his lips nervously. Why did this bastard never flinch, blink an eye, or something, Carlos wondered. He was in a quandary. If he folded with four sevens and three aces, and this son-of-a-bitch was bluffing, his reputation as a card player was ruined. But he knew if I had a winning hand, he was probably going to lose his job, and possibly his life. Carlos knew he had lost a lot of money to this cowboy in the last week, but he was fixing to get it all back.

Glancing nervously at his boss, he rolled his diamond ring over, a sign for four of a kind, and the boss winked. This was his sign for go for broke. Carlos raised my bet and raised the limit again. I never blinked. Reaching for my wallet, I began to count. I called the raise and countered with a raise.

Carlos called but couldn't find the courage to continue. Carlos had a sick feeling he was beat. Turning over his cards, he said, "Four Sevens," and bolstering said, "I'll just throw away those three aces."

I never changed expression nor said a word. I just began to turn over my cards. An ace, king, jack, queen and ten, all hearts. A royal straight flush, a once in a lifetime hand for a professional card player. It was never supposed to happen.

Looking quickly at the owner, a black scowl had settled over Carlos's face. Thumbs up was given and this was Carlos's sign to beat him, regardless of the chance you have to take.

This was a sign Carlos had only seen one other time. They had double teamed a rich Cuban and getting him drunk, had broke him by morning.

The game continued. I played conservatively, just playing the good hands. Folding on the not so good and not playing over a hundred dollar bet. Carlos was getting anxious. He had dropped about twenty five thousand on that one big pot, and had lost fifteen thousand earlier in the week, the day I got into town. This was forty thousand in a week. Carlos felt his stomach tremble and felt an urge to cry. Hell, he was cracking up, he thought. This bastard isn't human, Carlos concluded as they began another hand.

Carlos was pushing again. He stacked another hand. When Carlos ran the cards, I caught him palming another ace. I pushed the cards back and rather than make a scene, I just announced I was through for the night.

Carlos was desperate. This was exactly what I had done before. Won a big pot and quit. Without thinking it through, Carlos's temper ruled the moment.

"You can always tell a chicken shit by the way he wins a few dollars and runs," Carlos said.

I drew a deep breath and looking coldly at the gambler, I replied, "I usually quit when I catch a son-of-a-bitch dealing off the bottom, I ought to kill you for cheating, asshole, but it would be like shooting a baby duck in a rain barrel. Hell, no better than you play poker, you should be allowed to cheat!"

I stood up and turned to leave. Carlos had reached the breaking point. Screaming with rage, he challenged me to a duel at twenty paces, for ten the next morning.

Chapter 27

Flushed with anger, I strode to the *Flamingo Club* walking rapidly through the crowd, I was relieved that Ginny hadn't gone on yet. Shouldering a bodyguard out of the way, I shoved the dressing room door open. For a startled moment, Ginny seemed glad to see me, but regaining her composure, she candidly asked what she could do for me. I told her I wanted to talk.

She quickly countered that she had nothing to say to me. "You've made an agreement to die in the morning at ten, why should I get involved and be hurt again," she asked. "You have accepted a challenge from the most feared duelist in New Orleans, you hot headed fool," she said, and then began to cry.

I never could stand to see a pretty girl cry, and I reached out to put my arms around her and hug her. For a second she nearly yielded and then lashing out, she told me to get the hell out of her dressing room, and the rest of her life. All the hurt, fear and wrong that had been dumped on her from all the men in her life, flashed from her eyes. I saw raw hate in her eyes where love had once been. I knew I was responsible for part of this, but much of it I couldn't be blamed for. Something died in me as I saw my gentle embrace rebuffed by hate for all men in general. Turning I headed back to the *Orleans*.

If I had a date with death at ten o'clock tomorrow morning, I knew I needed a good night's sleep. Maybe I can figure out a way to win, I thought as I drifted off.

Dawn breaking woke me as the sky turned a chilly pink. Rising I shaved and took a long hot bath. I knew Carlos hated me with a passion. Without trying, I'd made a bitter enemy. I knew Carlos was under a lot of pressure over the money I'd won. Calculating the pressure and the hate he was carrying, I just might have a fighting chance. Walking to the bar, I began to make plans. I needed a second for the match and I needed to know exactly how the match would be handled.

The sheriff and the local judge had decided to preside over the duel. A deputy of the parish offered to be my second and explained the rules. The sheriff furnished the dueling guns.

It was decided we would stand back to back, step off ten paces each then turn and fire. Each man got a pair of cap and ball single shot pistols. They were loaded equal and I got to select my guns, because Carlos had extended the challenge.

This was all new to me. I'd have much rather drawn looking face to face, but I was in a strange land with strange rules.

Carlos and I walked to the middle of a field at the outskirts of town. The news had spread like wildfire. Carlos was much feared as a duelist and had killed a half a dozen men. Hate was brittle in his speech as he snarled a warning to me. "Let's see if you'll run from a duel like you run from a poker game," he growled.

Fanning his hate, I drawled real slow but loud enough for everyone to hear, "I hope you can shoot better than you can deal off the bottom of the deck, cause you can't cheat this time."

Carlos was purple with rage as he accepted his guns, and his hands shook as he grasped the handles of the guns. Taking advantage of the small emotional break, I backed up against him and bumped him before we started walking at the count of one. Breathing deeply, I listened to the count and tried to stay loose. I'd never held a dueling pistol, but the gun felt solid and comfortable to my grasp. I wasn't worried about it being a single shot, most of the times you never got but one shot anyway.

At the count of ten, I swung around, liquid in motion, leveling my right hand and fired. Blue smoke curled from Carlos's pistol as I fired and shot ripped through the arm pit of my shirt. Miraculously the ball only burned the inside of my arm and the side of my chest.

My shot struck Carlos halfway between his shoulder and elbow, shattering his right arm. The force of the huge ball, knocked Carlos backward and he dropped his second gun. It was laying ten feet from his prostrate body. Barely conscious, Carlos lay awaiting my second shot. I hadn't used all my luck at the card table. I raised my second gun to finish the killing, but something snapped in me. I knew I should kill him and get it over with, but bitter bile backed up in my throat and I was sick of killing and seeing people die. As much hate as he had in him, I knew I was leaving a bitter enemy, but he was probably going to lose that arm and that was punishment enough.

I handed the pistols back to the sheriff and left for the hotel. Ginny had made it plain how she felt and I knew I had no future in New Orleans. I'd booked passage on a streamer for Memphis. I thought I might try my luck there or maybe go back to Kentucky and see Eve. I worried about leaving Carlos alive, but hell, I didn't hate him, he was doing enough of that for both of us.

My thoughts returned to Eve as the steamer puffed its way up the Mississippi. I was trying to decide whether to get off in Memphis and buy me a horse or ride the paddle wheel to the Ohio and up to Cincinnati and then ride to Lexington. Trying to decide, I drifted off to sleep as the boat paddled north.

My mind was captured by the easy lifestyle on the Mississippi. Spring was in full bloom, and people sat along the banks of the great river fishing as if there wasn't a care in the whole world.

Large catfish were being snatched from the river as we paddled up the mighty Mississippi. Taking a pole from one of the boatsmen, I tried my hand at fishing. As the boat rolled along, my string filled up. Ten or twelve nice catfish were hanging on my stringer as evening approached.

There must be something relaxing about fishing. A strange peace had come over me as the sun played down. Purple shadows had descended on the river, and it looked like a giant mirror. As I sat there watching the sun set, my line was once again heavy with a big catfish.

I couldn't remember when I had been this at ease. My trouble seemed far away and I felt removed from the real world. Waco and the ranch were just a distant dream and I could hardly remember shooting Carlos.

I was worried about all the cash I was toting, and decided when we got to Memphis I would open an account there. I was carrying over fifty thousand dollars in my pocket. It seemed strange that two poker hands had really changed my life. I wondered what I would have done with this much money when I first got out of the Army. This brought my mind back to the missing cave and the Army's lost gold. How in the hell could a cave just disappear?

The ship bumped the dock at Memphis just as the day was waking up. Dock hands had began loading bales of cotton, racks of tobacco and barrels of molasses as I threaded my way through the freight. Carrying a briefcase in my left hand, my right hand was free and only inches from my gun. Life wasn't worth a lot on the Mississippi dock if you were toting fifty thousand dollars in cash with only your wits and gun for an insurance policy. Tough hard men frequented the river, and you had to be tough to make it.

My mind raced back to New Orleans. I knew I'd left a bitter enemy in Carlos Belyere and in thinking back I should have shot him between his eyes with my second gun and that chapter in my life would be closed. I knew if the roles had been reversed, that's what would have happened.

Hell I was just sick of killing. I guess I was getting soft but the list of men I'd killed was getting longer and I never set out to be a killer. I'd left that damned old buffalo hunter and his idiot son alive and I hadn't gone after that sorry assed nester that killed Willie and now I had left Carlos alive and wounded. Hell, I was getting soft and I'd probably live to regret it. Shaking my head in disbelief, I made my way up the street to the Planters Bank of Memphis.

I strolled into the bank and not wanting to deal with peons, I walked to the president's office. I introduced myself, and could tell he was offended that I just came in without knocking or making an appointment.

I dumped that briefcase full of money on his desk and his eyes flew open in surprise. I could tell he was curious about who I was and what I was doing. I had just deposited more money than most banks had at that time.

Scurrying around his desk, he asked me to have lunch with him and visit. Telling him I was leaving and in a hurry, he decided we could eat breakfast. He rushed around trying to make me comfortable as I explained what I was doing in Tennessee. I explained about my ranch and dispersing of my herds.

The banker was quickly laying out business deals available in Memphis. Various plantations and horse farms for sale, and several different businesses were available. He wanted my banking business. This felt strange as hell, from struggling to pay for some raw boned Longhorn cows to being courted by bankers. Not a damn thing I'd really done. Time and lady luck had done most of it, but I liked this end of the see-saw best.

I glanced hastily at my watch and knew the boat would be loaded shortly. Excusing myself, I folded my deposit sheet, and told the banker I'd be in touch. Rushing back to the boat, the captain was firing the boilers in preparation for leaving.

Boarding the boat I felt a lot more comfortable without all that cash. Funny how two poker hands had been worth more than a thousand head of horses and cattle. The boat bellowed a good-bye as we rounded a bend in the river on our way to Ohio.

Relishing the fried catfish, the ship cook had prepared yesterday, I opted for more. Reclining in an easy chair, I lolled the day away. Fully relaxed, I loved the Big River. By late evening I had caught enough fish to feed the whole boat. Turning the stringer over to a deckhand to clean, I went to my room and cleaned up. A fried catfish dinner was waiting for me when I returned.

I just fished and relaxed as the past drifted further from my mind and my life. We made it up the Mississippi to Cairo, Illinois where the Ohio River chugged into the broad Mississippi. I lay around Cairo for a week, sampling their hospitality and trying my hand at poker again.

Playing my style of poker, I managed to win more than it took me to live. If the cards were falling right, I'd play and bet them, but if they weren't, I'd go to bed. I never played anything but five card or seven card stud.

I was partial to seven card, I just liked those extra two chances. I guess I liked the fact that I was more in control. I could play five and throw away two, instead of having to play what I was dealt. Hell, I don't really know what made me like one better than the other, but that's all I would play. I knew how many tricks could be done with dice, so they were never tempting, I never played blackjack or any house game that was geared in their favor. I managed to win a couple of thousand dollars while in Cairo, but didn't hit any big hands, just tough hard nosed poker.

I woke up one morning and I was bored. Worse than that, I had dreamed about Eve and woke up hugging a pillow. I could nearly feel her soft creamy skin, and knew I was headed for Kentucky. I booked passage to Cincinnati, Ohio. I knew it was just a hundred and fifty miles from there to Lexington and Eve.

My heart started racing as I thought about her and wondered what would happen when I returned. Would she still be in love with me and would I be content to stay this time? A year had passed, and time changes everything, I'd been told. As I reflected back over the year, I recalled the changes in my life.

A lot had happened since I'd left Kentucky. We had killed those damn horse thieves in Arkansas, Bates and Willie had both died, Ginny had left, Wagner and I had killed those horse stealing Indians. Suddenly I was seeing dead horse thieves hanging from rafters and dead Indians and dueling pistols. I felt panic for a minute and decided my love for Ginny wasn't all that had died last year. I wondered about the ranch for a minute and missed the north range. I hated the thought of that rolling hills cow country being chopped up with barbed wire and turning plows.

Suddenly I needed to travel. Packing my bags and trunk, I couldn't wait for daylight. I loaded my baggage on the paddle wheeler. The crew was still loading and I was the first passenger aboard. I was tired of fishing and spent the whole trip restlessly walking from railing to railing and looking up river. I was anxious to get my feet back on the ground and a horse between my knees.

Damn, it seemed forever since I had felt the wind rush by my face as I loped a horse through the night.

Spending one night in Cincinnati, I was up early and took a ferry boat across the Ohio. I bought a horse from an Amish farmer and headed south for Lexington. The night was spent in the tiny town of Williamstown. It was just a stage station with a rooming house and store. Riding hard, I reached Lexington the next night and my spirits began to soar. The lights of *Shady Brook* twinkled in the early evening darkness.

I rode up to the expanse of the lawn and marveled at the beauty of *Shady Brook*. The white house and barns gleamed in the moonlight. Green manicured lawns, flowering beds of flowers were laid out in neat rows, as if by "God Himself."

Knocking softly on the door, I was greeted by the wild shouts from the house servants. I had become a favorite with them, while I was here before. My generous tips and kind treatment had put me in great favor. The maids and butlers were shouting, "Mr. Bill's back! Mr. Bill's back!"

Standing at the top of the stairs, Eve was dressed in a long slim, figure flattering, white dress. It was like the world stopped and a vacuum had sucked us together. Neither of us remembered taking the necessary steps. Kissing like drowning victims, neither of us came up for air. A strange, quiet descended on the plantation house, as maids and butlers faded back to their jobs and left Miss Eve and Mr. Bill to their privacy.

Knowing dinner would soon be served, she showed me to my old room and I was soon at home. After soaking away my travels in the huge tub, I dressed for dinner. Attired in my finest clothes, we cut quiet a figure as we sat down for dinner.

Eve smiled coyly at me as I sat down beside her at the table. Just the two of us and candlelight made the night more special. Eve couldn't keep her eyes off of me. She kept telling me how handsome I looked in my dark gray coat and pale gray slacks. I had on a white shirt, open a little the neck. I had knotted a black silk scarf behind my neck and it filled out the "V" in the neck of my shirt. She said the gray in my temples set off my black wavy hair, added to my Texas charm.

Eve was really a "bull shitter." She could talk "a rabbit into biting a bulldog." Something about her made me believe nothing was impossible if we both wanted it. I had on a pair of soft, black, calfskin boots that glowed in the dark. I could see her reflection in them they were so shiny. Her eyes misted over as she thought of all we had missed this last year. She said she looked everyday for a letter, but not knowing how I never wrote one, she had waited in vain.

Telling in minute detail the story of Jimmy and the race mare, she was spellbound about the attempted hijacking and the story of dispersing the ranch. I was careful not to include any mention of Ginny. Eve waited for the shoe to fall. I had never mentioned Ginny last year, and once again I excluded anything pertaining to this relationship.

Eve never mentioned the letter she had received from Ginny. The first part of the letter was openly hostile. Ginny had cursed Eve for stealing my love, then rambled off into a string of events, that left Eve wondering what kind of troubled person had written it.

Eve wondered if Ginny and I had been married as she claimed at the first of the letter. As the letter weaved its story, Eve had concluded that it was written by someone so consumed by hate and disappointment that the writer was on the brink of insanity. Eve just let me talk and was enchanted by the excitement in my life.

Never had Eve been so entrapped by a man's charm, she surmised. Eve would have given me the world that night, if only there was no tomorrow. Put it off until tomorrow her heart sang and her body was in perfect agreement.

After dinner, Eve and I danced to the soft music of the violin. We each basked in the feel of being in each others arms. Being bold once again, Eve stopped in the middle of a slow waltz and taking my hand, led me to her bedroom. Suddenly we became one and time disappeared. There was no past, no tomorrow, tonight was forever as we spent most of it making love. We hardly said a word, yet never was I so in tune with anyone. Both sated with the love in the night, we finally evaporated to sleep.

Slow spring rain was falling at *Shady Brook* as I awoke in the early morning. The night was vivid on my mind as I lay there drunk on the memories. I stretched and reveled in the luxury of the soft feather bed as Eve snuggled up to me. Dawn was still a couple of hours away. Stroking her soft breast, I nuzzled her neck. I drifted soft light kisses down her neck and back. She turned passionately toward me and the new day began as the old one had ended, in slow sensuous love making that made time stand still.

This last year had been a state of celibacy for Eve and except for the few times spent with Ginny before she left, I had not been with a woman. I grinned when I thought of the little red headed whore I'd picked to sleep with me. That had to be the easiest money she'd ever made. Hell, I was too drunk to do anything but snore. I realized it was the red hair that made me want her and tripped my trigger. No more redheads for me, I thought as I drifted back off to sleep.

Eve lay there in total ecstasy. Love was better this time than before, she thought as she simmered in the afterglow of satisfaction.

We arose as the servant finally knocked on our door. Breakfast was served in her spacious room and I was famished. Smoked ham with redeye gravy and grits was topped off by pancakes and fried eggs, cooked just right. It rained most of the day and we just snuggled and held each other most of it.

I told her of all my adventures since leaving last year. Tentatively at first, then finally the whole story about Ginny and her finding Eve's note and leaving. I went back to the beginning and told her about the Indian attack and about losing Old Blue. I relayed the mystery of the missing cave, the dead soldiers and the Army's lost gold. I told her about Deke Williams' bravery and about killing the buffalo hunters and rescuing Old Blue. I shared with her the Jim Wagner stories and how I envied Wagner with his family and their simple life. She was in awe as I told her about the card games, the pistol duel and finally getting to Willie. This was a part of my life I'd never shared with anyone, not even Ginny.

When I started telling Eve about Willie, and what made this old black man so important in my life, my voice cracked. As I relayed how a cowardly assed cracker had shot him in the back, I began to cry unashamedly. The night had an aura about it. I had never been or felt as close to anybody as I did this night. As the tears began to fall, a dam of emotions broke that had been walled off too long. Eve just held me and let me talk. I had never shared this part of my life with a living soul.

The first thing I could even remember was my mother and trying to be real quiet so my father didn't wake up and beat us. Life was hell for the Fowler family when Tollie Fowler was in a black mood. He was the white overseer of the Keytole Plantation, the largest plantation in Keytole County, Georgia. The Keytole Plantation was my earliest memories of life and the home I remember.

Many slaves felt the lash because of Tollie's black moods. Nearly anything could set him off when he'd been drinking, which was most of the time. Tollie Fowler was an over bearing bastard! He had appointed himself as chief stud for siring mulatto suckers. He took delight in breeding a wench in her bed, and making her man wait out on the steps till he was through with her. There was not a slave on the plantation that didn't hate his guts. None worse than Willie.

Willie had a young pretty high yellow wife. Hell, they didn't ever marry slaves, but I guess in God's eyes they were. I know in Willie's they were. He really loved her. Tollie had taken her for his personal whore and took great delight in performing his stud service in front of Willie. Tollie had a heavy hand with his women and liked to slap and whip around on them if they didn't perform as he wished.

Having Tollie Fowler's bastard baby, Willie's wife died in difficult breach birth delivery. Willie never forgave him. Tollie would make my mother have sex in the room with all us kids and woe if she refused. I had seen my mother beaten from the time I could remember and the years just kinda lumped together till I was fourteen. He had began to beat the little kids if I wasn't handy and I knew what lay in store for them.

Amber Keytole was the daughter of old Amos Keytole and his only child. Amos's wife had died at childbirth and Amber was his whole life. Amos not only owned Keytole Plantation but the little town of Keytole, Georgia. His main asset was the bank and furnished nearly all the planters' financing.

Amber had left the bank one day in her new horse and buggy he'd gotten for her sixteenth birthday. A storm was brewing and thunder began to roll and lightening flashed as she approached the plantation. The new horse became frightened and ran away. I had been fishing in the creek and was trying to reach home before the storm struck. I had just climbed up the bank and stepped into the road when the horse came thundering across the bridge dragging the reins. Amber was screaming and crying as I grabbed for the bridle and the horse thundered past.

When I grabbed the bridle, the momentum jerked me off my feet and flung me up in the air. As survival would have it, I flung my leg over the buggy stay and managed to climb aboard the run away horse and pull him to a stop. I reached down and picked up the trailing reins and soon had the runaway under control. Amber was petrified, so I drove her to the house and put the horse up for her.

Willie had seen the whole thing and between him and Amber they had painted a pretty picture for Amos. Amos had sent Willie to get me and bring me to the big house.

Willie had always been special to me. As bad as he hated my father, he was always kind to me. He'd take me fishing when it was too wet to work and on Sundays. Amos Keytole, never worked anybody on Sunday. This was the Lord's Day he'd say, and nobody did nothing.

Amos was loud with his praises and was surprised when I wouldn't take a reward. He knew I didn't have a quarter and wanted to reward my bravery. Shuffling my toe around and around, I told him I wasn't brave, I just didn't want Miss Amber to get hurt. Amos shook my hand and said, "Son, if you ever need money, or a friend, you get in touch with Amos Keytole, and I'm at your disposal."

Amos Keytole hugged his daughter with tears in his eyes. He was thankful for young Bill Fowler and decided right then as soon as I was old enough, he was going to make me overseer of his plantation and run my whore chasing daddy off.

Amos knew my ancestry was better on my mother's side of the family. Her dad had been a small farmer up on the Tennessee line. My mother had been the old man's only daughter and he'd left her two thousand dollars. She had sworn him to secrecy cause her sorry assed husband would have gambled it off. He had deposited it in his bank and in her and my name. He thought he might just add some to it, that boy deserved a chance, he concluded.

Chapter 28

I was trying to get the little kids to sleep before Tollie came home. My mother was heavy pregnant and had been sick a lot. She was laying across the bed, and I had just turned out the lamp. I had just dozed off to sleep when I heard a loud bang, and drunken cussing.

Tollie had tripped on the steps and fallen into the door. He had been to a dice game and was drunk and broke. Either would set him off. He began cussing my maw for not having supper hot for him. She had left fried ham and taters on the back of the stove but the fire had burned down. Grabbing her by the hair, he kicked her as he drug her to the kitchen. That brought me to my feet.

Something snapped in me as he kicked her swollen bloated body with his old hard rough brogan shoes. Grabbing a stick of stove wood, I slammed it into the back of his balding head. A river of rage and abuse flooded my strength and Tollie Fowler was dead when he hit the floor.

The young kids were all asleep. I helped my mother to her feet and wiped the blood from her face but was in a quandary. I knew if I was discovered, I'd hang. Only me and Maw knew the truth, but Tollie was a large man and we couldn't carry him. I wrapped Tollie in an old blanket and ran for the slave quarters. It was after midnight as I slipped up to Willie's door.

Willie lived alone since his wife had died and they had no children. Awakening softly, Willie looked up to see me standing there and he knew something was wrong. As he listened to my story, Willie walked to the tool shed for a shovel. Willie knew we had to get rid of the body.

Cutting across the field to the share cropper shack we lived in and called home, I formulated a plan. I decided we would bury him in the flower bed and tell everyone that Tollie had deserted his family and gone to Texas. One thing about Tollie, the world would want to believe the worst about him. Texas was a big country and no one would ever know whether or not Tollie was there.

Willie dug a grave right beside the house in my mother's flower bed. She always had a flower bed, which was out of place around the old run down house we lived in. This was her one link to the happy childhood she had known.

Placing the corpse in the hole was done in the pale moonlight. Willie was careful to put the red clay down in the hole first and keep the sand to put back on top. We spaded the rest of the flower bed up in the moonlight so the fresh dirt wouldn't show. Willie knew the soil and how each layer told its story.

By daylight, the flower bed was fresh spaded and the soil finely raked and seeded with flower seeds. Maw poured Willie and me coffee as the sun came up and sealed our grisly plan. It was never mentioned again.

We knew Tollie didn't have any friends. The rich tolerated him, the blacks hated him and our family lived in fear. Knowing there wouldn't be a big search for him was in our favor. Maw and I decided to go and explain his leaving to Mr. Amos Keytole and ask his advice on what to do.

Amos Keytole was neither surprised nor disappointed to hear that Tollie Fowler had left. "He was a sorry excuse for a man," Amos explained and then apologized to Maw.

Explaining about her father's little farm in Tennessee and a brother who lived close by, she asked about the money she had in the bank and Amos assured her it was available. He also told her Tollie had a month's pay coming, fifty dollars. Amos turned and handed her a hundred dollar bill, then walking over to me offered me the overseers job. I was surprised, but saying no, I quickly approached Mr. Keytole with my plan. I wanted to buy Willie and two horses and go to Texas. I lied and told him I wanted to find my father.

Amos started to argue the case, but remembering me saving his daughter's life, he promptly made out a bill of sale for Willie, two horses and two saddles. He also gave Maw a light wagon and harness and two mules to pull it, as a gift. Walking to the vault he withdrew my two thousand dollars and handed it to me. I have always been beholden to Mr. Amos Keytole for his fair business dealings.

I took the hundred and fifty that Mr. Almos gave Maw and I gave her the two thousand. She was going to need it with the youngins and a baby coming 'bout any time.

We was 'bout rich for share croppers, I guess. I went to the quarters and got Willie. I told him he was free now cause Mr. Amos had give him to me for saving Miss Amber from the run away. It didn't sink in for a few days, I don't think. He never acted any different. Willie and I selected two big geldings and a pair of matching sorrel mules that were real gentle. Willie picked out a little spring wagon that traveled light for Maw.

Night fell as all the packing was complete except the beds and the wood stove. After supper, Willie left and came back in an hour or so carrying a wild rose bush he had dug up behind the chicken pen at the big house. He planted the roses over the grave. "Ain't nobody gonna mess around no rose bush," he said as he finished his job. Willie slept on the porch that night, cause he didn't belong to the plantation any longer.

Maw fixed corn pone and fat meat for breakfast and she made real coffee with the last beans she had. Me and Willie loaded the beds and finished packing as the stove cooled down. The 'ol stove was the last thing we loaded, 'ceptin' the kids. Taking the reins, Maw tucked the kids in the seat beside her and left for Tennessee. Black pots, tubs and the stove was a rattlin' and the hens were cackling in their coops as she drove off without looking back.

I had the hundred and fifty dollars in my pocket and Willie and I mounted and headed for Texas and Tollie Fowler became history. Willie and I drifted around Texas before settling in Waco. Texas was fighting for her independence and Willie and I both joined the cause. I had Willie's papers fixed when we got to Texas, making him a free man so he was free to fight or stay, but Willie wanted to fight. We got to San Jacinto the day Santa Anna surrendered.

A man had homesteaded a place where the headquarters were in the fork of the river and wanted to go back to Missouri, where he was from. I traded my horse for his proving up the place and Willie and I rode double from San Jacinto to Waco. I bought the rest of the ranch from the state for a dollar an acre that we managed to scrape together.

Willie stayed and ran the ranch when the Civil War started and I joined the Confederate cause. I figured freeing Willie was the least I could do after the way Paw had done him, but you know, he never mentioned it one way or the other. I don't know whether I took care of Willie or Willie took care of me. We just kinda leaned on each other. Hell, we was family.

Eve kissed me softly as I finished talking. I felt like a huge burden had been lifted off my heart. I lay there a minute wondering about Maw and my family, but feeling no kindred in my heart, I drifted back off to sleep, unburdened for the first time in a long time.

Eve slipped out of bed as dawn streaked the sky. Damn, it was going to be harder than she thought, she argued with herself. Now she wasn't sure she could do it. Why in the hell had he ever left if he wasn't going to stay gone, she wondered. She felt like a yoyo. Just running up and down, never knowing when to stop.

Breakfast was a happy occasion as we feasted on fried ham, grits, eggs, and big fluffy cathead biscuits. Jo-Jo, the cook and unofficial house foreman, called the biscuits cathead biscuits. She said you pinched off a piece of dough 'bout big as a cat's head, and rounded it up to bake it.

I was as close to happy as I had ever been. Eve dressed for riding and we left for the horse barns. Walking along holding hands, the day was still new. Dew lay on the ground like a small rain. Roses were in full bloom and their fragrance filled the air. Stopping to pick one, I trimmed the thorns off with my ever present pocket knife and handed the rose to Eve.

"Beauty for the beautiful," I said and winked.

Eve looked off at the fog filled meadows and again decided this was not going to be easy. Our hearts beat as one, our emotions were as one, she thought, never had anyone been so in tune with her in soul, in mind or in spirit. Why in the hell didn't he stay last year, she wondered again. It would have been so easy then.

I interrupted her thoughts by pulling her close and kissing the end of her nose. The smell of her was intoxicating, fresh and clean and so feminine.

The mood was broken by Mose as he came hobbling into the barn. A stud had pawed him a few days back and he was pretty stove up he declared. Quickly, asking Bill's health and horse information, Mose asked about Jimmy. How was the boy? I had to set down on an old wood block and tell Mose the story of Jimmy and Moonshine.

Mose was all ears as the story unwound. Amening and shore 'nough'in at the wins and escapes. "Shore served da gambler right, poking' fun at da man's hat, and callin' that mare a dog. Sho nuff fish-eyed fool could see dat mare was a race hoss," he concluded.

"Jimmy shore dun fine wid da trainin'," he said. "Just right letten' the mare travel widda wagin whilst he rode on her back, and da walking behind da team legged her up fine. Jimmy was a race hoss man," he sighed.

And grinning a glad old toothless grin, he said, "Jimmy dun sired us a sucker while he here. My daughter, Lucinda, done got a boy chile from dat Jimmy boy, and I gonna make a race hoss man outta him for shore. You just watch dis boy," he chattered.

Mose was so excited about Jimmy that when he walked on down the shed row, he hardly limped. He was retelling the race horse stories all day, and every time he told it, Jimmy bet a little more and the little mare won by another length.

Chapter 29

Wanting to be alone and recapture the closeness of the morning, Eve and I rode out to check on the yearling colts and fillies.

The yearlings had been moved into the meadows and separated by sex. The fillies were in the pasture, the brook ran through that gave the horse farm its name. There were several by Domino Duke the roan horse I'd bought last year and I thought they really stood out from the herd. They had that roan flank and tail. The roans were carrying a little more muscle and were shorter and stronger across their backs.

I found myself wishing I had them back in Texas. Suddenly, I stopped and realized that I had colts by Domino Duke in Texas that I had never seen. For a minute I was homesick. Homesickness didn't last long this time. I realized that I didn't have a lot left at home. Ginny was just a haunting memory. Bates and Willie were both dead and those damn nesters had carved up the north range.

I needed to go home and fence the Childress Creek. All of the creek lay on my deeds but someone would be homesteading and claiming half the creek if I didn't fence it, like that redneck bastard had. I got sad thinking about Willie again. I just hated to fence it and not be able to ride where I pleased, but I probably can't now if I was back there, I decided.

My thoughts drifted back to the north range and the Brazos. I envisioned Jimmy Wagner and his little family. As I reminisced, I wondered about the cave and the missing gold. As we rode through the filly pasture, I surmised that Jim just might find the opening to the cave and the lost gold.

After spending several hours alone, both lost in deep thought, Eve and I decided to check on the three year-olds in training. Riding back toward the big house, we stopped by the track to watch. Mose was everywhere, talking and coaching. Hollering at a jockey for whipping a colt, "teach him what you want, don't whip him," he exclaimed. "Got to have mo sense dan da colt," Mose kept repeating.

The colts were fit and beautiful. They were speed merchants, I declared as we watched a couple work. I wondered back to last year and couldn't expect to put this much hot blood together again, even if you had a million dollars to do it with.

I decided guilt for betraying Ginny was the reason I'd left, but the longer it was since I last saw her, the less she crossed my mind.

As I studied Eve from the corner of my eye, I was once again struck by her beauty. I had seen a lot of pretty women, slept with more than a few, but never one with her class.

Catching Eve's elbow and leading our horses, I escorted her back to the horse barn. The smell of horses and bluestem hay greeted us as we approached the stable. We both stopped and inhaled like it was perfume. It was scary how our thoughts ran parallel. If nothing else in common, we both loved horses.

Eve contemplated everything we had in common and concluded we were the perfect match. Thinking of matches, Eve knew she had to break the news tomorrow, but couldn't decide how. Maybe it will be easier tomorrow she thought. She wanted to spend one more night of ecstasy, knowing this was going to end forever and dreading it.

I felt something was different but I couldn't put my finger on it. Eve gave herself so total, so complete. Never had I been so absorbed, by anything. I had finally found complete love. Never knowing love as a child and I had never really let Ginny love me completely. I had held back because of her past. Hell, I guess I just never did really trust her.

With Eve, It was spontaneous. I was head over heels in love this time. As we came back to the house that night, I stopped and just held Eve as we watched the sun sink behind the tree line. Just holding her brought a surge to my stomach.

She had to tell me, time was running out. She had sworn the house help to secrecy, but she knew it had to stop tonight. Dreading the time, she decided to wait till morning.

Dinner was served in splendor, the cook and waiters outdid themselves. The food was flawless, and I wondered how it would be to spend the rest of your life wrapped in this coat of luxury. My mind wondered back through the last year and I decided, I'd changed a lot. I wasn't homesick for Texas this time. I'd had a year to get over Ginny, I'd killed Running Bull and he'd never be a threat again. I had buried Willie, and Bates had died. Hell, I didn't have anything in Texas but money in the bank and some horses and cows.

Eve and I danced as if we were one. Eve was a great dancer, I decided. She was so nimble, even I couldn't step on her feet, and I sure wasn't a ballroom hero. I was totally enveloped by her charm. The way she smelled, the way her head lay on my shoulder, and the way her arm pulled me so close.

I just realized that I was totally in love for the first time in my life. I had a love for Ginny, but it was at first a lustful thing, and after the trial it was more of a protective, overseer relationship — but this was the real thing I decided.

Quietly taking my hand, Eve led me up the stairs. The violin was playing in the background and the butler blew out the candles and lamps as midnight descended. With no pretense of proper behavior, Eve led me straight to her room.

A million thoughts had raced through Eve's mind as the night drifted away. Was she making the right choice? Was reason overruling passion? Would her life be happy or just content? She had felt she'd never see me again when I left before she had spent a year wondering. She had gotten the letter from Ginny and not a word from me. This was the opportunity of lifetime, but yet, what was real life worth. She knew I was the love of her life, and yet would she be happy if I decided to go back to Texas. She knew the year had changed me. I wasn't as restless and I seemed more at peace, but did she really know?

I stretched out on the soft feather bed, a mountain of luxury and thought of the cold nights I'd spent laying on the rocky frozen ground at Palo Duro Canyon. It seemed for a minute, I could nearly feel the chill, but it quickly disappeared as I watched Eve slowly undress. I had seen the girlie shows at Galveston and New Orleans, but nothing compared to her naked beauty.

Eve was so different from any woman I'd ever know and I'd known more than a few. Real feminine, yet bold and deliberate in her actions. She undressed with no modesty, standing unashamed before me. She knew she was a beautiful woman, and had a beautiful body, yet she wasn't vain. She just accepted this as one of God's blessings she had inherited and didn't gloat on the fact. She was so relaxed and confident in her sexuality that it made me feel natural and this added to the excitement.

Eve left a single candle burning that cast dark shadows on the room and her naked body gleamed in the silky light.

Laying quickly beside me with a heavy heart, Eve decided when the night was over she would break the news. Determined to have the night to remember, Eve leaned over me and kissed me slow and sensuously.

Eve's long blonde hair caressed my chest as she leaned over and kissed me. Her embrace stopped the hands of time. There was no tomorrow, no yesterday and erased all the other times in our lives. Tonight was tonight. No tomorrows and no regrets. Time stood still. A life time was wrapped into one night, and damn tomorrow.

Neither of us slept as passion consumed us, and a pale pink dawn descended on our love nest. Eve rose first and after washing her face and brushing her teeth and long hair, she came back and sat quietly on the bed. I was dozing lightly as she softly kissed me. I remember how good she smelled, and reaching hungrily for her my world came to an end.

Eve grasped my hands in both of hers and began something I wish she hadn't. She told me she knew how different our lifestyles were and yet she loved me with all her heart. Tears spilled down her cheeks as she continued.

"When you didn't write," she said, "I decided you didn't love me and I was just another notch on your gun." She told me about Ginny's letter, saying she was my wife and she asked me if I was or had been married to Ginny.

I listened intently as Eve continued but my heart and mind were in a stupor. Just when I had came to grips with my feelings. Life had dealt me a new hand. I knew this was a game I couldn't win. Answering Eve about Ginny, I told her the whole story. I told her that I had loved Ginny, but in a different way. But whispering hoarsely, I told her never had I loved anyone like I loved her. I listened silently to the rest of Eve's story but my heart had died a sudden death.

Eve told me that after not hearing from me, she had decided she was just another string on my fiddle. Governor Ball's wife had been killed in a fall and after a year, he asked her to go to several state functions. She explained that Governor Ball was a handsome man in his late fifties, and they were of the same class. He had proposed and she had accepted his proposal. The wedding was set for next month. Governor Ball had been to England for a month, but would be back the first of next week.

Crying she told me, she just had to spend this time with me. Eve told me she would always love me, but she was going to marry Guy Ball next month. I felt betrayed, hurt and alone, but nothing could overcome the love and passion I had known this last week.

I wanted to beg her to change her mind, but I had too much pride. Bill Fowler had clawed his way form the cotton fields of Georgia to a rich rancher without begging and I sure as hell didn't intend to start today. Dressing quickly, I turned to go. Grabbing me and sobbing loudly, Eve held me close for a minute, and as I pulled loose and turned to go she whispered, "Bill I'll always love you," but I was already walking swiftly down the hall.

Jo-Jo hailed me, "Mr. Bill, breakfast is ready," but I hardly had an appetite for breakfast or life. I headed to the barn without realizing it. Mose was watching me come, and he said he knew by the way I walked, Mr. Bill was leaving and ain't a coming back.

Saddling my gelding, I was lost. Where in the hell was I going in such a hurry, I wondered. Sending a groom to the house for my clothes, I told the stable hands goodbye. Mose had to take me to his house and show me Jimmy's boy 'fore I left he said. It did look just like Jimmy, and was shore 'nough gonna be a race hoss man.

I rode swiftly away from *Shady Brooks*. I had suffered a lot of hurt in my life. Bullet wounds, frostbite, arrow wounds, and infections, abuse but nothing had prepared me for heart ache. It raged in my soul and devoured my mind. I contemplated murder, arson, kidnapping and suicide, but settled on liquor and for a month I lay in Cincinnati's finest hotel, too drunk to tell night from day. I'd sober up enough every few days to bath and eat a few bites and then get drunk all over again. I never cared for liquor. I'd drink a little beer sometimes when I ate, but too many memories of my drunk Paw was associated with the smell of whiskey.

This smell is what woke me from my drunken stupor. I had killed a quart of whiskey and left enough in the bottle to run out on my pillow in the night. This was the smell that greeted me as the sun rose. I looked around the room and was appalled at the sight. The room was littered with whiskey bottles, stale putrid clothes and scraps of uneaten food.

God, how long had I been here I wondered? I attempted to rise and my body wretched at the effort. My body was weak and my hands trembled as I tried to fasten my pants. I felt hungry and nauseous at the same time. Trying to remember when I had last eaten caused a violent headache.

Rubbing my face, I realized I had a full beard and mustache. Never had I gone without shaving if I could get to water, except the winter at Palo Duro Canyon. I stunk like a derelict and suddenly I hated myself for neglect.

I had always prided myself on being clean and well groomed. My hair was now real long and my face was gaunt and thin. A chambermaid passed in the hall, and I hailed her. Quickly greeting her, I ordered a new room with a hot bath and sent all my clothes to be cleaned and laundered. I managed to plod feebly down the hall to my new room. I tried to remember the last month. The calendar looked blurred before my eyes. I asked the chamber lady what day it was. It had been thirty-five days since I had checked into the hotel. It had just been a blur. I could only remember drinking and eating occasionally.

As I soaked in the tub of hot soapy water, I vaguely remembered leaving *Shady Brook*, after telling Eve goodbye. Hell, she told me goodbye. I never answered her. I guess I'm bad about that anyway.

Looking at the calendar, I knew Eve was Mrs. Guy Ball by now. The Governor of Kentucky's wife and born for the role. She was finally in her class at last. Once again, she was married to an older man, for less than true love, but secure in her social standing. I guess in her own way, she was as much a whore as Ginny had been. She just sold herself less often and for bigger stakes, I decided as I stepped out of the tub and began to dry myself off.

The full beard was next, as I attacked it with a straight razor. After cutting myself a half a dozen times in as many attempts, I retreated to a barbershop and let him finish my shave and cut my hair short. After a bath and shave, I decided it was time to put something in my stomach.

I ordered ham and eggs, but after a few bites, I gagged. After being drunk a month, my body was rejecting solid food. Drinking a couple of cups of coffee steadied my nerves and I managed to drink a glass of milk. I was suddenly real tired and I struggled back to my room and layed down. Sleep returned and long shadows lay in the room when I awoke again. I was starving for something to drink.

Pouring a glass of water from the pitcher, I ended up with more on the floor than was in the glass. I finally managed to turn up the pitcher and drank most of it without stopping. Water never tasted so good. I drank like a thirsty horse. Setting back on the bed to rest, I decided I needed some cow meat.

I trudged back down a block to the café again and ordered a small steak, rare, and a pitcher of milk. I kept it down but I had a real bad case of cramps most of the night. I rested and recuperated for about a week.

I would eat four or five small meals a day, and I couldn't get enough milk and water. My body started to replenish and my face filled out. I bought several suits of new clothes and began to play a few hands of poker in the evenings. Mostly, I slept. Sleep and eat. I didn't have any ambition at this point in my life. I just wanted to be alone. I was winning enough at poker to support my lifestyle and I was just floating.

I found a paper in the lobby of the hotel describing the wedding, where it had taken place, and who had attended. It read like a *Who's Who* of Kentucky. Deep in my heart I wished Eve the best, but a broken heart is a piss poor companion. Never had I loved so completely and never would I make the same mistake again. One night stands looked like the answer to me. Love them — sleep with them, till the new wore off and then disappear, I decided and headed back to the poker table for the night.

Suddenly I got the urge to travel and booked passage to Pittsburgh. I had never seen the East and one river town was as good as the next. I drifted from town to town, just following the rivers. Gambling which had no appeal to me for years now was a way of life. Drifting from town to town and gambling table to gambling table, I lived a life of leisure.

Never having a greed for winning, I played conservative poker. It was just a business for me. I harvested a crop when my luck was good and the cards were smiling. I never forced the cards. If they were cold, I'd change towns or casinos. It didn't bother me to get up and go to bed. I toured New York and places I'd just heard about. When the cards weren't falling right, I'd sightsee.

Chapter 30

Jimmy was training his best set of runners. He had always wanted to be a "race hoss man" and he had achieved. Building a breeding program around the roan stud and the ten Kentucky mares, he had achieved a lot of success. His greatest triumph was an accident. His little mare Moonshine got out and got bred to Old Blue. Jimmy was just sick about it, but it turned out to be the magic cross.

Blue Moon was a mare produced by the accident and the kind of mare a trainer dreams about. She could run short or long. Jimmy had won from Dallas to San Antonio with this mare. She was big as a boxcar, nothing like her little stunted mother, but they were both supreme race mares. Jimmy matched her from two hundred and twenty yards to a mile and a sixteenth and had never had her outrun.

He was now breeding all of his Domino Duke mares back to the "Old Hoss" as they had taken to call him. The first few years Mr. Bill was gone, he just bred the Old Blue Hoss to the saddle horse mares and raised ranch horses. His colts were in big demand for ranch horses and he'd cross him on some medium sized draft mares and raise buggy horses, but he was a sleeping giant. He was a race hoss sire, and Jimmy pampered him.

Jimmy had kinda let the ranch run itself. He kept most of the hands on but he couldn't boss folks like Uncle Willie had. The fields weren't producing like they used it, and Jimmy really didn't like the cattle. He was selling most of the bull calves to other ranchers so he had quit cutting his bull calves.

He kept every Hereford cross heifer but he needed to buy some new bulls. He was trying to build up the Hereford blood, but he kept forgetting to move the bulls around and they were getting awful inbred. Jimmy wasn't even sure what bulls had been on what cows the year before and the hands couldn't keep them straight.

The ranch sure wasn't making as much money as it use to, but the horses were making more. Jimmy was selling some high dollar race horses and he had won a lot of money betting on his horses. Jimmy had accumulated a lot of money in the last eight or ten years and a house full of kids.

Never selling a good mare, Jimmy had quiet a set of brood mares. He ran and sold mostly geldings. But the good mares, he'd always retire and breed. Jimmy never had a better racer than Blue Moon. He had thought Moonshine was the horse of his dreams, and she had answered a lot of his dreams, but Blue Moon was the dream.

A lot of people had tried to buy her but he would claim she belonged to Mr. Bill. Jimmy knew a lot of people would resent a black man owning this good set of horses, so he just passed it off as he trained for Mr. Bill Fowler. He just used me for a front. No one resented Bill Fowler having good horses, and as far as they knew Jimmy was a jockey and a trainer. Part of it was true, but Jimmy was getting rich in the meantime.

Jimmy had learned his lesson well about showing his money from Bill and Clara on the way back from Texarkana. Now he would have some in every pocket and make like he could just barely cover the bets. Sometimes he'd get money from Clara's bosom. She would set in the buggy with that same sawed-off shotgun and nobody fooled with Mrs. Clara — black or white!

He didn't put it all in the bank. He'd bring it home and hand it over to Clara and she'd put it in gallon jugs and pulling up the boards in the floor, she'd bury it. No one suspected how much money was under the house. Jimmy would always deposit Mr. Bill's part and some for him so no one was the wiser. Jimmy would get a letter occasionally from Pittsburgh, New York, Chicago, and foreign places like London and Paris. I had gambled on cards, horses and women. I sent my winnings to the bank. I had decided that horses, cards and women were universal entertainment and felt equally at home with each.

Jim Wagner had sent word to Jimmy that he needed another stud. Jimmy rode up the river leading a red roan two-year-old. He was by the roan stud from Kentucky and a daughter of Old Blue. His mammy was a full sister to the other stud Mr. Bill had given Jim Wagner. Jim had wanted some more of that bloodline. This horse could really run, but Jimmy had a stable full of horses that could and he didn't like studs. This horse was a short hoss, Jimmy thought. He was just like his daddy, but his daddy produced way over his head. This hoss would be perfect to raise ranch hosses, Jimmy decided, and thought him ideal for the Wagner's mares. When Jimmy showed him to Jim Wagner, Jim agreed.

Wagner insisted that Jimmy spend the night and they talked long into the night about how Mr. Bill had just left and about horses and horses and horses.

Jimmy retired to the hay loft and once again he recalled the story Mr. Bill had told about the Indian attack and how they had fired the haystack and he shivered at the memories.

Breakfast was eaten early the next morning before Jimmy left down river. No price had been established on the stud. They agreed to wait till Mr. Bill got back, like he was coming back tomorrow. Hell, Jimmy thought, he's been gone ten years, maybe he ain't never coming back. Riding home down the river, this thought kept plaguing Jimmy. What if he didn't, Jimmy questioned and grimaced at the thought.

Chapter 31

Ginny was the belle of New Orleans for several years. She was singing the long nights away, as drunk crowds roared their approval and clapped and threw money for encores. The smoke and abuse of her vocal cords began to take its toll. Ginny began having throat trouble, at first just hoarseness and then laryngitis. Sometimes she would be singing and reach for a high note and grow mute.

Fame is a fickle companion and the same people she was making rich one week, were sending her packing the next. Still a beautiful woman, she had no trouble drifting back into her old way of life.

For a year or two she was a kept woman by the owner of the *Flamingo Club* where she had sang. This was spoiled by a jealous rage when his wife discovered the affair. She killed him with his own derringer and was looking for Ginny when arrested.

Alone again, Ginny began to accept special clients at her cottage that he left her. As Ginny's age began to show on her lovely features, her clientele began to fade to the younger girls in town. Ginny had some money but was afraid of being an old broke whore. She had the money from the *Brazos Queen* in the bank. She had been adding her tips and "funny money" to it for ten years.

Thinking soberly she wasn't broke but she didn't have enough to live on the rest of her life. Looking at herself in the mirror, she knew she still looked good for her forty years but she also knew the road ran down hill from now on and real fast.

A plan was forming in her pretty head. She wanted her own bar and casino. She didn't want a big club, something small and elite, a private club with limited, carefully selected members. No one off the street admitted. She needed it secluded and she could do this reasonable if she used a lot of class. Deciding she needed six girls, no more, and all young and beautiful, she knew she could still sing the old favorites for a while if she didn't force her voice, just till she could afford to hire someone, she decided. She needed a bartender, who would also be the muscle if needed, and a dealer.

Carlos Belyere had been the best she had ever seen before his duel with Bill Fowler, and he could still do a lot with the cards but dealt one handed. His right arm was nearly ruined in the duel. People in New Orleans still talked about the duel. No one had ever came close to Carlos Belyere in a duel until that damn Texas cowboy out shot him and then insulted him by not finishing the duel by killing him. Ginny was glad he hadn't, cause right now she needed a dealer.

In short order, Ginny had made the rounds. By dark she had all six of her girls in tow. She had promised a family atmosphere and each girl was to have her own room. Commissions were to be paid weekly. They would eat here at the house and no, opium, no alcohol and no outside boyfriends.

Next she looked for Carlos Belyere. He was playing pot luck poker on the wharf, barely making a living for the last nine years. He was a far cry from the suave Fancy Dan gambler I'd shot. Ginny believed in long shots, and something about him reminded her of Bates.

She quickly cut him a deal. He could live at the *Palace*, as she had began to call her make believe casino and would receive ten percent of the winnings. She would furnish room, board, and laundry. He would leave alcohol, opium, and the girls strictly alone. This looked like heaven to a down and outer, who was having hell getting the first three items on the list and had no need for the last three.

Next she looked up Sam Levines. Sam had been the bartender at the *Flamingo*, till they caught him carrying home liquor and wholesaling it. Sam had been the best and most popular bartender in New Orleans. He had an uncanny memory and could fix your favorite drink after several years. People loved to be remembered and he was the best. She made him a deal, instead of stealing from me, you get fifteen percent of the bar profit, paid by the week, room and board and laundry. No drinking, no opium, leave my girls alone. From the dingy little dive where he was working, this looked like Utopia.

Next she needed a bouncer, and she knew just who to get. Sam Levines was tough enough to bounce anywhere, but she wanted him to mix drinks. Carlos Belyere was like Bates, you'd have to bury any trouble that came his way and either could ably assist if big trouble came along.

Ginny's idea was to stop trouble from ever starting and she knew just the man. Black Jack was the janitor at the *Flamingo*. He was a former slave and worked part-time on the docks. He could lift a hog sled of molasses and carry it over his head. She knew he could manhandle a drunk with enough power that you didn't have to hurt him. He could be the janitor and the bouncer. Black Jack was an easy hire. He just picked up his extra pair of overalls and followed Ginny home.

Now she needed a house to make into her *Palace*. A long deserted house on Canal Street had attracted her attention. The previous owners had died in the small pox outbreak after the war. The house had been sitting vacant for years but was still in relatively good shape. Ginny had a way of getting things done. After digging around at the courthouse a few days, she bought the house for back taxes and membership in her new club.

In a couple of days, Ginny had gathered a motley crew of carpenters from the down and outers. Drying them out and furnishing them room and board for staying sober, and a bonus when the job was done, she started work on the *Palace*.

After a month, the old house was no longer recognizable. A new clay tile roof had replaced the old. The old outside walls had been stuccoed in a gleaming white. Ginny expanded on the Spanish theme as she remodeled. She added new living quarters for her and the old bedrooms had been remodeled for the girls. The huge kitchen and dining room had been restored and converted into a bar and dining room. The carriage house and stable had been converted to make rooms for Black Jack, Carlos and Sam Levine. There had been a ballroom for dancing and this easily converted into the gambling room. The lawn was restored and all the flower beds reseeded.

The new stable had been built farther back away from the house, for customers' coaches and a tall security fence had been erected so no one could see in. Tall cane was planted outside the perimeter fence that grew thick and lush. This gave it the look of the swamp and further obscured anyone's view.

The *Palace* had quickly grown into a little work of its own, and nobody came uninvited. Suddenly it was the talk of New Orleans and the "who's who" were scrambling for membership invitations. Ginny knew how to manage people and what to put together.

A year passed like lightening and the *Pleasure Palace* was the night spot for southern Louisiana. The crew meshed and the whole operation was a machine. Gambling money had paid for all the repairs and remodeling and forbidding unseen disasters, Ginny felt confident that life's troubles for her were over.

Chapter 32

Awakening restless, I was in New York, and had been here a month taking in the shows, gambling and entertaining the ladies. Always a fool about pretty women, and now an ever so proper gentleman, with a lot of money, I was being pursued by the town's most notables. Winter had been cold and wet in the East. A warm south wind was blowing this morning and suddenly I was homesick for Texas and a ranch, I hadn't seen it in ten years. Dressing hurriedly I packed my trunk and stooping down to kiss last night's girlfriend goodbye, I booked passage on a ship for Galveston.

The day had warmed and the sea was calm and serene as we steamed out of the harbor. The city slowly disappeared as we slipped down the east coast and watched the rugged shoreline and lighthouses fade from view. We stopped at the main ports and usually would be docked for the night. I got to see a lot of country that was new to me.

The seasons were changing as we traveled south and as we steamed around the southern tip of Florida, it was a whole different world. Palm trees and glistening white sand beaches greeted us. I had been to England and Europe but never had the sea fascinated me like it did off the Keys of Florida. The beauty was breathtaking and the colors were nearly blinding.

Still a seafood lover, I gorged on lobster, shrimp and oysters at every port we stopped in. As we headed into the Gulf of Mexico, I knew we were going to stop in New Orleans. I wondered what lay in store. Having left two bitter enemies full of hate, the last time I'd been here, left me wondering what lay ahead.

The captain of the ship decided to lay over the weekend in New Orleans to restock supplies. There was a lot of freight to be unloaded and supplies for Louisiana and Texas to load. I hesitated about going ashore, I finally took a coach to the *Orleans* and registered for the weekend. Easing around the casino I learned that

Carlos had survived, but no one knew much about him. *The Flamingo* was closed and boarded up since the death of its proprietor and no one knew anything about a red headed singer.

Friday night just idled away as I entertained lukewarm poker hands. Win one, lose one. Bored with the game, I struck up a friendship with a cotton broker named Grant Archer and asked him about the city. Grant said there was a new place open in town called the *Pleasure Palace*. It was a private club and hard as hell to get in. He said he finally got an invitation to join and had bought a membership. Real small and elite, he said, but it was first class. Each member could bring one guest per week, and invited me to be his guest the next night.

This sounded good to me. I couldn't seem to relax here at the *Orleans*. I guess there were too many overcharged memories here from the past. Grant explained where it was located and sent his driver over with a note for reservations. He said it was kind of a big family operation but the gambling was sky's the limit.

The night approached as I dressed slowly. Suddenly I was apprehensive about going. I was ready to go home. I hadn't been homesick since Eve had broken my heart, but suddenly I was. I wanted to see the Wagners and Jimmy and Clara. I wondered if Waco had changed and thought about the cave that had just disappeared and the lost gold. Suddenly the broker was knocking on my door. Slipping on my coat, I greeted Grant as we stepped into the hall. Somehow I wasn't relishing the night.

Our carriage approached the *Pleasure Palace*. We were traveling along a tall cane field and suddenly a gate opened and we were at the *Pleasure Palace*. It was tastefully done, I concluded as we stepped down from the carriage. A huge black man greeted us at the door, attired in a black suit and tie with a starched white shirt and shinny shoes. This made me think about *Shady Brook* and Eve. For a moment my heart ached just like it had when Eve first broke it.

Grant Archer and I were ushered into a bright lit room where a couple of games of poker were in progress. I glanced around the room and didn't recognize anyone. Grant and I pulled out chairs and joined a two handed game in progress.

I won a couple of pretty good hands and the dealer excused himself from the game. We walked to the back and ordered a drink. I felt apprehensive as I was confronted by the sight of Ginny. She glided into the room, dressed in a long sleeved, white silk dress that flared at the waist. Ginny was still a pretty woman, but time had come a calling.

Her face was lined and she powdered it to cover and hide the little cracks and wrinkles around her mouth and eyes. Remembering our last visit, I steeled myself and waited defensively.

Ginny caught her breath sharply and thought, damn, I knew he'd show up someday. Forcing a smile she held out her hand and said, "Hello Bill." Turning to Grant, she made him welcome. Ginny played the perfect hostess. She knew the game was too young to spoil.

Walking back to my chair, a dealer had returned and was shuffling the cards. Something about his back looked familiar and my heart froze. Carlos Belyere was dealing, and I couldn't just walk away. Grant walked to his chair and not knowing the circumstances, began to chat nonchalantly.

Ice formed in midair as Carlos Belyere looked up and saw me. Turning gray around his mouth, he never acknowledged me, just dealt a hand of cards. Grant had three tens and I folded after the fourth card. I never called for all my cards for an hour or so. Every time I folded, you could see Carlos's jaw set.

Carlos was winning, Grant won a few hands, and a plantation owner who was setting in the fourth chair was cold. Nobody was winning or losing a lot. I studied Carlos closely out of the corner of my eye. He still had that minor twitch in his cheek when he hit, but I noticed Carlos looked bad. He had on good clothes, but his hands were rough and had seen rough work. His gun hand was nearly useless. I wanted out of this game. I felt like I was in a cave with a wounded rattler.

The bartender brought fresh drinks and said, Miss Ginny would like a word with me. I took a deep breath and figured, well here it is. But I was grateful for the reprieve. I pushed back my chair and a look of jealousy crossed Carlos's face. As if he needed another reason to hate me.

The bartender escorted me to Ginny's office. Quietly closing the door behind me, he returned to the bar. Ginny studied my face as I approached her.

Ginny's mind was buzzing. Damn, he's still a good looking man she thought and she smiled across at the stranger. She said, "Bill, I'd like to apologize for our last meeting. I've missed you," she said and tears welled up in her eyes.

Crying softly she said, "Bill, I've always loved you, even when I hated you, I loved you, but you'll never know how my heart broke when I read Eve's note."

I held her for a minute, but the love was gone. I felt something for her but the fire of love was out. As Ginny opened the door for me, she asked where I was staying. I told her the *Orleans*.

Returning to the game, my mind was whirling. I sat down heavily. Ginny had stirred something. It wasn't love, but we had been friends before we were lovers and I felt something for her. Carlos dealt the cards.

Two down around the table and the first cards up was a jack of clubs for the farmer, and a queen for the cotton broker. I caught a red ace. I picked up my down cards and was shocked to see two aces under, both down. Carlos caught a king of clubs. He checked his down cards and his cheek flinched ever so slightly. I knew Carlos had something going.

Ginny had shared with me that she had put all this together with her savings and her nest egg from the *Brazos Queen*. I knew she couldn't stand a big hit. I checked the ace and Carlos bet five hundred. Everyone called. Fourth cards came quickly. The planter caught a ten, Grant caught another queen, and damned if I didn't hit my other ace.

Damn the game, I thought. Four aces and I couldn't bet them. I was watching Carlos and a king fell for him. His cheek jerked and I knew he was sitting on four kings. Knowing the hate and jealously that was possessing Carlos, I figured he was a fixing to lose Ginny's casino. I knew he had hit his fourth king.

Grant was sitting there holding a full boat, and the planter had a flush. This was fixing to be a gut shooting. I checked the aces, and grabbing the house chips, Carlos bet a thousand. The planter folded, Grant called. He'd bet a full boat every day. It was back to me. I was torn between greed and loyalty for lost love. Ginny needed this new start. She was getting older and time had been drawing interest from her account. I looked Belyere in the eye and I knew this bastard was not going to back off.

Turning my two aces over, I shoved them into the discard stack and folded. Ginny had walked up behind my chair and was watching the game. As I folded and pushed back my chair to rise, she picked up my two down cards and saw the other two aces. She stared at the pair of aces in her hand and glancing at the two I'd discarded, she knew I had folded with four aces.

Carlos turned over his four kings as the hand wound down and raked in a sizable pot. Ginny sat there with tears in her eyes as she slowly shuffled the cards. She knew that I had given her back the *Pleasure Palace* because we both knew Carlos would have lost it on that hand.

I didn't look back as Grant and I walked out. Too many emotions were grinding me as we made for the door. Grant had seen me burn those four aces and was wondering what in the hell was going on. I explained in the carriage as we made our way through the winding streets to my hotel. Shaking his head in bewilderment, Grant bid me farewell as I stepped out of the carriage.

Retreating to my room, I packed my trunk and waited for dawn to get here and the boat to leave. I could nearly hear the Brazos flowing in my mind. A light rap on my door awoke me. Slipping on my pants and pulling and cocking my gun, I softly opened the door.

Ginny was standing outside my door and quickly walked in. In a voice choked with emotion, she told me she knew I had thrown the game and why. She told me she knew I could have won the *Pleasure Palace* and was thankful I had given her back the casino.

In a choking voice she thanked me. I sank back on the bed and not knowing what to say, just said nothing. Ginny began to remove her white silk dress. Pained silence was haunting the room. Clearing my throat awkwardly, I quietly said, "Ginny you don't have to do this."

Ginny replied, "Bill, this isn't a whore paying a debt. This is for me. Hold me, and make love to me one more time."

As she slowly stripped in the soft dim light of New Orleans, I marveled at her body. Still small and tight waisted, her hips and buttocks would be the envy of a lot of thirty year-olds. Her breasts were still large and firm without any sag in them.

I don't know if it was nostalgia or passion, but as she lay down beside me, I wanted her like the days of old. I was trying to decide if I had let passion overrule greed when I threw in the cards, but as her body enhaled me, I decided this beats the hell out of poker. Consumed by desire, the night melted into the past.

For a minute I thought I had drifted back in time. I awoke to the clean, slightly lilac smell of Ginny. Her porcelain white body felt like satin as I stroked her breast. Remembering how this used to arouse her, I gently stroked and rubbed her large breast, rekindling the flame that had long lay smoldering. As day replaced the night, Ginny's moans could be heard in the hall, but I'd already started thinking again of Texas.

When the sun rose across a foggy, swampy sky, my ship was backing away from the dock and steaming for Texas. I stood at the rail and waved goodbye to Ginny. For a little while things had seemed like they used to be. I guess love is something you can't keep from happening, or make happen. I thought about just taking her back to the ranch and starting over, but it wasn't but a little while and I was glad I hadn't suggested it.

Ginny stood on the dock and sadly waved goodbye as the ship turned out to sea and was Texas bound. Looking down at her wrinkled dress, she had to wear again to see him off, she wandered if he was disappointed about last night. Ginny had a glow in her cheeks and a sparkle in her eyes that had been absent for a long time. Saying a silent prayer for his safe passage, Ginny stood and waved till the ship was just a speck. Maybe, just maybe, he still loves me, she thought, as the ship dropped over the horizon.

Chapter 33

Time seemed to stand still for me as we stopped at every port and picked up and delivered freight. Any other time, I'd have enjoyed the hullabaloo of the docks and sin dens but all I wanted was to go home. I was homesick for Texas soil. Maybe seeing Ginny had jolted me back to the past. I'd have given everything I owned to have stepped back ten years and Willie and Bates would have been alive and Ginny and I would have still been in love.

For a minute I could see the teams coming and going to the fields and Willie shouting orders. Old Blue would be grazing in the pecan trees' shade, with the mares. Chicken was frying in the kitchen, and Ginny was standing in the door. A shrill blast from the ship's boiler jarred me back to reality. It's funny how your mind can just go on a vacation of its own. Damn, it felt so real for a minute but daydreams don't last. As I looked up the lights of Galveston was shining in the distance and I knew we'd be docking soon.

The ship docked in about an hour and I was thrilled to hear the dock hands say the Brazos was on a rise and a running strong.

A boat was leaving at ten the next morning and soon as the ticket office opened, I was standing at the counter with my trunk. I was the first passenger to board, and as the paddle wheeler pushed off, I was standing at the front rail looking north. Texas fields and pastures slipped by as the boat paddled north.

Night came swiftly as storm clouds built in the sky to our north. A norther blew in about midnight, and a cold rain started falling. Dawn broke cold and crisp. This late spring norther had some bite but the sun came out and the day was cold and clear. The cold wind blew in my face as I stood on the deck and watched the Brazos roll by. My mind started drifting back to the lost cave and the Army gold, and I decided I'd ride up that way to see Jim Wagner and look one more time for that cave.

The wind had laid by the time we reached Waco. March was a

trading winter for spring and the last cold spell had lost its bite by the time we got docked and unloaded.

Waco had changed in the last ten years, grown a bunch. The Army had gone and the Texas Rangers were in control of the fort. The Rangers were a great bunch of men. None of this pulling rank like the Army. Just a bunch of no nonsense law officers that covered every inch of the ground they stood on. Feelings about the war had kind of mellowed and the Indians had nearly all been trailed to the reservations. Streets were being bricked and the town was sporting lots of new homes and businesses. The *Brazos Queen* was still competing with the *Cotton Palace* but they both looked a little used as I rode past.

I rented a buggy and horse at the livery stable and headed for the ranch. Winter grass was thick and tall along the river banks and I knew the grazing should be good this year.

Riding up to the ranch I was shocked to see the house so dilapidated. The porches were rotted out, the steps had fallen in and the lawn was over grown with weeds. Tall grass and weeds covered Bates' and Willie's graves. The graves had sunken and the whole place had just run down.

The stables were in some better shape, but the corrals were ragged and needed repairing. I could tell Jimmy didn't have his uncle's knack for bossing people. I drove through the mare pasture and baby colts lay sprawled out asleep in the lush grass. The mares were fat and a real good set of girls. At least Jimmy had been taking care of the horses.

Opening the gate, I drove into the Brazos bottom to check the cow herd. Last year's calves were still following their mothers and some had big yearlings sucking and a fresh baby calf following along behind trying to suck. The calves hadn't been worked. Red necked half blood bulls were running on the cows.

I was disturbed at the neglect of my cattle. There were dead carcasses laying under several trees, where yearling heifers, that bred too soon had died trying to calve. Shaking my head I recalled the days when Willie was alive and I could leave for a year at a time. Everything would just keep a running like I was there.

Jimmy was a grinning from ear to ear as I drove up to the horse barn. "Mr. Bill you home," he said. "Sho'e is good to see ya back. You stayin' this time?"

Looking around, I knew good horses and Jimmy had a barn full, mostly blues and roans. Jimmy led Blue Moon out of her stall and explained her accidental birthing and her successful race career. He said he had won three races at three different distances at the State Fair in Dallas last year.

Jimmy explained how every colt out of Old Blue crossed on Domino Duke mares were automatic race horses. The roan stud crossed on the Old Blue fillies were good but they run short, he babbled and told me about loaning Jim Wagner the little roan stud.

The night was spent in my old home and ghosts of the past seemed to ramble all night. I awoke with visions of Ginny's naked body on my mind and thought back to all the nights we had spent here. I could nearly smell her fragrance, and I wondered if I should have brought her home and started over.

Jimmy saddled Old Blue for me the next morning and I decided to go see Jim Wagner. The stud was fresh and I counted off the years. Old Blue was just as sound as a four year-old but he must be sixteen or seventeen. He sure felt good as I loped him through the river bottom. I saw a lot of neglect in the cow herd as I loped past. There were top cattle and I recalled the struggle I had been through to get my start.

Good Shorthorn and Hereford blood flowed through this herd. The Shorthorn Hereford cross cows were as good as I'd seen anywhere, big red motley faced and red roans with white markings and lots of milk. Damn, Jimmy for not taking care of them. I guess he was just a "race hoss man."

Stopping suddenly, I looked around and made a final decision. I'd been contemplating for several years. I decided to sell the ranch and cattle. The more I pondered about, I decided to sell the broodmares too. I first thought I'd keep the race mares, but I decided to give them to Jimmy. Jimmy had developed them and he deserved them.

I decided to ride through the north range I had claimed so long. It sure didn't look the same. Barbed wire fences cut zigzag patterns across the prairie.

I crossed Childress Creek and thought about that rednecked bastard shooting Willie in the back. My blood started boiling. I wondered what ever happened to the poor pregnant woman and those half starved kids. It's hard to imagine how a coward could leave his family in that condition.

The buffalo trail was dim and finding it I followed it to the river crossing. Stopping to let Old Blue drink, I recalled the Indian attack and Deke Williams valiant defense. Dusk was gathering as I rode up to the Wagner house. I was surprised that it was twice the size it had been when I left. The barn had been enlarged too, and a couple of more built. Jim Wagner didn't have a lazy bone in his body, and the neat little ranch showed it.

Who was the proudest to see one another was hard to tell. I sure set a heap of store by Jim Wagner and he acted awful glad to see me. Little Jim was twelve-years-old and Henry was ten. Henry was still a nursing when I left. Two more little boys were underfoot, one four and one six. They had a new little girl, two years-old, that stole everybody's heart.

Talking low and far into the night, Jim and I discussed horses and strange towns. The boys stayed up to listen but one by one drifted off to sleep.

The house was pretty full, so I just got me a blanket and climbed up in the loft. Spreading it on a soft pile of hay, I rolled up and let my mind wonder. Thinking back to the Comanche attack, I recalled how close they came to burning us out. I could still see the one I killed in the hall of the barn. Screaming and hollering with war paint etched on his face and body. The hate burned in his black eyes. I shivered as I drifted off to sleep.

The last thing I remembered before dozing off was how good life had been then. Nostalgia nearly smothered me and I longed for the old slow life we had lived then. A trip to Europe was the last thing on my mind as the Indians came a calling that day so long ago.

A rooster crowing roused me from a troubled sleep. I had fought Indians, stole studs, and helped Deke back to the cave in my sleep. I was sleeping with beautiful blondes as I awoke and was mad at that damn rooster for spoiling that part of the dream.

Little Jim and Henry wanted to help me hunt for the cave. I saddled two roan geldings for them that had been weanling colts when I left. I saddled Old Blue and told them the story of the old black stud stealing their geldings' mamas and how their Dad had to walk home.

I thought back to everything that had happened and realized how time just flies by. We rode up the creek and I told the boys the story of the lost cave and Army gold. I told them about crawling out of the little hole and never had been able to find it since.

We spent the day looking for the cave, the lost gold and the little hole in the brush to no avail. I spent the night again, and Jim and I got down to the business I had come to do

I explained that I was no longer a rancher, but a drifting gambler, and I wanted to sell the ranch. Jim tried to pay me for the young stud he had got from Jimmy, but I told him it was a token of our friendship. Without stopping for air, I explained that I wanted to sell him the ranch and my cows. I explained the neglect of the cowherd and the shape of the ranch. Jimmy had the horses and race barn in excellent condition, but he just wasn't a rancher.

Jim was taken back by the offer but he said he'd put too much of his heart and soul into this ranch to leave it. He said he would like to buy twenty five or thirty cows. He said he had that much cash saved. Since I had left he'd managed to raise about a hundred cows.

I studied a minute and suggested that he just pay down what he could and I'd sell the rest of them on a note. Pay what you can each year, I said, and this way I'll know the place and the cows are being taken care of. I also told him I wanted to sell him the ranch mares and colts, everything but the race horses. Grinning at the boys, I told Jim, this would make sure these rascals had plenty to do.

Finally a deal was struck and Jim leased the ranch for ten years, with an option to buy. He was to repair and restore to the original condition. Keep the fences up and operate it.

Jim took me home in a wagon and surveyed all he'd bought on credit. Jim and I slept in the old house again and were up at dawn counting cows. This took all morning. There was five hundred plus cows and bred heifers, not counting Willie's cows. They were branded different.

We penned all the cattle the next day and sorted them. We let all the cows, heifers and purebred bulls back out to pasture. We culled all the maverick bulls, yearlings and weanlings into the feed pens. When we got through with the sorting, there was a little over three hundred head of yearlings to three-year-old and older bulls to be shipped.

Jim made me a deal to drive them to Fort Worth and to take all the draft mares and colts and farm teams along on the drive. There was also a big group of yearling to five year-old-geldings that were raised by the ranch mares that needed shipped.

These were things Willie had always done, second nature, but Jimmy didn't get around to. I guess I shouldn't even compare them because Jimmy was as good at what he loved as Willie had been at what he did best. Jimmy was just a "race hoss man," but danged if he wasn't one of the best.

Jimmy was relieved to be rid of the ranch. He hated cattle and farming. Never good at bossing anyone, he let me dismiss the hands and shut the operation down. I'd already given Jimmy the two hundred acres and the horse barn and now I signed over all the pedigrees on the race mares and the roan stud.

I couldn't give him Old Blue. I'd sworn when I rode him out of Palo Duro Canyon, that no one would ever own him but me, till I died, and I wasn't a fixing to die. I told him he could use him till he died or I asked for him back, if he would turn him out and let him run with the mares. He loved to herd the mares and hated to be penned up. Hell, I guess we had something in common.

Early next morning found me at the bank. I went over my financial affairs, and was pleased to find things satisfactory. Jimmy had mismanaged the ranch but the race winnings he deposited for my share, more than offset that weakness. The lawyer recorded some legal transactions regarding the lease purchase of the cows and ranch. He also made a clean and precise transfer of all the race horses to Jimmy.

I made sure that the title was straight on the two hundred acres I'd given him and made arrangements that if ever he couldn't pay the taxes on his place they would draft them out of my account. Times had changed a lot since the war but there was still a lot of people that resented a black man having property and money, much less the best race horses in Texas.

The Brazos was again running bank full as I walked to the boat dock. The boat was leaving for Galveston in a few minutes, and as usual I boarded and left without telling anyone goodbye.

Galveston bound, the paddle wheeler steamed back out into the swift current. With a mighty blast of the steam whistle, it turned and headed down river. I stood on the deck and stared up the river, as Waco grew small and faded into a speck in the distance. Home wasn't home anymore. I guess I'd given up more than ten years of my life, when I left before.

Once again, my mind returned to the disappearing cave, and the lost Army gold. How in the hell could a cave just disappear and take two dead soldiers and a shipment of gold with it. Shrugging my shoulders, I turned and headed below deck, and into the first day of the rest of my life.

Epilogue

1961

The spring rains had turned the world green and White Rock Creek had been running bank full. The creek had slowed to a trickle now and fish were feeding in the shallows as the sun warmed the chilly water.

Spring break was in full swing and the Kotch and Williams boys were exploring the creek. Bill Kotch, the oldest of the group at twelve was the leader. Everyday was an adventure. The Kotch boys' dad had bought the old ranch and it was a hot bed of activity. The back pasture was being cleared for pasture and a dozer could be heard in the distance, as it pushed and stacked brush and trees. The pasture was thick with virgin cedar and native oak.

Mexican labors were cutting the cedar posts and staves for fencing, and then the dozer would clear and stack the down brush and trees in long windrows. The five boys drifted toward the roar of the bulldozer.

Rambling, with nothing particular on their minds, just being kids, they climbed up out of the creek bank and drifted toward the dozer. One of them stopped and hollered for the others as he stared at a hole in the ground. The dozer had scraped the dirt down to solid rock and kneeling down, they could see that the hole opened into a cave of sorts.

Quickly backtracking to the house, they began to gather up flashlights and ropes to go down in the cave. Mr. Kotch heard their plans and quickly forbade it. This was rattlesnake country and this time of the year they would still be denned up. He told them under no condition were they to go near this cave unless he was with them. They knew he meant business. He was the best Dad in the world, but his no meant no. They abandoned their adventure and as kids do, drifted off to another project.

Rain was falling slowly as eleven o'clock approached. Mr. Kotch was startled from a sound sleep. On a rural ranch, most people are asleep at this hour, he cautiously opened the door. The three Mexican labors that were cutting cedar stood at the door dripping wet and terrified. They were all talking at once in rapid fire Spanish with just a little English thrown in.

Mr. Kotch spoke very little Spanish, but by slowing them down and quieting their fears, he concluded that had also found the hole in the ground. They told him that they had gone down in the cave, and it had bad spirits in it. They said there was some writing on the wall that they couldn't read and the bad spirits had followed them home. The house they lived in was about a mile from the work site and cave and real secluded. They were terrified of ghost and evil spirits from the cave.

They asked him to take them to Waco to spend the night with some friends. They had been drinking and he wasn't sure of all they were trying to tell him, but he was sure they had gone down in the cave and thought the ghost or spirits were after them.

The rain had began to fall harder, and not wanting to get up and drive forty miles to Waco and back in the middle of the night, he told them tomorrow, he would and they turned and disappeared into the night.

Rain continued to fall over the weekend and Monday morning about daylight he went by to pick them up for work. He was going to another ranch and he was going to get them to fix water gaps. They weren't at the house. Thinking they had already gone to cut cedar he went on without them.

About dark Tuesday, he went back to the house where they were staying and discovered they were gone. The house was empty. An old iron wheeled wheelbarrow was sitting in the front yard. It had always been in the barn before. As he investigated, the tracks from the wheelbarrow went to the creek and back about a mile away. The return tracks were pretty deep in the soft ground and you could see where they had stopped periodically to rest. At first he thought they had used it to haul their tools out, but on further checking, the tools were still at the work site. He wondered about the wheelbarrow tracks and laughing said maybe the fat one made the two little ones push him to the house. The strangest thing was they had a month's wages coming for each laborer and they never came back for their money.

Mr. Kotch went back the next morning to look at the cave and see what scared them so bad, but the dozer had ran the day before and had evidently windrowed brush and dirt over the hole. No one has ever been able to find it. Everything looked different with the trees gone. Now the pasture has been converted into a large cotton field.

The Mexicans were never been heard from again. They never came back for their wages and this was highly unusual.

1975

Gus's Hardware was located just off the square in Hillsboro, Texas for many years. It was one of a kind even for hardware stores. You could still buy horse harness and walking plows, new coal oil lamps and butter molds and churns in 1975. Every kind of hardware was available.

I had bought the ranch that lay between the Kotch Ranch and the river. I was building some corrals and needed some hinges. There was some old hinges on some of the gates that were still good and I was trying to match them. Gus's was the local "spit and whittle" club. All the old men in town would gather everyday to swap "wild west" stories and reminisces. Lots of coons had been treed, bumper crops made and lost, and a fight or two embellished on in this old hardware store.

An old man named Henry Wagner struck up a conversation with me as I browsed through the hardware hinges. He asked where I lived, and I told him Aquilla, a small town nearby. He asked me where from Aquilla and I stopped and started giving him directions. A contented smile crossed his old face as I named the ranch, and he said, "Why I know exactly where it is. That was part of the Hudson outfit."

He wanted to know if the old house was still there between the White Rock Creek and the Brazos River. I told him it was just a shell, and he told me he was born in that house, ninety-two years ago.

He told me he spent a lot of time up and down that old creek and river. When he was a kid, he said an old man used to come and ride up and down that creek looking for a lost cave and a cache of lost Army gold that was stashed in it. Mr. Henry said when the old man quit coming, he and his brothers took up the search and spent countless hours searching the creek bed and bluff.

I was real busy that day and I didn't pay a lot of attention to the old man. But several days later, I slowed down a little and started rethinking his story. As I thought back, I recalled the Kotch and Williams boys from the sixties finding the hole in the ground. How the Kotch and Williams boys nearly went down in the cave the day they found it. I remembered the Mexican laborers fear of the haints or spirits and the mysterious wheelbarrow tracks.

Were the bad spirits ghosts of the two dead soldiers? Did the loaded wheelbarrow hold the mystery of the lost gold? Did the removal of the gold raise the ire of the ghost? And was the gold why the labors never returned for their wages.

I guess no one will ever know for sure. The White Rock Creek still flows lazily to the Brazos on its way to the Gulf and water still puddles in the buffalo wallows when it rains. Cotton now grows in the cleared field and closely guards it. I never was able to locate Henry Wagner again. Gus died and the hardware store closed shortly after my purchases and I have since sold the ranch. But I guess I'll always wonder if we were ever so close to finding "Bill Fowler's" lost Army gold, and does someone in Mexico know the answer.